Pla

A Neighb

by

R.L. Mathewson

Playing for Keeps © R.L. Mathewson 2011. All rights reserved.

http://www.rlmathewson.com

Edited by Maura O'Beirne-Stanko, Lieve Van den Heuvel & Christi Main-Ehrlich

eBook ISBN-13 9780983212539

ISBN-13 9780983212546

This book is dedicated to everyone who was willing to take a chance on me. Thank you.

Also, to my mother, grandmother, and cousin Jamie who keep me entertained with online Scrabble games.

And of course to my children who will always be my inspiration and my little buddies.

Chapter 1

"Oh, no, no, no, no, no!" Haley murmured in disbelief as she watched her pink, white, and yellow tulips being yanked viciously out of the ground. She shoved back from her computer desk and stormed towards the front door. She was going to kill him this time there was no doubt about it.

After five long years of juvenile nonsense he'd finally gone too far. Her college roommate hadn't been able to aggravate her this much, even when she went through her six month period of not showering or using deodorant to "save the planet."

Five years ago she'd been proud to buy her first house at the ripe old age of twenty-four. She'd worked her butt off to buy her dream home, a one level two bedroom ranch. The experience of owning her own home was better than anything she could have ever imagined.

She spent hundreds of hours picking out the perfect color scheme for each room, cleaning, organizing, and hitting every yard sale within a thirty mile radius, trying to turn wood and plaster into a real home. None of that work could even begin to compare to the hours she spent on her lawn and garden. With countless blisters, cuts, bee stings and back aches she turned her dull yard into a paradise.

Her enjoyment lasted for all of four months. That's when *he* moved into the house next door. At first she was excited to have a new neighbor, one that wasn't elderly and well, cranky. All of her enjoyment ended the moment she met Jason Bradford.

Within the first ten minutes of his arrival he'd backed into her mailbox, spilled fast food wrappers from his car onto his property, which quickly made their way onto her immaculate lawn, and relieved himself on the great old oak tree in his front lawn with a sheepish smile and a shrug in her horrified direction.

The man was a barbarian.

For the next five years he turned her picturesque life into a nightmare. She wasn't sure how one person managed to take so much control over her happiness, but he did. Over the years she dealt with paintball pellets decorating the laundry hanging on her clothesline and splattering the side of her house. Haley had endured loud music, parties, twice she found naked people trying to climb the fence to skinny dip in *her* pool, three a.m. drunken basketball games, women throwing hissy fits on his front lawn and sometimes on *hers* when the jerk refused to come out and deal with them.

What made it worse was that they both worked at the same private high school, in the same department, with adjoining classrooms, and adjacent parking spots. It didn't take long for him to turn her dream job and house into a nightmare. At work she had to deal with him constantly "borrowing" things from her room like paper, pens, books, and even her desk one time.

He seemed to think that he was the most charming man on earth and had no problem with using it to get his way, leaving her with extra work and responsibilities while he got to be the laid back teacher. It didn't take her long to figure out that she would have to suck it up at work. There was no way at her age that she was going to be able to land a better job. She'd been lucky to land this one. So the only option left for her was to move.

After the first year, she tried to sell her house, unsuccessfully. Every time a prospective buyer came around, he scared them off by just being Jason. She gave up the idea of selling her house for the next two years and put it up again last year when he took up golf and shot out three of her windows. He managed to scare off fifteen prospective buyers by walking out to get the mail in his boxers, a particularly memorable fit of rage when he threw his computer out the window accompanied with a loud roar, and of course there was the upkeep, or rather lack thereof, of his property.

His lawn was covered in crab grass and weeds. He only paid the neighborhood kid to mow it once a month. The rest of the time it was the chosen habitat of little woodland creatures. The house needed a serious paint job, or at the very least, a cleanup of all paint chips that had fallen to the ground over the years. If he didn't personally scare someone off, his house did the job. She gave up the dream of moving away five months ago and settled for praying that he would move soon, very soon.

Now he was going after her babies. This was not happening. Enough was enough. Over the last five years she'd bitten her tongue, too afraid to complain. She'd always been like that, even as a little kid.

She was always the shy quiet girl with her nose buried in a book, hoping no one would notice her. It wasn't so much that she wasn't a very social person, she was. It had more to do with the fact that she was a huge chicken. When the other kids picked on her or pushed her around she cowered, unable to deal with confrontation. That nasty habit followed her into adulthood.

It was made even worse with good looking men like Jason. His ebony hair, ocean blue eyes and chiseled good looks made her nervous. She just wasn't any good at handling people. Throw good looks onto a guy that was being particularly jerkish and she turned into a blubbering idiot. Pushy people just sucked and it really sucked that she never learned how to deal with them.

When she caught her roommate, Angel, stealing her papers, food, and money what did she do? She avoided her room until well after two in the morning when she knew Angel would be asleep and then hurried the hell out of there before she woke up in the morning.

The same could be said of the few boyfriends she did manage to have over the years that took advantage of her. Instead of throwing them to the curb like she should have done she pulled back into herself, knowing they would get bored eventually and move on. Yes, she was a chicken. That was the only reason why Jason Bradford had gotten away with his behavior for the past five years. No more. The flowers were the last straw. Her grandmother had given her the bulbs from her own garden when Haley bought the house and she loved them.

She spied the rolled up hose and made a snap decision. This ended here and now. The days of being the world's biggest pushover were done.

* * * *

"What the hell!"

Jason jumped to his feet as a torrent of ice cold water hit him.

He didn't know what he expected to see, but it certainly wasn't his timid little neighbor and co-worker aiming her very long hose at him. Clearly she'd lost her damned mind.

"Step away from my tulips," she ordered in a tone of authority.

He really couldn't help grinning at her. She looked so damn cute standing there with her long bronze hair pulled back into a twisted pony tail, green eyes full of fire hidden behind large glasses making her look adorable, and of course her rather tight black tee shirt with the word "Nerd" written across her very decent size chest made her look hot. His eyes dropped to the cute little shorts that revealed short, but very nice, shapely, tanned legs, very nice indeed.

Of course he knew his quiet neighbor was stunning. It was the first thing he noticed about her the day he moved in. The second was that she was a very shy, very nervous, and easily frightened female. He still winced when he thought back to that day. After five hours on the road and three Big gulps he was in desperate need of a bathroom. Unfortunately the realtor hadn't left the keys where she said she would and he had to make a split second decision, piss his pants or water the tree. In the end the tree got a healthy amount of recycled cola.

She hadn't even given him a chance to explain or apologize. Her face reddened before she practically ran into her house. From then on she avoided him at all costs. If he waved or said hello to her, she would mutter something or ignore him. If he, or one of his asshole buddies, broke something on her property she didn't say a word. If he was a jerk he could have easily gotten away with not paying for all those broken windows or paintball streaked sheets, but he wasn't that big of a prick. He learned she would never speak up for herself so as soon as the shit hit the fan he made a call and replaced whatever he fucked up. It would just make him feel like an even bigger asshole to take advantage of the situation.

It always bothered him that she never spoke up. He couldn't remember someone disliking him so fast and intensely before in his life. No matter what he did she couldn't be bothered to speak to him. Hell, he would have kicked his ass years ago, or at the very least called the cops on him like the other neighbors did or file a complaint with the principal like so many of his other co-workers had. Hell, she never even signed any of those numerous petitions demanding that he move that the rest of the neighborhood liked to give him every few months. He checked each and every time.

It wasn't like he was purposely being an asshole. It just came naturally to him. Everyone understood and accepted it. Probably because even though he was an asshole, he was a likeable asshole.....most of the time.

As happy as he was that she finally came off her throne to talk to him, he was also pissed to be soaked to the bone in his favorite shirt and khaki shorts in seventy degree weather. Apparently he didn't move fast enough because she sprayed him again.

"Are you fucking insane?" he demanded.

She gestured with the hose for him to take a step back. "Get away from my flower bed.....Now."

"Your flowerbed?" he asked in disbelief.

"Yes, my flowerbed!" Another short spray. "I planted these flowers five years ago, before you moved in!"

Jason ran frustrated fingers through his messy hair. "Then you should have checked the fucking property lines before you wasted your time!" he snapped.

Her eyes narrowed on him. "The flowerbed is my property!"

"I don't think so, sweetheart. Go check your deed if you don't believe me. This flowerbed is one hundred percent on my property," he said harshly. He pointed to the two feet of space that separated their houses where the flower bed continued until it came to the large wooden picket fence that started at the corner of her house and continued to the back, separating their backyards. "You have five inches out from the wall of your house. Your property ends two inches before *my* flower bed! That's why the stupid, little, white picket fence starts against your house instead of on the other side of the flowerbed."

He watched as she glared at the small space that separated their houses. Whoever built them was a real prick. Both of their master bedrooms were built less than two feet apart. Yet, there was more than thirty feet of space between each house and the other neighboring houses. There was no privacy with the way the identical houses were designed. He had no choice but to place his large bed directly at the window and from what he could see neither had she. Taking the smaller bedroom was out of the question. His bed would never fit in it.

It felt odd sleeping less than two feet away from a woman who thought him less than dirt. During the summer they both refused to open their windows until the heat became oppressive, leaving them with no other choice. Forget about bringing a woman to his bedroom. He'd never been one for PDA's never mind having sex in public and having sex in his room would definitely feel like a public performance.

No matter how many times he tried to remind himself that they were in separate houses and separated by more than just a stupid little flower garden he couldn't bring himself to allow a woman in his bed. Not that he did that normally. He never invited a woman to his home. That was one of his top ten rules of dating. The only time they ever came to his house was to bitch him out when he moved on and that was done from the outside.

He never in his entire adult life shared a bed with a woman. That was too much intimacy and sent the wrong message. The few times he made the mistake of relaxing in a woman's bed after a quick lay proved to be serious mistakes. They wanted to cuddle and always asked the questions that made him cringe, "What are you thinking?", "Do you love me?", "Where do you see this going?", "Are you as happy as I am?', "Why do you keep calling me by my sister's name?", or his personal favorite "I wonder what our babies will look like." No, sex was best kept at a woman's house, hotel room or better yet in the backseat of a car.

Thank God his neighbor seemed to share the same attitude. He hated the idea of waking up to the sounds of another man grunting and moaning. With his luck the sounds would filter into his dream and he would end up having a gay dream. Thankfully that never happened otherwise he'd be sleeping on his couch.

It wasn't as if his beautiful neighbor was without male attention. He'd seen several losers sniffing around her in the last five years. She was easily out of their league, at least physically. Personality wise, well even from afar he could tell they were all pricks. He wasn't a prince, not by any measure, but he found himself eager to deck a few of them over the years with the way they treated her. They never hit her otherwise he would have killed the bastards. He didn't go for hitting a woman no matter what. Sometimes he felt like they were using her, or not treating her right. He didn't know why he cared, he just did.

Haley eyed the fence and then the remaining length of the flower bed. She sighed heavily. "Fine. If I made a mistake I'm sorry, but I replaced the last flower bed with the tulips from my Grandmother's garden."

He nodded in relief, glad that it was settled. The damn flowers were out of here and not a moment too soon. He couldn't take another night like last night. Besides, he was running out of cornstarch.

"I'll just move the flowers over into my five inches of space," she announced.

His eyes widened with that announcement. "The hell you will!"

Chapter 2

Haley's eyes widened in total disbelief as Jason threw himself back onto the plants, tearing them up like a man possessed.

"Stop!" she shrieked. He ignored her and continued to rip the tulips from the ground, making sure those damn bulbs came with them. He tossed them far onto his property so she couldn't get her hands on them to re-plant them.

She squeezed the nozzle, sending a full blast of cold water on him. Still he continued to tear up the flowerbed.

"Stop! Please stop!" she cried. He only slowed down when he reached the tight space between their houses.

Jason had to shift his shoulders so he could lodge himself into the tight space. Thankfully she gave up on squirting him. It might be April, but they were in New England and that meant a bright sun with a cold breeze. His body shivered violently as he reached forward to grab handfuls of tulips. Suddenly something clamped around his ankles.

"What the hell-*oomph*!" He was pulled off balance, landing face first into the thick mud she created with her little water meltdown. Before he could push himself up, she was crawling over his back to get to those damn flowers.

Haley used her small frame to her advantage. After quickly crawling over Jason she began digging up as many tulips with her hands as she could and setting them gently, yet quickly, against the side of her house.

"Hey! Stop that!" he demanded as he leaned over her to grab her hands.

"Get off of me!" she snapped, digging faster.

"I wouldn't be on you if you weren't on my damn property!"

She threw back an elbow to dislodge him. He cursed under his breath as he pushed himself in further until her entire body was snuggled tightly beneath his. She instantly froze beneath him. He took advantage of her stunned reaction and grabbed as many flowers as he could.

"I said get off me, not crush me!" she clarified. It was all she could do to control her breathing. She was going to hyperventilate and pass out. No doubt about it. A large muscular man was on top of her!

Her senses went into overload as she tried to focus. But all she could think about was how the feel of his strong, hard stomach felt pressed against her back. Suddenly a shiver shot through her body that had nothing to do with the cold water seeping through her clothes.

Then realization sank in. A very large man was on top of her! "That better not be what I think it is," she hissed between clenched teeth.

"It's not." It was. "Don't flatter yourself, sweetheart," he snapped, trying not to groan or grind into her. He was a little shocked himself. Not that he ever had a problem getting it up. He didn't. Of course these days his interest in sex had waned a bit. Hell, he couldn't remember the last time he had sex, which in itself was pathetic.

He made a half assed attempt to pull out more flowers. That seemed to distract her enough from her pert little ass being snuggled against his lap. His eyes closed as he nuzzled against her neck and inhaled slowly. She didn't seem to notice so he did it again. He would swear on his life that she smelled like blackberries and cream. It was damn enticing.

She groaned her irritation. "I don't know what your problem is. I made a mistake planting them on your property. Just let me move them over a few inches and everything will be settled."

That snapped him out of his daze. "No!" He reached past her and began ripping flowers out. She swore under her breath as she crawled out from under him to save whatever flowers she could. He simply followed her, assuming the same position each time and frustrating the hell out of her.

"You're being a jerk! I just want my bulbs!" she said, trying to not to cry. These were her Grandmother's bulbs. Her Grandfather bought them for her Grandmother after the war to celebrate the success of their first business.

"No, you're not going to plant them here! They can't stay!" he said, digging faster.

"Why?" she demanded, coming closer and closer to frustrated tears. "I don't understand you! You do nothing with your property at all. Why do you care if there's a flower bed here or a few inches over? They're not hurting you!"

"The hell they're not!" he snapped, thinking of all the spots on his back and neck that still throbbed.

She scoffed. "They're just flowers. What could they possibly do to aggravate you to this level?" She heard a buzzing pass her ear and absently waved it off.

"Bees!" he said, trying to back up, but couldn't. His large frame was trapped between their houses.

"Yes, it's a bee," she said slowly as if she were talking to a child.

He groaned as he tried to twist his large frame loose. When that didn't work he tried to shove backwards. His arm snaked around her waist, trying to pull her along with him.

"Hey, get your hands-"

"It's a fucking nest and we just disturbed it!" he yelled.

Haley's eyes shot forward and then widened. Sure enough, two feet in front of her the end of what appeared to be a very large ground nest was now poking out of the ground thanks to the flowers they yanked up. Yellow jackets began swarming just above the nest. It wouldn't be long before they descended on them.

"Move!"

"I can't!"

Haley clenched her teeth as she slammed back as hard as she could against him. He groaned low in her ear, but didn't stop trying to move back. She moved forward and slammed back again, and again. Each time was met by a groan and a gain of a few inches.

"One more time!" he grated out.

She moved forward and this time when she slammed back into him she pushed up with her shoulders, dislodging him. Jason used the momentum to pull them both back several feet. He kept his arm snaked around her waist as he dragged her away from the nest.

"They're swarming!" Haley cried.

"Shit!" Jason looked frantically around for a safe place.

"My house!" she said, gesturing wildly towards her front door.

"Good idea," he said as he ran towards the house, dragging her along. The buzzing sound became louder and louder as the swarm began circling them. Once they reached the front door he opened it, relieved that she'd left it unlocked, and they ran inside, slamming the door shut behind them.

"Bees!" Haley cried, gesturing to the bees that had followed them inside.

He quickly released her and grabbed two magazines from a small pile on a coffee table and threw one to her. Without a word, they rolled the magazines up and began to attack the dozen or so bees that managed to follow them inside. Neither spoke until the last bee was squashed.

"Five nights….in….a….row…..stung…," Jason bit out while he tried to catch his breath.

"You knew there were yellow jackets and you still tore up the flowers?" she asked in disbelief. Her grandmother had taught her well. A ground nest was not something to mess with. It could be as small as a stack of quarters or several feet long.

Jason gestured in the direction of his house. "I was trying to kill them."

She shook her head in disbelief. He knew there was a nest and he didn't tell her?

"Why didn't you tell me there was a nest? You know I work in that flowerbed," she said, working hard on keeping her tone even. They could have been killed!

"I did!"

"No, you didn't!"

He threw his hands up. "I've been trying to tell you for the last few weeks, but whenever I approached you, you ran off!"

She opened her mouth to argue, but shut it as quickly and winced. Yeah, that really did sound like something she would do where he was concerned. "Oh," she finally said.

"Yeah, *oh*," he snapped. He peeked out the window and groaned. "They're still swarming."Haley sighed. "They're going to be a problem for a few hours. We need to call an exterminator."

* * * *

Man he was freezing. He was soaked to the bone and it didn't look like he was going to be able to go to his house anytime soon to change. Normally, he'd strip down to his boxers, but his neighbor was already skittish around him. He didn't want to give the poor thing a stroke. He looked down at her very clean and obviously well cared for wood floor and cringed.

"Shit, maybe I should step out the backdoor and dry off," he said as he raised his eyes to look into her adjoining kitchen. His brows flew up as he watched the windows darken.

"I don't think that will be happening for a while," Haley said softly as she rubbed her forehead. "Why don't you go take a shower and I'll see if I can find you something to wear. While you're taking your shower I'll call for an exterminator."

"If you're sure," he said, hoping she wouldn't change her mind. He was freezing his balls off. Hell, at this point he'd squeeze his ass into a dress to get warm.

She nodded absently as she watched the bees swarm around her backyard. "Yeah, let me show you where the bathroom is."

Ten minutes later the shivering finally stopped and he was really enjoying his shower. Never in his life had hot water felt so good. This was the best shower ever. It didn't hurt that his little shy neighbor shared his appreciation for the simple things in life like a normal bar of soap, none of that overly perfumed expensive shit that never lathered properly and always left a rash on his skin. It also didn't hurt that the bathroom looked like a bathroom and wasn't covered from head to toe in lace and makeup. This was a bathroom a man could comfortably use without worrying about his masculinity.

He was just pulling on the tee shirt she'd left him when he heard her scream, "No! Don't do it!"

Jason was out of the bathroom in less than a second, running towards her and ready to kill whatever bastard was trying to hurt her. He came to a skidding stop in front of her.

She smiled sweetly as she said, "God, I love you."

His brows nearly shot through his hairline as his heart pounded. Shit, this was worse than he thought. She hadn't been avoiding him all these years because she was shy. No, she was head over heels in love with him. Shit. This was awkward, especially since he was stuck here until an exterminator could come. Now he hoped it was soon.

Really soon.

He opened his mouth to say something only to find himself gestured impatiently out of the way with a dough covered wooden spoon. He stepped back, frowning, afraid of getting dough all over him, and wondering what was wrong with the woman professing her love for him one moment and shooing him out of the way the next.

"Never come between me and the man I love," she said, snapping him out of his thoughts.

Jason followed her gaze and chuckled. "Derek Jeter?"

She frowned as if questioning her love for the man was stupid. "Of course."

He couldn't help but grin. Damn. How had he missed this? She had a huge television. Bigger than his even and that was really saying something since his television was the one thing he'd really splurged on.

"That's a really big TV for such a tiny woman," he said teasingly.

"Well, how else am I supposed to watch my games and feel like I'm there?" she countered back. "Plus, this way I get to see my future husband better."

"Does he know?" he asked, looking back at her.

She scrunched her face up adorably. "Not yet, but I can wait," she said with a smile that made her face go from utterly adorable and sweet to heartbreakingly beautiful in less than a second.

Damn.

He shifted his feet awkwardly for a moment while she watched the game with rapt attention.

"Are you a Red Sox fan?" she suddenly asked.

"Hell no!" he said, insulted by the question. He may live knee deep in Red Sox territory, but that didn't mean he was a betraying bastard. Yankees were his first love and they would be his last.

She sighed with obvious relief. "Thank God." She sent the game one last look of longing before returning to her kitchen counter where he noted with a chuckle that she had a small flat screen with the game playing. This woman really loved her Yankees, or at least one in particular.

What the hell was it with women and Derek Jeter?

He took a moment to look around her house. The damn bees were still covering all of her windows, but his attention was elsewhere. Her walls were covered in Yankees memorabilia. He wasn't too surprised when he spotted a signed photo of Derek Jeter above the television.

"Looks like we're stuck inside until after dark," she said, pulling his attention back to the kitchen. "The exterminator said he has to wait for the nest to calm. That will happen when the sun goes down. He'll come spray them and remove the nest if he can."

He ran his fingers through his damp hair and sighed. "I guess you're stuck with me for a little while."

She shrugged. "It's fine. There's a good game on so it should help pass the time."

"True," he agreed.

"I'm making homemade pizza. I hope you don't mind. I was planning on ordering pizza today for the game, but with the bees and all.....," she trailed off, shrugging.

"No, that sounds great. I'm sorry that I'm intruding," he said, feeling like an ass. This woman spent the last five years avoiding him and now he was being forced on her by Mother Nature.

"Not a problem," she said and he got the feeling that she was lying. She never liked to be around him before. Whenever he stood too close to her at work or went to sit next to her, she found an excuse to move. Now she was forced to have him in her house. That couldn't make her all that happy. His eyes drifted to the television when she sighed dreamily. Then again, her attention was elsewhere at the moment.

"Beer?"

"What?" he asked a little confused. "Beer," she said, gesturing towards the fridge without taking her eyes off the television.

"Oh," he said with a chuckle as he retrieved two bottles. He handed her one and she took it with a mumbled thanks and then a few choice words for one of the players.

Jason leaned back and watched the show. Not really the game, but Haley as she cooked and ranted. Soon it became obvious if the vegetables were going to get cut and not mangled every time she didn't agree with a call, he'd have to do it.

For the next six hours they cooked, watched the game, ate, laughed, swore and screamed at the television, and got into an hour long fight with the exterminator over the insane amount he wanted to charge them before the argument shifted back to the game. By the end of the night, Haley seemed to have come completely out of her shell around him and he counted himself fortunate to have another buddy. One who actually knew the stats without messing up or having to look them up. Not like several of his friends that he wouldn't mention. It didn't hurt that she was incredibly hot. That was just a bonus.

A nice bonus, but a bonus nonetheless for him from his newest buddy.

Chapter 3

"Is this 32 Long Point Road?" the short husky man who smelled like he bathed in a gallon of cheap cologne and garlic asked as he climbed out of the beat up Taurus parked across Haley's driveway, blocking her in.

Now, normally Jason would either just ignore the asshole or give him a quick nod and continue minding his own business as he pulled the keg of beer out of his backseat, but not today. Today he was going to do his normally shy neighbor and co-worker a favor. After yesterday he was pretty sure this wouldn't piss her off and send her back into hiding.

Okay, maybe he wasn't a hundred percent sure, but he just couldn't help himself especially when the jerk actually shoved a condom in his pocket and gave Jason a conspiratorial wink.

Fuck it.

At that moment he didn't care if this sent her running for the hills and she slapped a restraining order on him, he was getting rid of the asshole.

"You're not here for Haley, are you?" he asked, pulling out the keg and setting it on the ground.

The man frowned. "Yeah, why?"

Jason made a show of cringing as he quickly looked back at Haley's house as if he was making sure that she wasn't watching them.

"I really don't think that's such a good idea," Jason mumbled.

"Why not?"

He gave the man an "Are you kidding?" look and had to stop himself from laughing as the man shifted nervously.

"Surely you know....," he said, purposely letting his words drift off.

"No, my friend set me up with her," he said, shooting a nervous glance towards Haley's house. Did the curtain just move?

Jason rubbed the back of his neck, sighing wearily. "It's really not my place, but I'm not sure this is such a good idea."

"What?" the man practically whined.

After a pause he shook his head. "I'm sorry, but I really don't like talking about it. All I can tell you is that you really need to be careful." He gave the man a pointed look as he stressed, *"Really careful."*

The man's eyes widened as his mouth dropped open. He took several steps back, shooting nervous glances towards Haley's house. When he reached his car he said, "I, uh, just suddenly remembered I have somewhere I'm supposed to be." With that he practically jumped into his car and sped away.

Jason chuckled as he made his way to Haley's front door. He knocked on the door and wasn't too surprised a moment later when there was no answer. He pushed aside his disappointment and knocked again.

Just great.

It seemed last night had been a fluke and his shy neighbor was here to stay. He really liked spending time with Haley last night, more than he thought possible. Feeling like an idiot, he headed back to his house and keg.

A loud, wet hacking cough had him pausing halfway down her small walkway. The front door slowly opened as Haley said, "I'm sorry I took so long," another hacking cough, "to answer," another cough, "the," cough, "door. But, the doctor said I was still," several loud and disturbing coughs later, "contagious, so I--Oh, it's only you," Haley said with a relieved sigh.

His lips twitched as he took in her outfit. On her head was one of the ugliest puke green knitted hats he'd ever seen. Her oversized ratty bathrobe was worse, but the large wadded up ball of tissues in her hand was a nice touch. There was no doubt in his mind that she was faking it considering that he'd hung out with her last night and she'd been the picture of health. Right now she looked well enough, just frumpy in those oversized ratty clothes.

"Love the hat," he said, smiling as he walked over to her.

Laughing, she pulled the offending hat off and chucked it at him. He caught it before it hit him in the face. "What's this all about?" he gestured towards her getup with the hat.

"Nothing," she said quickly.

"Looks like date repellant to me."

With an innocent doe-like expression she said, "I have no idea what you're talking about. I'm sick," cough, "really sick." And just to backup her story she sniffled.

It was sad, adorable, but sad.

He couldn't stop himself from rolling his eyes and chuckling. "I don't know why you can't just admit that you were ditching the love of your life. But, as much as I'd love to listen to your denial I'm afraid that I have to go since you're sick and all."

"I *am*," she stressed. "Really sick. I might very well be dying as we speak," she said as she pushed her cute little glasses back up her nose.

With a shrug, he took a step back towards his house. "That's a damn shame because I was hoping you'd come to my party today, but since you're sick......."

She pressed the back of her hand against her forehead. "Hmmm, what do you know? I'm all better. What time is the party?" she asked with the cutest shy smile he'd ever seen.

"Eight o'clock, you little faker," he said, chuckling when she let out an excited little squeal as she ran back into her house.

* * * *

Maybe this wasn't such a good idea, Haley thought as she stood on Jason's doorstep with a plate of brownies. With an inward groan she berated herself for being an idiot. What kind of geek brought brownies to a kegger? Okay, she was assuming that this was a kegger since she'd witnessed some rather scary behavior over the years during his little gatherings and never witnessed that type of behavior at any party or get-together she'd ever attended.

Some of the things she'd heard and seen had scared her, but some of it had intrigued her. Not that she'd ever admit it, but on more than one occasion she'd wondered what it would be like to go to one of Jason's parties, which is why she'd jumped at the chance today. Jason's parties had to be the equivalent of the parties the popular kids in high school used to throw and somehow forgot to invite Haley, but now she was about to rectify all that.

Maybe not, she thought, worrying her bottom lip as she looked down at the overflowing plate of brownies. She was going to look so stupid bringing brownies to a kegger. Figuring that probably no one heard her knocking over the loud music, she decided a quick stop at a package store was in order. She was just about to make her escape when the door opened.

"What do you want?" the woman glaring at her demanded. Haley frowned as she quickly took in the woman's sleek black hair, perfect features touched up by flawless make-up and the killer short dress and decided that she was severely underdressed for this party in her jeans and baby pink Yankees long sleeve tee-shirt.

Haley opened her mouth to make an excuse so she could leave, knowing she was in way over her head here, when the woman snorted.

"You're the next-door neighbor," the woman said, sounding amused. "What do you want?" Her eyes narrowed on the plate in Haley's hands.

"I just-"

"Amy, who is it?" Jason's voice came from somewhere behind the woman apparently named Amy.

Amy rolled her eyes. "It's just your neighbor dropping off brownies." She reached forward to take the plate from Haley. "I'll just take them so she can g-"

"Brownies?" Jason said, suddenly filling the door, causing Amy to stumble back out of the way.

"Hey!" Amy snapped, but Jason didn't seem to hear her. His eyes were glued to the plate.

"Are those," he noticeably swallowed, "brownies covered in peanut butter frosting?"

Did he just whimper?

"They're chocolate chunk fudge brownies with peanut butter frosting," she clarified automatically as her eyes caught the murderous glare Amy was sending her way. She was just about to hand the plate over to Jason and leave when everything in her stilled.

After last night she was through with getting pushed around and being intimidated. She was sick of missing out on things because she was too scared to do anything about it. She was a grown woman, damn it, and if she wanted to party it up at her first kegger then she was damn well going to do it and she was going to have fun doing it. Even if it killed her, and judging by the mascara glare being sent her way that was a good possibility.

"Let me just take those off your hands so you can grab yourself a beer," Jason said, taking the plate from her, gazing down at it lovingly as he stepped back inside the house, leaving Haley to follow him.

"Hey, those look good! Can I have one?" a man she'd seen hundreds of times around Jason's house asked, reaching out to take one.

"Back the fuck off! She brought them for me, you bastard!" Jason snapped.

Haley automatically took an anxious step back, fearing getting caught in the middle of the fight that was most definitely about to happen. But instead of yelling at Jason or getting mad like she'd seen a lot of guys do in bars over less, the man just rolled his eyes and turned his attention to her.

"Hi, my name is Brad," he said, holding out his hand.

After only a slight hesitation, she hoped he hadn't noticed, she took a step forward and shook his hand. "Haley."

"Haley, it's nice to meet you," he said with a charming smile. "I apologize for my friend's rudeness, he just learned how to walk upright last year," he said dryly, earning a soft chuckle from her and most everyone around them.

Jason threw him a dirty look before making his way towards the kitchen, making sure to glare at anyone that came within touching distance of the brownies.

Brad gestured towards the kitchen. "There's pizza, chips and plenty of drinks in there, as long as Jason doesn't get to it first, and a volleyball game going on in the backyard and of course video games in the living room until the game comes on. Make yourself at home," he said with a warm smile.

"Thank you," she murmured, taking it all in. This was it? she wondered as she took in the laidback party. Something must have shown on her face, because a few seconds later Brad leaned in. "Were you expecting *Animal House*?" he asked, chuckling.

"No!" she said quickly, too quickly. She had in fact been expecting something along those lines. She definitely hadn't pictured any of this. *This* she could definitely handle.

He chuckled. "Come on outback with me so I can introduce you to my wife," Brad said, smiling. "I promise you'll have a good time."

For the first time since she walked over here she thought she might just fit in with Jason's friends.

* * * *

"Who's the hottie kicking Mitch's ass?"

Without looking up from loading his plate with pizza he said, "Amy." At least he hoped it was Amy. Her clingy behavior was becoming annoying and he hadn't missed the bitch act she put on for Haley or the dirty looks she'd been sending his neighbor all night. He knew when he saw Amy heading towards his house earlier that he should have sent her away.

"No, the cute little thing with glasses."

Frowning, Jason looked up and followed Pete's eyes towards the couch where Haley was sitting next to Mitch, playing a game on the Xbox.

"She's my neighbor," he said, not liking the expression on Pete's face one bit.

"Is she here with anyone?" Pete asked, never taking his eyes off Haley.

"No."

"Good," Pete said, looking back over his shoulder, grinning. "I won't even bother asking to use your room since we can just mosey on over to her place."

Jason sighed heavily. It seemed he was going to have to save Haley from two douchebags in one day.

Pete turned to look at him. "What was that about?"

"What?" Jason asked innocently.

"That little sigh you just did," Pete said, gesturing lazily towards him.

"Nothing," he said with a shrug, returning his attention to piling food on his plate, "I just didn't think you were into that, that's all."

"Into what?" Pete demanded, sounding a little unsure. Considering the man's reputation, there probably wasn't much that he wasn't into, which was why Jason decided he would not do for his shy little neighbor. It took him five years to get Haley to climb out of her shell. He wasn't about to let this jackass send her back there for good.

"Just forget I said anything," Jason said, grabbing a cold soda from a cooler on the floor.

"But-"

"I don't want to get involved in this," Jason said, cutting him off. He moved to step past the man only to pause. "Just....just make sure she takes her medication and you should be safe, I mean fine." Jason quickly walked away before he burst into laughter at his friend's horrified expression.

Damn that felt good. He should have done that years ago when he spotted the first asshole sniffing around Haley. Did this make him her wingman? he pondered that as he walked over to the couch and shoved Mitch off so he could sit down next to his new little project. That was fine with him, he decided, because by the time he was done with her, she'd be living a much more entertaining and asshole free life.

Chapter 4

Haley took a deep breath and said, "I'm gay."

"You're gay?" the obnoxious guy who'd been sniffing around her and bugging the heck out of her in line for the past ten minutes repeated. "Are you sure?"

She bit back a laugh. The guy looked truly upset. She hated pulling out the gay card, mostly because she wasn't, but sometimes she had no choice. If he'd been nice when he was hitting on her she would have politely declined, but no, he had to be a complete pig the entire time.

He actually used the old line, "That dress looks great on you, but it will look even better crumpled on my bedroom floor in the morning." Yeah. It was truly sad, especially since they were in a coffee shop and it was barely half past seven in the morning. Between dirty comments, overcrowding her and staring at her breasts she was starting to get a little irritated. Plus his B.O. was really turning her stomach. If she didn't need a caffeine fix so badly she'd leave, but she did and couldn't or she was pretty sure she'd die.

Jason and some of the guys had been over last night to watch the game. Since it went into extra innings and she was a dedicated fan she stayed up until two in the morning and of course she had to watch the post game wrap up. With barely four hours of sleep, here she was, practically getting mauled by the poster boy for deodorant.

After three weeks it was still funny how she went from being completely intimidated by Jason to thinking of him as an oversized teddy bear. She felt silly for her behavior. Jason could still be a pain in the ass, but a really nice pain in the ass. He still "borrowed" things from her classroom, but now he left her funny notes that had her laughing until she was crying and scaring the heck out of her students.

She couldn't help but wonder how many good friendships she'd missed over the years because of her shyness. Part of it, of course was because after years of building up defenses she'd been judging people like Jason a little harshly. He was still a bit wild and a ridiculous flirt, but he was a big sweetie as well. He treated her like his buddy. It was actually rather nice to be treated like one of the guys. That being said though sometimes first impressions were dead on, like with her current problem.

"Yes, I'm sure."

He looked thoughtful for a moment. "Well, do you think the two of you would want to-"

"No," she said firmly.

"But what if I-"

"No."

"Come on, you won't let me finish. I have this camera-"

"No."

"It would be fun-"

"No."

"But what if-"

"She said no," Jason said as he cut in line and threw his arm around her shoulders in that lazy way of his.

"Hey! I thought you said you were gay!" the man said accusingly.

Without missing a beat Jason said, "She is. I'm just her bitch."

The man sent a narrowed glare at Jason's arm and then to her. He sent another glare at Jason and she could tell the man was deciding whether he wanted to push it any further. Based on the man's small size and Jason's large muscular build he wisely chose to drop it.

"So, what are you buying me this morning?" she asked Jason.

He scoffed. "Me? Why am I buying?"

"Because I helped you win fifty dollars off Brian last night."

He rolled his eyes. "I would have won it without your help."

"Uh huh," she said absently, stepping up to the counter to place her order. She added a chocolate chip muffin, knowing Jason was going to steal hers. He seemed to have a thing for stealing her food.

"I would have. I didn't need your help you know," he said more firmly.

She grabbed her order while he was waiting for his and headed for the door. "See ya."

"I won that bet on my own!" he called after her, making her smile. Sometimes he was like a big child. It was rather cute.

* * * *

Jason bit back a smile as he watched Haley tell Headmaster Jenkins that she couldn't chaperone the dance tonight. A month ago his shy friend would have simply stared at her coffee and nodded no matter what her plans were. Now, she was telling the man no, firmly yet gently.

He took some pride in it. It was because of him after all. It took some work, but she was coming along rather nicely. Who knew there was a little tigress beneath all that cuteness? He sure hadn't, but it was nice to see her stick up for herself for once. The staff might bitch at his methods and his easy going relationship with the kids, but at least he never ganged up on a woman like Haley and took advantage of her by making her chaperone this or organize that.

"But, Haley, we really need you to chaperone. John has tickets to a play tonight."

"I'm sorry, Tom, but I have plans already tonight. I really wish I could help you out, but I can't break my plans at the last minute. You understand," she said politely yet firmly.

Her self-esteem was clearly on the rise and it made the whole package even better and he wasn't the only one to notice either. Other teachers were showing her more respect and the men were definitely noticing her. Oh, he took a hundred percent of the credit for his little protégé. Yup, he was the master. It was probably about time that he used his greatness for good.

He spotted the table where she left her coffee and muffins as well as three men, losers in his opinion, who were eying the seat next to hers. Without any hesitation he sauntered past them and sat down at her table, earning killing glares from the other men. Too bad. In his opinion if a man didn't have the balls to make a move he didn't deserve the woman he desired. Not that he desired Haley. He didn't. She was his buddy and turning out to be one of his best friends. No, what he desired was that piping hot chocolate chip muffin with extra butter he saw her buy earlier.

He sighed happily as he fished the muffin out of the bag. "When will she ever learn?" he mumbled as prepared the stolen muffin.

"Please, help yourself," Haley said dryly as she sat down and added a sugar to her coffee.

"Thank you, I think I will," he said happily as he slathered more butter onto his muffin.

"What are these amazing plans you have for tonight?" he asked between bites.

"Date," she said.

"I guess that means our love affair is over," he said with a pout.

"I guess so."

"I'm hurt."

"You'll survive....with therapy of course," she said with a wink and a grin.

"Is this another loser?"

She looked away and mumbled something.

"I'm sorry I don't speak mumble," he said while eying the piping hot apple muffin with streusel topping that she just took out of the bag. Hell, how had he missed that delicious little morsel?

His hand seemed to have a life of its own as it crept towards that tasty little treat. With a gasp, Haley's hands came down to protect her muffin.

"Control yourself!" she hissed as she broke off a small chunk and ate it. His eyes went back to the muffin. He knew he was pouting when Haley rolled her eyes and continued to eat. Damn it, where was the love? He was a hungry man. With a sigh he opened his bag and pulled out one of his three coffee rolls and began eating all while keeping his eyes on that muffin.

"You're pathetic," Haley muttered with an eye roll. She pushed the last half of her muffin over to him. With a huge grin he popped the large half into his mouth and savored it. It really was as good as it looked.

"So, what is it that you don't want me to know, my little grasshopper?" he asked, stirring his coffee. The last date she had was a loser in his opinion at least and really, wasn't that all that mattered? The loser was not worthy of all his work. They'd work on that until she dated guys that he approved of. Someone cool with a cabin in New Hampshire for fishing trips or a house down in Florida would make him very happy. He really could go for some deep sea fishing in the winter.

"Stop calling me that!" Haley hissed softly. "For the hundredth time, I am not the Daniel-son to your Mr. Miyagi."

He simply shrugged. "If that's what you want to believe…"

"It is and I do."

"If I could get everyone's attention before you head off to homeroom?" Jenkins said, holding up his clipboard to get everyone's attention in the teacher's break room. "We need one more volunteer for tonight's dance," he said, throwing a hopeful glance Haley's way.

"Wax on…..wax off…." Jason whispered, earning a rather indelicate snort form Haley.

"Did you say something, Miss Blaine?" Jenkins asked Haley, drawing everyone's attention to her.

Jason leaned back in his seat and watched Haley as the blush crept up her cute little face. She nervously pushed her glasses up her nose. Ah, seems his protégé still hated drawing attention to herself. Well, she'd have to get used to that if they were going to be friends since he had a rather nasty habit of drawing attention to himself pretty much everywhere he went.

"Yes, Miss Blaine, did you have something to say?" Jason asked in an amused tone.

She shot him a narrowed glare before turning to look at Jenkins. The glare was gone only to be replaced by a rather sweet and innocent smile. He was so focused on her smile that he almost missed what she said.

"No, Mr. Jenkins, that wasn't me. Mr. Bradford was volunteering to chaperone tonight," she said cheerfully.

"What?" he said, too late.

Jenkins grinned at him. "Well, that's excellent! Very good. Make sure you're here by seven o'clock and it goes until eleven. Thank you, Mr. Bradford." Jenkins said. It didn't escape Jason's notice that the man didn't bother double checking with him and that he practically ran out of the room before Jason could refuse.

His attention immediately turned to the little traitor. "You betraying bitch," he gasped.

Her smile went from innocent to wicked in less than a second. "Have fun at the dance." She stood up and placed her hands together in front of her as if she were praying and bowed.

Smartass.

She betrayed him. Damn that hurt. He couldn't help but grin. She really was coming along rather nicely.

* * * *

"Oh God, I love him!" the girl, Cindy or something, wailed loudly, making Jason shift nervously. He'd never dealt well with emotions, especially female emotions. He looked around nervously and damn near sighed with relief when he spotted a small group of girls descend on the girl.

"He's such a jerk!" one of them said.

"Don't say that! I love him!" Cindy cried.

"Oh, I know you do. He's not good enough for you," a slightly chubby girl said as she put her arm around the girl.

Good. Everything was fine. He could go back to chaperoning a bunch of hormone driven teenagers to god-awful music. Yup, he was truly going to kill Haley. He stepped away.

"Mr. Bradford, why would he do this to me?" the girl demanded.

He froze mid-step and looked around nervously, hoping another Mr. Bradford was standing close by and willing to handle this. No such luck.

He cleared his throat. "Do what exactly?"

She scoffed at him with a look of utter disbelief that told him that she thought he should be very aware of everything in her life. Considering he'd never paid much attention to any woman's life, she was in for a hell of a rude awakening. Thankfully, one of her friends took pity on him.

"Marc Griswold. They ate at the same table two times in the last two weeks, he talked to her during study hall, and asked to borrow her notes. Now he's here with *her*," she said with such distaste that he couldn't help but follow her glare.

He spotted Marc dancing with a very pretty brunette. Her name he remembered, Janie. She was a smart girl and funny as hell. If memory served him correctly, Marc had been in love with the girl for the last two years. The poor guy who was normally so sure of himself and easy going turned into a stuttering fool when the girl was around. He'd been wondering when the kid was going to work up the courage to finally ask her out.

"Hmmm, good for him," he mumbled, earning a collective gasp of outrage.

"How could you, Mr. Bradford?" the girl wailed even louder, making him cringe.

Oh, he was going to kill Haley for this shit.

* * * *

"I had a really nice time," Jonathan said, probably for the tenth time.

Haley forced herself to smile and of course lie. "I did, too," she said, hoping he wouldn't ask her to elaborate on what she found nice, because she would be hard pressed to find something nice about this evening, except of course that it was nice that it was ending.

This was absolutely the very last time she went on a date with any man Mary, one of her oldest and dearest friends, suggested. One would think after Mary set her up with the taxidermist who cross dressed she would have learned her lesson, apparently not because somehow she agreed to go out with this loser.

It didn't start off badly. In fact, he was on time and she thought he was rather cute in a nerdish way. He was tall, a bit thin, but still, he looked nice. His clothes were clean and he smelled good. The first clue that something just wasn't right occurred when they made it to the restaurant.

That's when his mother called for the first time. Yes, the first time, as in there was more than one call from his mother. In fact, during their four hour date, it lasted that long because he took so long to eat, she called a total of twenty-three times. Yes, she was very sure it was his mother since he sat at the table when he took the calls and the speaker on his phone was rather loud.

The reasons for the calls ranged from, she missed him, wanted to know if he'd rather come home and eat what she cooked, reminded him to clean his room tomorrow, and her personal favorite, she wanted to know if he was still with *"her"*. Judging by her tone and the amount of calls, his mommy was not a happy camper about her little boy dating. Granted her little boy was thirty-five years old and according to him had never lived on his own. Why would he when he lived with his best friend? Meaning, mommy dearest. Of course, he did spend a good amount of time complaining about how unfair his mother could be. Who knew that a thirty-five year old man could still be grounded for not picking up his dirty socks? She certainly hadn't.

She could not wait to get inside her house and change into a pair of jeans and a tee shirt and have a good laugh about this with Jason. That is of course, only if Jason had forgiven her for her little jest earlier. Hence the large piece of chocolate cake with peanut butter frosting in the doggy container she was currently holding. Jason was a big baby, but a big baby that could be bought with food.

"Well, here we are," she said brightly as they pulled into her driveway. "It's been fun. Thank you again," she said quickly as she practically ran from the car.

"This is a really nice house," he said, from somewhere close, too close. Haley looked back and bit back the curse that threatened to leave her lips. The man was following her to the door. She wanted to cry, really, she did. When would this nightmare end?

She walked up to her door and plastered another fake smile on her face. "Well, thanks again."

"You're welcome." He gave her a shy smile before he leaned in to kiss her. Thankfully she saw that one coming and turned her head in time to receive a rather wet kiss on her cheek. Ew....

She barely stopped herself from wiping her face. She'd scrub that off in a matter of minutes in a scalding hot shower.

"Oops. Sorry," he mumbled as he leaned in to give her another kiss.

Faster than even she thought was possible, she had the front door unlocked and opened. She stumbled back, saving herself from more slobber.

"Well, it's been nice but-"

"Can I come in for a cup of coffee?" he asked eagerly and then of course had to add, "I can stay out as late as I want tonight." Oh, she knew he was lying. Someone was going to be in so much trouble when he got home. She mentally *tsked* him.

She opened her mouth to politely refuse when the yelling began.

"Help me!"

Haley jumped. What the hell? It sounded like Jason was right in her house.

"Help me, please! Somebody please help me! Why won't somebody help me?"

"What's that?" Jonathan asked nervously.

Haley didn't stop to answer. She was already running towards the direction of the screaming. Her room? She threw the door open and nearly tripped as she came to a halt five feet into the room which put her right in front of her bed.

"What the hell...." Jonathan stopped behind her.

"Oh, thank God you're here, Haley!" Jason said, sounding happy for someone who was tied to her bed, wearing only a pair of boxers. "I know you said it turns you on knowing I'm tied to your bed waiting for you, but I really need to use the bathroom and stretch my legs before we begin....," his voice trailed off when he caught sight of Jonathan.

Jason sighed dramatically. "I thought we agreed that you would tell me ahead of time before you added someone to our bed." With a roll of his eyes he said, "It's fine this time. Lucky for you I think we have plenty of lube." He looked thoughtfully at Jonathan, who was still staring at Jason dumbly. "I hope you're not a screamer. The last guy screamed his head off every time I-"

"You're sick!" Jonathan cried, cutting Jason off. "Stay away from me and don't try to call me either. I'm telling my mother about you!"

Haley didn't spare Jonathan a glance as she glared at the man with the huge shit eating grin tied to her bed. She was vaguely aware of her front door slamming shut and the sound of tires peeling out of her driveway.

"Is that for me?" Jason asked, looking pointedly at the styrofoam container in her hands.

"Mmmhmm," she said as she walked around the bed and placed the container on his chest and opened it. She didn't miss his eyes widening in pleasure.

"Is that-"

"Peanut butter frosting, yup," she finished for him.

He licked his lips as he stared at the huge dessert. "You are the best, ever. Untie me so I can dig in," he said absently as he continued to stare at the cake, probably trying to decide which end he was going to attack first.

"You can't get free?"

"Nope."

"You did this yourself?"

"Yup. Now cake, woman."

"Uh huh....." She stepped away from the bed and headed for the bathroom.

"Wait, where are you going?"

"I'm just getting something to untie you with."

"Hurry."

"Sure thing," she said, glad he couldn't see her shit eating grin.

Chapter 5

"I said shut up!" Jason snapped as he stole the ball from Brad, his oldest friend, and tossed the basketball into the hoop.

Brad wiped the tears off his cheeks as he struggled to stop laughing. He failed miserably and fell to his knees when he was no longer able to stand.

"Shut up!"

"I can't….I can't….believe….she….shaved….your legs!" Brad said between gasps and laughter. The bastard. Thankfully Jason was wearing a shirt to cover up his now hairless chest and armpits. Oh, she was going to pay for this.

"She ate my cake, too!" Jason said, which in his mind was the more serious betrayal. She wouldn't even let him lick the spoon clean and he had asked, several times. Damn tease. That cake had smelled so good. His stomach rumbled just from thinking about it.

"Man, for someone so obsessed with food you're lucky you're not fat," Brad said as he continued to struggle with his laughter. Thankfully he was now able to stand so Jason could kick his ass in this game.

"It's not luck. I have a high metabolism and I work out," he said, taking another shot.

"How long did she keep you tied up?"

Jason shot a glare at the man. "I don't know why you find this so funny. You're supposed to be my best friend. This should outrage you that someone would take advantage of me like that. Where's your loyalty?"

Brad abruptly stopped laughing and arched a brow. "You hired two strippers at my bachelor party to give me a Brazilian bikini wax when I passed out."

Jason chuckled. Oh, that had been a very good night indeed. In fact, he was pretty sure that he had the pictures around somewhere in his house. During the entire ceremony Brad fidgeted at the altar while he tried to discretely scratch himself. From what Jason heard his wife loved it so much she'd been after Brad to have it done again. To say Brad was reluctant to allow hot wax near his goods again, was an understatement.

"Nothing you can bitch about will be any worse than what you've done to everyone else over the years. In fact, I believe Haley is now my hero."

"She's dead to me," he said with a sniff.

"Uh huh," Brad said, stealing the ball and making a shitty shot.

"What's that supposed to mean?" Jason demanded, taking the ball back.

Brad shrugged. "It just seems that you like her."

"I do like her," he said easily before adding, "When she's not betraying me she's my buddy."

"She's a very hot buddy in a very cute way I would say," Brad added.

"There is that, too," Jason said, dribbling the ball. "It's nice to have eye candy around for my enjoyment." He looked Brad over. "It wouldn't kill you to pretty yourself up if you're going to be in my presence."

"Yeah, I'll get right on that," Brad said wryly.

"See that you do."

After a few minutes of playing, Brad asked, "So, is there anything going on between you and Haley?"

Jason just barely held back a laugh. "Come on! She's my buddy. I don't see her that way!"

"Uh huh."

"I don't."

"Sure."

Jason shoved the ball at Brad. "What the hell is that supposed to mean?"

Brad shrugged as he took another shot. "Nothing. Just noticed how you watch her sometimes."

"Oh? Enlighten me. How do I watch her?"

Brad looked down at the ball as he bounced it once, twice, and then looked up. "Like you want to devour her from top to bottom and you'd kill anyone who got in your way."

Jason snorted. Then for good measure he snorted again. "No, I don't."

"Yes, you do."

"It's all in your head."

"Whatever you say," Brad said easily, pissing Jason off more.

He didn't want Haley. He didn't look at her in any special way. She was his friend, his buddy, his amigo and he saw her as that and not some tasty morsel he wanted to devour. Okay, so yeah, she was hot and those glasses made her look utterly adorable and he noticed that she had really nice legs and big breasts that he was sure would cradle his head very nicely, but who wouldn't notice that? She was also short, which made him protective of her, and he liked putting his arm around her, because she felt good against his side and fit perfectly under his arm. So what? It didn't mean anything more than friendship.

"Oh, here comes the object of your desire now," Brad said, chuckling.

"Shut up!" Jason snapped before he turned his attention to Haley, who was in a new green silk blouse and a dark skirt. It looked like she was going to work, not hanging out on a Sunday. She held a foil covered plate in front of her.

"You look nice. Where are you off to?" Brad asked.

Haley sighed, "Barbeque."

Both men gaped as they looked her over. "You're going to a barbeque like that?" Brad asked. Jason kept his thoughts to himself since he still wasn't speaking to her. Who went to a barbeque like that? What happened to jeans and a tee shirt or a tank top? Clearly they still had much to work on.

"Family barbeque, don't ask," she said before turning her attention to Jason. "Are you still mad at me?"

He grunted before walking off.

"Oh, come on! I eventually let you go!" He flipped her off without looking back. "Come on! That cake wasn't half as yummy as it looked. It left me uncomfortably full!" she yelled, earning a laugh from Brad and a second one finger salute from Jason.

"What do you have there?" Brad asked.

Haley sighed as she pulled back the foil, revealing large chocolate chunk cookies. "I made these for the big baby so he would stop his little tantrum."

"Wow, those look really good! Can I have one?"

She shrugged. "Sure, since the baby doesn't want one."

Brad picked up a cookie and brought it up to his mouth. It was inches away when a large tan hand grabbed it. Jason snatched the plate from her before sending Brad a killing glare.

"How dare you touch my cookies, you bastard!" Jason said in utter disgust before popping the cookie into his mouth and heading back to his house.

"Damn those looked good, too," Brad grumbled.

Haley sighed. "Don't worry I have a second plate on my counter." The words were barely out of her mouth when Jason abruptly changed course and headed towards her house.

"Well, there was," she said, watching Jason walk into her house like he owned it. A minute later he walked out of her house, carrying both plates and the gallon of milk she had in her fridge. He headed back to his house, but not before he glared at Brad. "You cookie thieving bastard," they heard him mutter.

Brad rolled his eyes, chuckling. "And people wonder how I lost weight rooming with him in college."

Haley just laughed as she locked up her house and headed for her car. For a moment there she forgot the hell that awaited her.

* * * *

She ignored the glare of the parking attendant as she pulled around her parent's mansion and parked her own car. She tried not to roll her eyes, but she just couldn't stop herself. Leave it up to her parents to go overboard for a family barbeque.

Why they bothered, she would never know. It wasn't like the rest of their family didn't know they were rich. It wasn't like the rest of the family wasn't also rich. They were always trying to prove they were the best and richest. Kind of pathetic if you asked her, no one did of course. She was just expected to show up at family functions, act perfect and bite her tongue. Yup, this was going to be so much fun.

For the next four hours, and that was the time her mother told her she absolutely had to stay or she'd throw a fit to end all fits, Haley was going to have to endure looks of pity over her marital status, childless state, job, and looks. Yup, this was going to be great, just great.

Why couldn't her damn reliable car have stalled on the way over here or better yet, run out of gas leaving her stranded at the mercy of the wildlife that would maul her and save her from this hell? Was it really too much to ask?

She ran a hand over her shirt to smooth it down as she approached the front door. Before she could knock, the door was opened. Jameson, their snotty butler of ten years, looked distastefully down his nose at her.

"Your mother expected you a half an hour ago, Miss Blaine," he said with a sniff. It hadn't escaped her notice that he called her sisters by their first names and even smiled when he did it.

She wasn't about to stand here and argue with the man. "Where is she?"

Another sniff. "Madam is in the backyard. She's very exhausted. She's been working day and night on this barbeque. She was up at the crack of dawn and hasn't rested since!"

"Uh huh," Haley said absently as she walked past a lot of people she didn't know. Funny how family barbeques in her family really meant bringing everyone they wanted to impress or schmooze. It seemed she was the only one that hadn't brought an entourage. She had friends that she really cared about and could have brought, but well, it was because she cared about them that she couldn't inflict this upon them.

"Haley, so nice to see you!" her cousin Jacob said. "You should come to the Vineyard this summer and stay at my new cottage. It's fabulous, you'll love it!" he said loud enough to draw attention to himself. She had no doubt that it was the for the benefit of the crowd around him considering he absolutely hated her. It might have something to do with her putting Nair in his shampoo when they were kids. Ah, whatever.

She simply gave that fake smile her mother drilled into her head and made her way to the backyard where she found her mother working hard at sipping a Martini and gossiping with her sisters, a few aunts, and her grandmother snoozing in a wheelchair a few feet away under her own umbrella.

Her father, brothers-in-laws, several uncles, cousins and men she didn't recognize sat on the opposite end of the large brick patio that spanned the entire length of the mansion. On the lawn, professional caterers were barbequing on huge gas grills while others set up food on tables and chairs around tables that now covered a small portion of the ten acre backyard.

It didn't surprise her that there were no kids at the family barbeque and to suggest bringing a child here would send her mother into a snit. A social queen her mother definitely was, a mother and grandmother? Not even a little bit. She was hardly there for their childhood. Why do it when she could pay someone else was her mother's motto. Nannies and maids raised her and her siblings until the age of ten when they each in turn went to a private year round boarding school. From then on it was obvious they were only guests in this house.

Some might think it was a pathetic upbringing and to a point she would agree. Since her parents only saw children as an accessory they really had no business having them. It would have been a horrible childhood if her grandparents hadn't bought a house close to her school the first week and took Haley to live with them. Thanks to her grandparents she had a wonderful childhood. She loved the life her grandparents had given her, which is one of the reasons why, at eighteen she took over her life and decided to pursue her own dreams instead of following in her family's footsteps.

"Oh, Haley! There you are, dear!" her mother said cheerfully. Was she trying to smile? Yup, it appeared she had Botox done once again. Her whole face looked completely frozen.

"Hello, mother," she said, giving her mother a barely there kiss on the cheek as her mother gave her one.

"Have a seat, dear!" Her mother gestured to the seat next to her. Haley's sisters, Martha and Rose gave her smirks as they picked up glasses or fluffed back their hair in attempts to show off whatever new trinket their husbands, more likely husbands' secretaries, bought them.

"It's so nice to see you, Haley," Rose said with a cool smile as she jiggled her diamond bracelet.

"It's nice to see you too, Rose. How are your children?" Haley asked.

Rose gave her a rather bland look. "How would I know?"

Haley opened her mouth to point out that they were in fact her children, but decided against it.

Martha leaned in, trying to look discreet. The fact that she raised her voice kind of wrecked the effect. "You poor thing! I see the diet didn't work." She pouted. "Did you get dumped again?" She shook her head as if it was of no consequence and pulled out a business card that she probably had ready for this moment. "Here's the name of a good doctor who does wonders with removing fat and cosmetic surgery."

Still smiling, Haley accepted the card. Since she'd lost a few pounds in the last couple of weeks and didn't consider herself fat, especially since her stomach was flat, she knew her sister was delicately as ever pointing out that Haley was not stick thin like the rest of them. Flat breasts and looking skeletal was in apparently. Since she would never look like them or want to, she simply left the business card on the table.

She had no problem with how she looked. She was comfortable with her curves. In fact, she had the same body type as her grandmother had when she was younger. The same grandmother out cold in her wheelchair and the one that everyone here, but her, feared to piss off. She could be a little hellion to deal with. They all looked down on her for her middleclass ways, forgetting that it was her hard work and sacrifices that made the family what it is today.

"You know they can reduce those things these days," Rose said distastefully, pulling Haley from her thoughts.

"What things?" Haley asked, distracted by one of her cousins eying their grandmother like a vulture. She had no doubt he was counting her breaths. Hell, the little prick was mouthing the words. These people were pathetic.

"Your breasts, dear. They're….well….they're so lower class. They make you look like a waitress or something," her aunt said sympathetically.

"I think you would look great with less….curves," Rose added.

Smile. "I'll keep it in mind, thank you. Now, if you'll excuse me."

"Oh, wait, dear!" her mother said, holding up her hand. "I wanted to ask you how your little hobby was going."

Her little hobby, meaning her job. Smile. "It's going great. Thank you for asking. We'll be breaking for the summer in two months. I'm thinking of traveling, or renting a cabin in New Hampshire for a few weeks."

"Honestly, dear, I don't know why you do it. If you're so determined to work you should go back to school and get a real degree in law or medicine like your father. Is it because you're trying to meet a man?" her mother asked, sounding hopeful.

Smile. "No, I'm not looking for a man. I enjoy what I do."

Her mother's answer was a frown; well it looked like she was trying to frown. Actually, everyone at the table was frowning now. They couldn't understand why she worked since none of them had ever worked a day in their lives. Personally, she thought the whole bunch was rather spoiled and she was wondering why she came here in the first place. Then she remembered. She came here for Grandma. She couldn't leave Grandma to these vultures and it didn't hurt that Grandma threatened to take her over her knee and spank her if she didn't show up.

"Sweetheart!" her father said, smiling hugely as he leaned over and kissed her on both cheeks. Smile. "Happy Birthday, sweetheart. I'm sorry it's a couple of weeks late," he said sheepishly.

"Thank you, Dad," she said, taking the birthday card. Smile. Her birthday had been five months ago. Yes, her entire family had forgotten, well except Grandma of course. She called at five in the morning, waking Haley up on her birthday, demanding that Haley should knock some sense into her parents. Haley calmed her down and thanked her for the gift she'd sent the day before. The next day she went and saw Grandma. Her old nannies sent her birthday cards and gifts. Her friends made her a dinner and they went out, so it was okay.

"I can't believe my little baby is twenty-five already!" he said.

"I know." She couldn't believe it either since she was twenty-nine, but hey if he wanted to make her younger who was she to argue?

"She's twenty-nine, you fool!" Grandma said. "She turned twenty-nine in December. How I raised fools is beyond me," Grandma grumbled.

Smile. "Thanks, Dad. It's fine."

His smile wavered and for the first time in her life he truly looked embarrassed and ashamed.

"I'm going to call you later this week," he said firmly.

"Dad, it's okay," she said, letting him off the hook.

"No, it's not," he said before he forced the fake smile back and turned to respond to someone calling his name.

"Honestly, Haley. There is no need to create such drama over nonsense," her mother said, trying to save face. Everyone sent her mother pitying looks and eye rolls at Haley as if it was Haley's fault for simply living.

Smile. "Sorry, if you'll excuse me," she said, taking her card with her and sticking it in her purse. She walked over to her grandmother and sat down.

Grandma huffed. "I don't know why you put up with such nonsense."

"It's fine."

"The hell it is!"

For the first time since she arrived, she let out a real smile.

"Deborah, what are we eating today?" Grandma demanded of Haley's mother, her least favorite daughter-in-law.

Her mother smiled, well tried to smile. "We're having Salmon with broiled spinach leaves, a nonfat mock potato salad and some nonfat sugarless flourless soy French delicacies that are simply to die for."

Grandma's eyes narrowed dangerously as her hand went for the cane. Haley discretely wrestled the cane away from her grandmother.

"Hey, that's mine!" Grandma snapped as Haley put the cane next to her chair, away from Grandma, while rubbing the back of her hand. Damn, Grandma had a firm grip.

"Behave," Haley hissed, making Grandma smile. Out of all the children and grandchildren, Haley was the only one who treated Grandma as a human and not an old responsibility they got stuck with.

Grandma turned her attention back to Deborah. "I want a burger, a hot dog and some real potato salad."

"Mother dearest, we simply don't have that here!" she said as if the very idea of having such basic food items in her house was unheard of.

Grandma glared at her for a moment longer before turning her attention to Haley. "You?"

"Me what?"

"You have those things in your house, don't you?"

Haley nodded. "Yes." In fact her freezer and pantry were filled to the brim with staples for barbeques since she lived for barbeque food in the summer, probably had something to do with Grandma raising her. The woman simply lived for barbeque food.

"Good," Grandma said firmly as she gestured to Chris, her helper. The man was just entering his fifties, but he still worked hard to take care of Grandma. "Let's go, Chris."

Chris nodded and walked over obediently and began pushing Grandma around the house. Without looking back Grandma said, "Let's go, Haley!"

Haley stood. "Go where?"

"To your house. Where else? Now come along before the parasites try to crash our party."

Haley hid her smile as she obediently followed her grandmother out the door. No wonder she absolutely adored the old woman.

Chapter 6

"I'm hungry," Jason grumbled as he stared at the empty plates on his small coffee table.

Brad groaned, "You practically ate both plates of cookies. How in the hell are you hungry?"

Jason shrugged leaning back in his chair to watch the game. "I just am. Leave me the hell alone! I'm a growing boy, damn it!"

"Yeah, a growing thirty-one year old boy," Brad mumbled.

"I'm still growing damn it so shut the hell up and feed me!"

"Order something and stop bitching!" Brad snapped.

"You order something. I'm too weak to move."

Brad rolled his eyes. "I don't know how Haley put up with you for the last few weeks. I would have killed you by now."

"Haley worships me," he said with a snort.

"Yeah, okay," Brad said, laughing. "That's why she dates other men and screws you over just to laugh at you."

"Exactly."

Brad looked over at him. "You are a seriously fucked up man, aren't you?"

"Probably," Jason said unconcerned.

"I thought so."

A soft knock at the door drew both their attention. Brad cringed. "This isn't another one of your girlfriends coming for revenge is it?"

Jason rolled his eyes as he jumped to his feet. "I think calling any of them my girlfriend is a bit of an exaggeration. I rather you stick with referring to them as 'the women who agreed to having a good time with no strings attached who got really pissed off at me when I got bored and left them for someone hotter.'"

"Wow, that's a mouthful," Brad murmured. "And surprisingly none of them has killed you yet."

"It is, isn't it," Jason agreed.

He opened the door, knowing no angry ex-lovers would be there. It had been a while since he took a woman to bed and to the best of his knowledge all the previous women already told him off. So, at least for now he was good.

Standing outside his door was Haley in a cute pair of cut off jean shorts and a tank top. Her hair was pulled back into a messy loose bun and some of the strands escaped and teased her nape. It didn't hurt that those glasses of hers made her look like a sexy little bookworm.

She smiled sweetly. "I am so glad you're here!" He couldn't bite back the smile from that declaration. Maybe it was time to forgive her. It was pretty funny after all and those cookies were damn good, not to mention that smile she was giving him made him happy.

"Brad, do you think you could give me a hand? I could really use a man's help for a few minutes."

His jaw dropped. He could hear Brad trying to stifle his laughter.

"If you need a man, I'm right here!" he snapped.

Haley blinked and then blinked again. "Oh, sorry I didn't think of you. I need a guy with muscle and you...." Her voice trailed off while she looked him over and then shrugged. "Well, you know," she said innocently.

"Know what?" he demanded.

She ignored him and focused back on Brad. "Do you think you could give me a hand? I'm having company and I can't get the barbeque out by myself. It's kind of heavy." Brad chuckled as he came to the door. "Sure. I was on my way home, but I can give you a hand since there's no one around here strong enough to help you," he said, sounding amused with a twinkle in his eyes.

"The hell you will!" Jason said as he grabbed Haley's arm and practically dragged her towards her house. She threw a wink over her shoulder to Brad, who was still laughing and shaking his head in disbelief.

Brad strolled to his car while Jason gave Haley a lecture on his manliness and something about her being a bad grasshopper, whatever the hell that meant. He looked back over in time to catch Jason giving Haley's ass an appreciative look without breaking from his lecture. His buddy might not know it yet, but he met his match in that little lady. If any woman could bring Jason to his knees it was that woman.

* * * *

"That's not enough," Jason scoffed as Haley tried to put away the package of frozen hamburger patties and hot dogs.

"There are only three of us. How much food do you think we need?" she asked as she tried to sidestep him to put the food away. Jason swiped the packages from her and took out more food.

"What the hell?"

He shrugged. "I'm hungry."

"You're not invited."

"Since when do I need an invitation?" he asked as he doubled the amount of hot dogs on the plate.

"Three weeks and we already have a set history? For five years I contemplated manslaughter."

He merely shrugged.

She growled.

He smiled, making her knees tremble. Damn him.

"Tell me who's coming? It can't be any of your friends because you wouldn't care if I was here since they all think I'm a prick and you get a kick out of watching them bitch me out."

She sighed. "It entertains me so."

"As it should. I am a very entertaining guy," he said with a smile as he snuck a forkful of the potato salad she made yesterday. She considered bringing it with her today, but she knew how well it would have been received and decided to leave it here.

"Damn, that's good, woman," he practically growled.

"I'm glad you like it," she said casually, but in truth it was really nice to have someone to cook for occasionally. Her friends were constantly on diets and glared at her when she offered them cookies or other baked goods. It seemed Jason hadn't found a food that he didn't like. She really was surprised that he wasn't fat.

"So?"

"So what?"

"So, tell me why you stayed less than an hour at one barbeque only to come home to have one of your own? Food suck or something?" he asked while sneaking another bite of the salad before she returned it to the fridge. "Or was there a family smack down?"

"It's complicated," she finally said.

"What's so complicated about a family barbeque?"

"Just drop it. My grandmother is coming here with her helper. Actually, she should be here by now, but knowing her she stopped at the grocery store to get all her favorites."

His brows flew up. "Your grandmother's coming here? I didn't think any of your family ever came to visit you."

She gave him a sly smile. "Been spying on me have you?"

"Not really. I just picked up on things. I'm an observant guy after all."

"Well, my grandmother comes here several times a year. I usually invite her when I know you'll be out of town."

"Afraid I'll embarrass you?" he asked teasingly.

"Nope. Afraid she might kill you."

"Puhlease, she'll love me. Every woman loves and wants me," he said sincerely.

She chuckled softly. "I'm glad to see you're so humble."

"That I am," he said as Haley began to load his arms up with plates of food to take out to the grill. "So, you mentioned inviting her down. I'm guessing you're close to her."

"I am. She raised me off and on until I was ten and then took over full time," she said, opening the screen door for him. "Anyway, I decided to cut my visit to my parent's home short today."

"Why?"

"Because I told her to. That's why," a woman's crisp voice said.

Jason looked up to see an old woman in a wheelchair being pushed towards them by a wiry man with thinning gray hair. By the look of the man he was Haley's grandmother's helper or caregiver.

"Are you my Haley's boyfriend?" her grandmother demanded. Wow, she was a no nonsense woman. Just like Haley, once she was out of her shell of course.

* * * *

Haley felt her face burn as she waited for the earth to open beneath her and drag her under. Prayed for it was more like it.

"No, Grandma, he's not my boyfriend. He's my friend from next door."

Grandma's eyes narrowed on Jason. Haley was about to tell her grandmother to cut it out. That look had sent many friends and boyfriends running scared, but to her complete surprise Jason didn't cower.

He reached over and shook her hand. "My name is Jason Bradford. I'm the neighbor from hell."

Grandma's lips twitched. She looked over at her companion. "Chris, be a dear and go get the items we picked up."

"Yes, ma'am," he said, leaving Grandma with them. He sent Haley a smile before he hurried away. No doubt he was expecting Grandma to tear into Jason. Hell, that's exactly what she was waiting for.

"You also work with my granddaughter, Mr. Bradford. Isn't that correct?"

Without asking, Jason pushed Grandma carefully to the table and locked the chair. "Yup, I make her life a living hell there as well."

"You sound proud," Grandma noted.

Jason walked over to the grill and started placing the meat on it. "I am," he said, smiling.

Grandma did something she'd only heard when it was just the two of them. She laughed. It was soft and musical and immediately brought memories of a happy childhood to her mind, making her smile in return. Jason caught her eye and winked.

"I like you," Grandma announced.

"Thank you, Mrs.-"

"You may call me Grandma," she said in a tone that let him know she would not tolerate him calling her anything else.

Haley sat there stunned. She was the only one allowed to call her Grandma. The rest of the grandchildren called her grandmother when they started to take after their parents.

"Okay, Grandma it is," Jason said with an easy smile. Wow, the man really did have a way with women.

Chris stepped out from the house, no doubt where he just put away an enormous amount of groceries that had nothing to do with a barbeque. It was one of Grandma's sneaky ways of helping her out since she refused to accept financial help from her family. Grandma had her ways.

"I'm sorry to interrupt, ma'am, but it seems some of the guests from the last barbeque have followed us here," Chris said softly.

"Who is it?" Haley asked.

"Your cousins and a few aunts. I believe one or both of your sisters as well, Miss Haley," Chris said.

Grandma waved a dismissive hand towards the front of the house. "Well, they can leave because there isn't enough food," she said even though she hadn't looked at the grill.

"I can put some more on if you want," Jason offered.

"No!" Haley and Grandma said at once, startling Jason.

Chris cleared his throat. "They're rather insistent about joining, ma'am."

"Tell them to go away or I'll write them out of my will in the morning," Grandma said firmly.

Chris hid his smile as he turned to do just that.

Jason gave them all a curious look before shrugging. Apparently he really didn't care enough to be bothered, which was a good thing for her. She earned her way in life and didn't want anyone thinking any differently. All her friends knew she came from money and none of them cared. She was just Haley to them and she planned to keep it that way.

"What did you think of your father's birthday gift, Haley?" Grandma asked.

Jason frowned. "I missed your birthday?"

"It was months ago," Haley said with a shrug.

"He just remembered today?" Jason asked in disbelief.

"It's no big deal," Haley said, giving him a tight smile.

Jason scoffed. "If you say so."

"I do."

"Fine."

"*Fine.*"

"Ah, children? If I may interrupt? Haley, have you looked at your gift?" Grandma asked.

"Not yet." There was no rush. She already knew what was in there since her father thought she was twenty-five there would be twenty-five hundred dollar bills in an unsigned card.

"Well, go get it," Grandma said.

With a sigh, she went into the house, rolling her eyes at the overfilled bags of groceries that covered her kitchen counters and retrieved the envelope from her purse. She carried it out and sat down with it.

"Well, open it!" Grandma said.

"Why are you so eager for me to see this gift?" Haley asked suspiciously.

"Because I'm the one that suggested your gift," she said with a dismissive wave of her hand.

Haley bit her lip so she wouldn't cry. Not only had her father forgotten her birthday, but Grandma had to be the one to finally remind him and most likely ordered her gift.

She opened the card and wasn't too surprised to see the card wasn't signed. Surprise, surprise. Her eyes shifted to the gift and froze there. It was a full minute before she began breathing again. In another ten seconds she was up and around the table, hugging her grandmother and kissing her.

"You are the best, ever!" Haley said between kisses.

Grandma laughed. "I'm glad you like it. I wanted to give those to you but you're so damn stubborn about no one helping you so I used your father's stupidity. Now you have to accept them," Grandma said with a firm nod.

* * * *

Jason stood up and flipped the burgers before he added the hot dogs. He turned back in time to see Haley jumping up and down and giggling like a school girl.

"Well, don't leave me in suspense," he said, earning a loud squeal from Haley.

Apparently she was beyond words, so she pushed the card into his hands. He looked down, blinked and blinked again, before stumbling back into a chair. Did he just wet himself? Ah, who cared? He was holding four tickets to the Yankees vs. Red Sox at Yankee Stadium for this Friday and they were without a doubt the best seats in the stadium.

His eyes shifted from Haley to the tickets and back again before he made a split second decision and made a run for it. He didn't make it five feet before his little grasshopper tackled him to the ground and ripped the card from his hands.

He spit grass out of his mouth. "Fine. You can come with me I guess," he said, earning a knee to the ribs.

Chapter 7

"I love you, Derek!"

Jason tried to drag Haley back to her seat, but she fought him tooth and nail. "I love you, Derek!"

"He knows, woman! He's known since the first inning. Let the man focus," he said, finally managing to drag her a foot when that bastard Derek Jeter went and waved to Haley. That did it. She tried to break free and make a run for the field.

Trying not to drop her as he burst out laughing, he readjusted his grip and pulled Haley back with him until she was sitting on his lap. He kept one arm around her waist as he retrieved his beer from Brad.

Brad threw him another triumphant grin. For three days Jason taunted the man with the two extra tickets. He already knew he was going. There was an unspoken understanding between him and Haley. If she tried to leave without him, he would burn her house down, plain and simple. This was a Yankees/Red Sox game for Christ's sake.

On the third day of taunting, the betraying bastard had his wife call up Haley. Fucking tattle tale. Since Haley's friends hated anything to do with any sport she invited Brad and another friend of his, Mitch. Mitch was a good buddy and had an obvious crush on Haley, one that she didn't seem to return. That was fine with him, because he didn't think Mitch was good enough for his sweet little grasshopper.

"Come on! He was safe! Get your head out of your ass and pay attention!" Haley screamed as she bounced on his lap, desperate for freedom, no doubt to rip the umpire's head off.

Okay, he thought, chuckling, maybe sweet was a bit much. His little grasshopper was a fire cracker.

"Calm down before you get us kicked us out of the stadium," he said, laughing.

She huffed and crossed her arms over chest as she leaned back into him. "Cheating bastards," she muttered.

"Because they're winning?" he asked, already knowing the answer.

"Yes!"

"Relax and I'll buy you a foam finger," he said, absently caressing her stomach with his thumb while she thought it over. Today she wore a tight pink tank top under an open Yankees jersey and a pair of shorts that gave him and every guy a look as those golden beauties that she called legs.

"I already have a foam finger at home," she pointed out sullenly.

"Then what would my little grasshopper like?" he asked, fighting back the urge to press a kiss to her back.

She glared over her shoulder at him. "I'm not going to call you Mr. Miyagi you know."

"Yes you will, but that's not important at the moment. What do you want?" he asked as his eyes dropped to her pouty little lips. What the hell? He pulled his gaze away in time to catch Mitch's dirty look and Brad's smirk.

Haley stole his beer and took a sip. She returned it to him with a grimace. "That's warm."

"Well, it did take me over twenty minutes to drag you back here to prevent you from jumping the wall," he pointed out.

"Whatever, you're just messing with fate," she said as she stood up. He reluctantly let her, but he was ready to pounce and drag her back if needed. Judging by the looks the security guards around them were giving, they were ready as well. Damn, his little grasshopper was making him proud. He idly wondered if she'd be able to cause a riot.

"Where are you going?" he asked, wanting her to sit back down. He'd been comfortable damn it.

Haley rolled her eyes. "I'm not going to start a riot or anything. I have to use the bathroom and I want to get a cold drink."

"Oh," he said, going to stand up the same time Mitch did. Jason shot Mitch a glare, but the man ignored it and jumped to his feet.

"Want some company?" Mitch asked, giving Haley his best smile.

Haley laughed softly. "No, I'll be fine."

Mitch reluctantly sat down. The two of them watched her walk away as Brad sat there smugly. They sat there silently for a few minutes before Jason spoke.

"Don't even think about it," he said firmly.

Mitch snorted. "Just because you think you own Haley doesn't mean that you speak for her."

Jason took a sip of his drink, nodding slowly before he placed his cup on his knee. "How about this then? I know you and there is no way in hell I'm letting an asshole like you, near her."

"So, let me get this straight. I'm good enough to be your friend, but not date Haley?"

"Exactly. Glad we're on the same page."

"Why is that exactly? You don't like the idea of some other guy swooping in and getting her first?"

"Because you sleep around, don't care about any of the women you fuck, and treat them all like shit. I'm not letting you do that to Haley. She deserves a nice guy."

"Oh, like you?" Mitch snorted. "You treat women worse than I do."

Jason barely held back his temper. "No, not me. I'm not interested in her like that. She's a friend, nothing more."

"Yeah, okay. Keep telling yourself that, buddy. Anyone with two working eyes can tell you're getting ready to pounce."

"That's bullshit and you know it. If I wanted her I would have had her by now," he said through gritted teeth.

"Yeah, whatever," Mitch mumbled. "She's a grown woman. If she wants to go out with me she can. You have no say in the matter."

"We'll see," he said, knowing if Mitch tried anything he'd beat the shit out of his friend.

"See what?" Haley asked as she squeezed into the small aisle, juggling her beer and a tray full of food in her arms.

"If the Yankees can get this game back under control," Jason said smoothly.

"They will," Haley said firmly. Jason had a funny feeling that if they didn't, she would go beat the shit out of someone.

She sat down next to him. He placed his piss warm beer on the floor and took hers while she settled her tray in her lap. He took a sip of her cold beer while she took a bite of her hot dog topped with sauerkraut. She closed her eyes as she savored the treat.

"That is really good," she nearly groaned in delight.

"Give me a bite," he said.

Haley nodded absently while she watched the game. She held out the hot dog for him. He took a big bite. While he chewed he sat back and couldn't stop smiling as Mitch frowned at him. For the next ten minutes he held the beer for her to sip while she held food out to him.

Jason wasn't even sure she realized what they were doing. Her focus seemed to be on the game itself. When their beer was empty he put it down and turned to find another beer vender.

"Oh shit!" Brad yelled as he jumped to his feet the same time Mitch did.

He turned in time to see Haley jump to her feet and then jump onto her seat, holding her hands out as she mumbled, "Oh no, oh no, oh no!" He jumped to his feet the same moment as something white slammed into Haley's hands. She held onto the thing for dear life as she lost her footing from the impact of the ball and from several guys trying to grab it from her.

Before he could push the bastards away from her, Haley was jumping up and down on her seat while hugging the ball to her chest. Her smile was intoxicating when she looked down at him and proudly showed him the ball.

"Look!"

He placed his hands together in front of him in a praying gesture and slightly bowed. "Very good, grasshopper." He straightened up in time to catch her in his arms. He whirled her around as she hugged his neck tightly.

"I can't believe I caught it!"

"You did great!" he said, kissing her cheek. The action was so sudden that it took him back. He carefully placed a very happy Haley on the ground. She sat down, still grinning while hugging the ball.

After a few minutes she said his name tightly.

"Yes?"

"I think I broke my hand," she whimpered.

* * * *

"You sure you don't want to go with us?" Mitch asked, giving her a puppy dog expression.

Haley forced herself to smile. She liked Mitch, not as much as Jason, but she didn't see it going any further than friendship. Mitch was becoming rather persistent over the past week. It was getting kind of annoying.

She held up her hand and ice pack. "Sorry. I think I'm going to go relax. You guys go have fun. Hit the clubs or bars or whatever you guys do. No doubt Jason's going to want to hit the all male review."

While the other men laughed Jason stuck his tongue out at her. Haley looked at the front desk. "Ah, guys, did you remember to check in earlier?"

Jason waved it off. "We have the room reserved on a credit card. It will be there by the time we get back."

Haley didn't think it would be. Hotels had a tendency to give rooms away when the holders didn't show up and since it was now nine o'clock she didn't have high hopes that the room the guys reserved was still available. She didn't say anything, knowing it would come off as bossy and she was sick of being a worrier. She didn't want to nag the guys and wreck their good time.

"Alright, have fun, guys," she said before making her way to the elevator.

"Haley! Wait up!" Mitch called. She almost groaned.

"What's up?" she asked him, feeling her patience fraying.

He shrugged. "I was going to ask if you wanted company. I know your hand must hurt so I figured I'd keep you company," he said with a charming smile that probably worked on most everything female.

Her eyes shot past him to see Brad grab Jason by the arm and hold him back. What the hell was that about? She gave herself a mental shake and focused on Mitch.

"That's really sweet, but I'll be fine. I'm just going to watch a movie and go to bed. I'll see you tomorrow." She didn't give him a chance to respond before she headed off towards her room.

She might not have the best track record in dating, but she knew the womanizers by sight and Mitch was definitely a womanizer. She didn't feel like being just another notch on any man's bedpost.

A few minutes later she was closing her hotel room door behind her. She walked to the first double bed and searched her bag for aspirin. Her hand was throbbing like crazy. When she couldn't find any she called room service for a bottle and a large ice cream sundae.

Twenty minutes later, she was sitting comfortably in a bubble bath while eating a decadent hot fudge sundae. Her mind wandered to Jason and how good it felt to have him hold her most of the day. Then she reminded herself that they were just friends and forced herself to smarten up.

Nothing was ever going to happen between them. Jason was a buddy, a real good friend and she wouldn't ruin that for anything in the world. Friendship was one of the things she valued most in the world and she would not risk their friendship. It wasn't worth it.

Besides, he was probably with some bimbo at the moment. The idea turned her stomach. She placed her half-eaten sundae on the floor and groaned. Sometimes friendship sucked, she thought as she dunked herself under the water so she could let out a frustrated scream.

Chapter 8

"Come on, guys! Let's go back. Those women were hot!" Mitch said for the hundredth time since they'd left the club.

"No," Brad and Jason said in unison.

Mitch let out a frustrated sigh as they walked into the hotel foyer. "I know why Brad doesn't want to, he's married, but why don't you?"

He shrugged. "I just don't want to. Is that okay with you?"

"All night you turned girls down. What the hell is wrong with you?" Mitch demanded.

"Nothing," he mumbled. He wasn't in the mood for this conversation or for Mitch. All night he resisted the urge to punch the asshole. When he wasn't thinking about punching Mitch he was kicking himself for leaving Haley. He should have stayed and taken care of her. She was cool enough to bring them with her to catch a really great game and they ditched her like a bunch of ungrateful bastards. Plus, if he was going to be honest, he probably would have had a better time with her just sitting around watching a movie than going to a club and having a bunch of women rub all over him.

"Problem, guys," Brad said as he walked back to them from the desk clerk.

"What is it?" he asked.

"They gave our room away since we didn't check in and there are no more rooms available."

"Shit."

"Yup."

"Hey, where are you going?" Jason asked Mitch's retreating back.

Mitch stopped and gave him a "duh" look. "We don't have a room. I'm going back to that club to find a warm body and a bed for the night."

That son of a bitch.

He'd been trying to get between Haley's legs for a week and wouldn't stop. Now he was trying to get laid, just for a bed. Jason had no doubt come morning he'd be back sniffing around Haley.

"Are you coming or what?" Mitch demanded.

He shook his head in disgust. "No, you go have fun. I'm going to bed."

"Whatever," Mitch muttered as he headed out.

Jason nudged Brad. "Let's go beg for mercy."

Brad looked relieved as he nodded and gestured for Jason to lead the way.

They walked up to Haley's room and knocked. After a few minutes they knocked again. Finally the door opened, revealing a sleepy eyed Haley.

"What is it?" she asked, trying to stifle a yawn.

"They gave away our room," he said with a pout.

She rolled her eyes. "Well duh, you didn't check in this afternoon."

"You don't have to rub it in."

"That's not me rubbing it in, trust me. If I was doing that I would give you an evil little laugh and shut the door in your face."

"Good point," he said, wincing, while hoping she didn't do just that. He was exhausted and didn't feel like fighting with Brad over the backseat of his car.

"So what do you want?"

"Mercy?"

She rolled her eyes. "You want to sleep here? There isn't enough room for all four of us."

Obviously she hadn't noticed Mitch's absence.

"Mitch went elsewhere for night. It's just me and Brad."

Something in her expression shifted. Was she upset that Mitch wasn't here? The idea pissed him off more than he wanted to admit.

"Alright, guys. Come on in," she mumbled as she made her way back to the first bed. Jason of course took the time to note the cute little tank top and matching cotton shorts that hugged her round backside rather nicely.

She climbed onto the bed and flopped down beneath the covers. Obviously she was all set to go to sleep and wasn't giving them a second thought.

"Ah, Haley?" Brad said hesitantly.

"What? Please tell me you two don't need me to brush your teeth and tuck you in," she mumbled into the pillow.

"Ah, no," Brad said, smiling. "Is it alright if I sleep in my boxers? I don't want to make you uncomfortable."

She waved a hand at him without looking. "Knock yourself out."

"Okay, good night," Brad said, heading for the bathroom.

Jason looked around the room, noting only two beds and no other furniture except for a chair and shrugged. He yanked off his shirt, pants, and shoes and began to climb into bed with Haley.

Her hand came up in a stopping motion. "Hold up there, buddy," she said, turning to face him. She pointed to the other bed. "Have a good night."

Jason frowned at the suggestion. "You can't expect us to sleep together."

"Yup."

"Nope," he said, climbing onto the bed quickly and flopping onto his stomach. She pushed him, well tried to anyway. He did outweigh her after all.

"Out."

"No."

"You're not sleeping in the same bed as me."

"Yes, I am. Unless you're planning on sleeping with Brad and I don't think you want to do that. His wife will kick your ass."

She groaned.

He smiled.

"Look, I'll stay on my side and you stay on your side. We'll both sleep. Problem solved."

"No way."

"Afraid you won't be able to keep your hands off of me?" he teased.

Haley rolled her eyes and dropped back onto the pillow. "Fine, but just so you know, anything that comes over this way will be chopped off."

"Duly noted," he said, snuggling deeper into the bed.

"Oh, and if you snore I'll kill you in your sleep," she mumbled.

"Ditto."

* * * *

"Ah, guys?" Brad said.

Haley buried her face deeper into the warmth while she tried to block out Brad and the sunlight streaming into the room.

"Go. Away," she muttered.

"I'm hungry. Let's go grab some breakfast," Brad said, a little louder this time, earning a groan from her cushion of warmth.

"Fuck off. We're sleeping," Jason mumbled as he pulled Haley closer. Surprisingly she went willingly. Her head rested on his chest just under his chin, her arm laid across his stomach, and one leg was thrown over one of his.

She felt so good in his arms. He'd never held a woman like this, never cuddled with one never mind spending the entire night in her bed. Normally when a woman tried to cuddle he felt cornered and irritated. With Haley he felt comfortable, relaxed, and even happy. She felt like she belonged with him. He wasn't about to look too far into that at the moment.

"If you weren't the best mattress ever I would totally kick your ass for moving onto my side," Haley mumbled against his chest.

"Actually, you're both in the middle," Brad pointed out.

"Why is he still here? Sleepy," Haley grumbled adorably.

Closing his eyes, he waved his hand towards the door. "Go eat with Mitch or something. We'll be up in a little while."

Brad sighed unhappily. "Fine."

A moment later the door was closed and they both drifted back to a beautiful deep sleep.

* * * *

"Stupid pillow," Haley muttered, trying to punch her once comfy pillow into submission.

Last night had been the worst night of sleep she'd ever had. She spent the entire night tossing and turning and trying to get comfortable only to finally fall into a restless sleep around five this morning. Now it looked like she was in for a repeat performance.

She looked over at the alarm clock and groaned. It was nearly two in the morning. She buried her face into her pillow and screamed. This sucked! She was so tired. All day she kept herself busy with grading tests and homework, and even cleaned her house, thinking that by the time she went to bed she'd be too exhausted for anything else but sleep.

It looked like that plan was failing miserably.

"So tired……." She nearly whimpered.

Damn Jason. Somehow he wrecked sleep for her. She'd never slept in the same bed with a guy before. Sure she cuddled with a few boyfriends in front of the television after a heavy make out session, but it always felt awkward. With Jason if felt so good. He was a thousand times more comfortable than her bed or down comforter.

How was she supposed to get comfortable on a pillow top mattress after sleeping in his arms? She couldn't. There was no way she was going to be able to manage work tomorrow on less than two hours of sleep in forty eight hours, but she couldn't call in because they were preparing for finals.

"Move over," Jason said, startling her.

She jumped up, clutching her chest, trying to catch her breath as she watched Jason push up her window screen and climb into her room. He closed the screen behind him and lay down on her bed.

Still gasping, she sucked in a breath and said, "What the hell is wrong with you? You just scared the hell out of me!"

"Look, woman, I don't know what you did, but I haven't been able to sleep since we got back from New York. I'm tired and bitchy and all I want is some sleep so cuddle your ass up with me or so help me I will kill you," Jason snapped.

"Wow, you are bitchy," she mumbled.

"It's your fault."

"Whatever."

"Let's go," he said, holding out his arms expectantly. When she hesitated he wiggled his fingers. "You know you want to."

"Just for tonight," she clarified.

He nodded quickly. "Just for tonight. Now, let's go, I'm cranky."

"I hadn't noticed," she said dryly, but she did as she was asked. She was too exhausted to do anything else at the moment.

It didn't take long for the beating of Jason's heart to lull her into a deep and peaceful sleep.

The alarm went off, waking Haley from a deep comfortable sleep. Instead of feeling jumpy and attacking the alarm clock after only getting five hours of sleep she felt oddly well rested.

Jason yawned as he sat up and shut off the alarm. He rubbed his eyes and turned around to lift up the screen.

"I'll see you at work," he mumbled.

"Okay," she said, getting to her feet. "This was a onetime deal," she said, more to remind herself than him. She could quickly become dependent on the comfort and warmth he offered and that wasn't a good idea with a guy like Jason.

He gave her one of his lopsided smiles. "Of course. It was just a onetime deal."

Chapter 9

Monday Night

10:35 P.M.

Haley rolled onto her side, facing the wall and wondering if she should just suck up her pride and go ask Jason to come sleep with her. Did that make her a sleep slut? At this point she was willing to beg for it. Just as she feared, she was addicted to Jason's body. Thank God they never had sex. She'd hate to think how bad the addiction would be then.

She felt the bed dip behind her before a strong arm curled around her waist, pulling her back into a strong warm body. Jason's inviting scent enveloped her as strongly as his body did. Her bottom was cupped by his pelvis. He was hard again, but like usual he didn't make any move on her. It was just his body's reaction to being pressed against a female. Just like her body was reacting to being held by a strong man. Neither cared enough to comment or act on it. In a matter of minutes they were fast asleep.

Tuesday Night
11.30 P.M.

"That was a great game and a really great dinner," Jill, Brad's wife, said.

Brad stole another brownie off the plate and groaned while he nodded his head in agreement. He reached for another brownie only to find the plate gone and Jason glaring at him.

"Brownie thieving bastard," he muttered as he stalked off to Haley's kitchen counter.

The three of them watched with humor as Jason placed the brownies in a large zip lock bag that he no doubt planned on taking with him to work in the morning. Halfway through transferring the brownies he turned to glare at Brad and mouthed the words, "Thieving bastard," before returning to the task at hand.

"Anyway," Haley said, drawing Brad and Jill's attention away from Jason's rather disturbing affection for her baked goods. "It was nice to have you guys over."

"Yeah, you guys are coming over next week, right?" Jill asked as she frowned at her husband who held up the last bite of brownie, but didn't eat it. His eyes were fixed on Jason.

Both women watched as Jason turned around. Brad made a huge show of putting the brownie in his mouth. He closed his eyes as if it was the best thing he'd ever eaten and moaned.

"That was a damn good brownie," Brad finally said.

"You betraying bastard!" Jason gasped.

"I'll bring you an entire pan of brownies next week, Brad," Haley said, knowing it would take the glare away from Brad.

"Traitor," Jason mumbled as he lovingly stroked the bag of brownies.

"It's so not right that he isn't fat," Jill said. Haley had to nod in agreement. The man put away three helpings of lasagna tonight, a salad, and a ton of garlic bread, not to mention about a dozen brownies and cookies. With her one helping of lasagna and two brownies, she was probably going to gain five pounds. Sometimes life simply wasn't fair.

They said their good nights and walked Brad and Jill out the door. She shut the kitchen light off, knowing Jason would shut off the living room light. Still neither spoke of the sleeping arrangements and she didn't know how to bring it up. So instead, she quietly said good night, rolled her eyes as Jason mumbled "I love you" to his brownies and headed off to her bathroom.

After a quick shower she pulled on a small tee shirt and panties. Yawning, she walked into her room and wasn't surprised to find Jason on his stomach, wearing nothing but boxers, in the middle of her bed. She flicked off the lights and crawled in bed. She laid her face on his shoulder while her hand rested on his other shoulder and her leg entwined with his. In a matter of seconds she felt Jason relax and drift off to sleep.

Wednesday Night

10:45 P.M.

Jason felt bone tired as he pulled into his driveway. He waited until Haley pulled into her driveway before getting out. It had been a very long day and judging by the adorable little whimper Haley made as she climbed out of her car, she was feeling it as well.

"I am so tired," she mumbled.

He yawned loudly. "That was a parent-teacher meeting for the records," he said.

"Too much drama. Who knew parents of spoiled rich kids who were failing could become so damn dramatic? I had one woman sobbing hysterically because her son got a B instead of an A."

He chuckled. "I was offered a blow job to make a D into an A."

Haley's face squished up prettily. "You had a woman offer you a blow job during parent-teacher night?"

"Nope, a man. Seems the guy is desperate to get his son into Harvard."

She laughed softly. "Obviously." She yawned loudly. "I'm off to bed. Goodnight."

"Me too. Goodnight," he said as they walked along the small patch of grass between their properties. Just before she veered off to the right he put his arm around her shoulders and steered her off towards his house.

For the last three nights they'd slept at her house. It wasn't that he missed his bed. He just wanted to see if the bed made the difference or if it was Haley. Plus, he'd been imagining her in his bed all day. Whenever his thoughts turned sexual he forced his mind out of the gutter. It was becoming more and more difficult as time went by.

He'd never had a female friend before and this level of intimacy was new and a little frightening for him. He made himself a promise today. He would get her into his bed and if he didn't sleep as well as he did in her bed or that hotel bed he would go out and buy a bed matching hers and the problem would be solved. If he still slept like a baby with her then.....well, he didn't really want to think about that just yet. He was pretty sure part of the problem was sex.

Maybe he'd go and get laid and then see if he slept as well with Haley snuggling him all night. Part of him was scared that it wouldn't make a damn bit of difference what he did. Haley was quickly becoming his world and for some strange reason, that was fine with him, hence the reason he was scared shitless.

They didn't say anything as they walked into his house. He could tell she was nervous. Hell, he was nervous. He'd never had a woman in his bed before. It didn't matter that there wouldn't be any sex involved. This was a big step for him. He didn't even know if he could tolerate having Haley in his bed. Every time the panic started to surface he shoved it back down. He knew if he couldn't handle it that he could make some excuse and they'd go back to her bed. With that in mind he led her into his room.

Still neither spoke as he handed her one of his old favorite tee shirts. She gave him a shy smile and disappeared into his bathroom. He pulled his shoes off and waited for her to come out. He heard his shower turn on and he gritted his teeth as a wave of lust poured over him.

He frowned down at the rather uncomfortable tent in his pants. "Stop causing problems." It didn't listen of course. It never did where Haley was concerned. He kept telling himself that eventually his body would come to accept that Haley was just a friend.

"All yours," Haley said softly as she stepped out of the bathroom ten minutes later wearing his tee shirt. The hem of the shirt ended just above the knee, giving the illusion that she wasn't wearing anything underneath. He swallowed. Hard.

He nodded woodenly and walked past her to the bathroom where he proceeded to take an ice cold shower. As he was drying off he spotted her little glasses folded on his sink counter. He picked them up and smiled as he put them back. They looked like they belonged there.

The bedroom light was already out by the time he stepped out of the bathroom. Light streaming in from the street illuminated Haley. She lay on her back on the right side of the bed waiting for him. He walked over to her side of the bed and raised the covers. Without a word he climbed onto the bed and slowly lay on top of her so that his lower stomach rested between her legs, keeping his errant erection away from her as best he could. She opened her legs wider to cradle him.

Jason laid his head between her breasts and closed his eyes, releasing a sigh of contentment. She felt so good, so right. After a moment's hesitation he felt her move. He wasn't sure if she was about to shove him off or hit him. He was taking liberties in their sleeping arrangement, but he couldn't help it. He needed her so badly.

Instead of shoving him away, she wrapped one arm around his shoulders while she gently ran her fingers through his hair. That's how he fell asleep in the cradle of the woman he trusted and cared about the most in the world. It was absolutely perfect.

Chapter 10

"No! I'm not going and you can't make me!" Haley said as she tightened her grip on the edge of the kitchen sink.

"Haley,-"

"I'm not going!"

Jason tried not to smile as he placed his hand on Haley's round little bottom, but failed miserably.

She went completely still.

"What the hell are you doing?" she demanded as she tried to shift away from his hand.

"If you don't let go of the sink and get your ass in the car in thirty seconds you'll leave me with no choice but to spank you," he said, enjoying having his hand on her ass more than he should, but clearly she left him with very little choice in the matter.

Sure, he could easily pick her up and throw her over his shoulder, but where was the fun in that?

"You wouldn't," she said through clenched teeth, glaring over her shoulder at him.

He squeezed her ass.

She gasped, jumping away from him and ran towards the front door. "Bastard!" she yelled over her shoulder before throwing the door open and leaving.

Jason followed her at a leisurely pace, whistling happily, half hoping that she refused to go a half dozen more times before he got her in the car. He stepped out of her house, locking the door behind him, and nearly groaned in disappointment when he spotted her waiting for him in his car.

Damn.

There went his plans for her ass.

He climbed into the driver's side seat and sent her a huge grin, knowing it would piss her off. Her eyes narrowed on him before she looked away mumbling all sorts of unpleasant things about his manhood that he simply chose to ignore.

"You'll pay for this," she promised.

"Haley,-"

"Rot in hell, you betraying bastard," she hissed.

He couldn't help but chuckle. "It's just a family dinner. I really don't understand why that has my little grasshopper all riled up."

"I. Hate. You," she bit out.

"You love me," he said, turning on the radio.

"*Hate*. I hate you."

"Uh huh," he said absently, searching for her favorite radio station, hoping it would calm the little demon down.

Since this morning when her grandmother called asking him to join her family for dinner tonight, Haley had been on edge. He wasn't sure if she was pissed because her grandmother had called him before her or what. All he knew was that when she overheard her grandmother ask him to join them at dinner she went a little insane.

It hadn't mattered that they were standing in line at the bakery. Haley jumped up and tried to snatch the phone out of his hand. He'd been too surprised, and admittedly laughed his ass off when she tried to take him to the ground, to give it much thought. Of course it did surprise him that her grandmother wasn't shocked to hear her granddaughter scream all sorts of threats of violence to him.

Jason really didn't know what the hell was going on, but he liked Haley's grandmother and didn't want to disappoint her by saying no, so of course he accepted the invitation and tried not to wince when Haley kicked his shin.

From that moment on she'd been royally pissed at him. She'd ordered the last four apple fritters, knowing he looked forward to his apple fritters every Friday and didn't offer him one. Even worse, she gave away his delicious treats during the morning meeting. He spent the entire meeting glaring at the bastards who ate his fritters.

It only got worse after that.

During their lunch break not only did she refuse to eat with him, but she somehow managed to steal his lunch, toss it in the trash and made sure there were no delectable treats in the staff refrigerator for him to steal. When he went to buy lunch in the student cafeteria he discovered another lovely surprise.

She'd somehow lifted his wallet.

By the end of the day he'd been so pissed and hungry that he decided she was damn well going tonight, whether she wanted to or not. When he arrived home, he wasn't too surprised to discover that Haley had barricaded herself in her room. That was more than fine with him. It gave him plenty of time to recoup his strength. After devouring everything in her fridge, he broke into her room.

She'd put up a good fight, but eventually he managed to drag her into the living room where she pretended to hurt her ankle. When he released her to check, she shoved him, knocking him flat on his ass, and took off for the backdoor. She made it as far as the kitchen sink before he was on top of her.

"Are you still mad at me?" he asked as he turned into the parking lot of Harrington's, the five star restaurant her family was dining at tonight. He was glad he finally found his wallet during their little wrestling match since this meal was most likely going to give his credit card a workout.

Haley sighed heavily, shifting to look at him. "No, I just don't want to do this."

"Really? I couldn't tell," he said drily.

"I'm really sorry," she said, as he pulled up behind a short line of luxury cars.

He shrugged, thinking she was apologizing for starving him. That reminded him that they'd need to stop by the grocery store after this to refill her fridge otherwise she might be pissed to discover that he left her with only three eggs, a jar of olives and some expired girly yogurt that he wouldn't touch with a ten foot spoon.

"I'm sorry if I hurt you," she said, sounding serious.

He had to bite back a smile at the thought of his little grasshopper kicking his ass. "I'll, ah," he just barely stopped himself from laughing, "I'll survive."

She nodded regally. "I know. I held back."

"And I really appreciate that."

* * * *

"You know you're going to starve here, right? Even I have to hit the drive thru at Burger King after coming here," Haley pointed out desperately as Jason dragged her from the safety of the car.

Jason simply sighed, wondering if she really knew him at all. As if the prospect of eating two dinners would upset him.

Puhlease.

"Fine," Haley said, giving him a sly, little smile as she stood up, straightening her lavender shirt and dark skirt. "If you take me home right now I promise," she said in a sultry tone, reaching up to run her fingertips down his tie, "that I will fulfill every single sexual fantasy you've ever had and some you didn't know were possible."

With a bored sigh, he simply grabbed her arm and gently tugged her towards the front entrance, ignoring the valets as they choked on their tongues. If he thought for one second that she was serious, he would have hauled her ass back into the car and been going ninety to the nearest pharmacy, all while he had his hand shoved up her skirt.

Not that he really wanted to do that.

Much.

"B-but I'm offering you sex! Lots and lots of sex!" Haley hissed urgently as they stepped into a lush foyer.

"You would have had more luck offering me meatloaf, my little grasshopper," he informed her, catching her arm as she tried to make another escape.

Haley exhaled heavily as she pushed her glasses back up her nose. "I was going to offer that, too." She gave him a hopeful smile. "What if we go home and I   cook-"

"Too little too late, my little grasshopper. Besides, there's nothing in your fridge to cook anyway."

She frowned up at him. "But I just went shopping the other day."

"I got hungry," he simply said, ignoring her adorable glare.

"You better not have touched the last piece of pumpkin pie," she warned.

He had to laugh at that. "It was the first thing to go," he informed her as they stepped up to the maître d's podium. She sent him a glare that promised all kinds of retribution. Where Jason could eat just about anything, and often did, his little grasshopper was a pumpkin pie junkie.

"Welcome to Harrington's. My name is Elizabeth, how can I help you?" the woman asked them both as she sent Jason an inviting look that let him know he'd be getting offered more than just appetizers tonight.

He looked down at Haley, wondering if she caught the look and what she thought, not that he wanted her to be jealous or anything. He had to smile when he caught Haley gazing longingly at the exit sign.

"It won't be that bad," he said, taking her hand into his, mostly to keep her from bolting again.

"Yes, it will," she sighed pathetically.

Jason turned his attention back to the woman who was now frowning unhappily at their entwined hands.

"We're joining the Blaine party," he said, tightening his grip on Haley's hand when he felt her trying to pull away.

"Right this way," the woman said with a tight smile.

As they followed the woman through a richly furnished sitting room, Jason couldn't help but wonder why Haley settled for the losers that she did when she was clearly used to so much better. He'd seen some of the losers she'd dated over the years and doubted they'd pulled out their wallet for much more than Denny's and even then, only if they had a coupon.

She should be dating someone who was willing to bust his ass to show her how much she meant to him. He'd have to work on it with her, but that was for later. Right now he had to focus on dragging her alongside him.

* * * *

"What are you doing?" Jason asked, smirking as he glanced down at her.

"Nothing," she said quickly as she tried to discretely shift so that Jason was blocking her from the left side.

"Doesn't look like nothing," Jason noted, quickening his pace, probably to annoy the hell out of her.

"It is *nothing*," she bit out between clenched teeth even as she hurried to keep up with Jason again, angling a little to the right so that her entire body was blocked by Jason's massive body.

She dared a peek behind Jason's back and nearly cried in frustration when a pair of smoky gray eyes that she was all too familiar with met hers. She sent him a polite smile and did her best to ignore the determined glare he sent her way.

"Who's that?" Jason asked as they continued to follow the hostess through the spacious aisles and around larger tables that surrounded the small dance floor.

"No one," she lied. Tonight was going to be difficult enough. She didn't want to get into the drama of ex-boyfriends who still took her refusal to sleep with them as a challenge, one that Robert seemed hell bent on winning no matter how many years passed.

The man was a self-professed playboy and truly believed he could have any woman he wanted. He hadn't always been like that. When they started dating at fifteen he'd been shy, sweet, and down to earth. It wasn't until their senior year when his skin cleared up, he put on some muscle and he inherited about thirty million dollars from his grandmother, that he started to change.

He went from the sweet guy she could watch Indiana Jones movies with to the guy screwing around on her with every bimbo he could find. When she confronted him about it he denied it left and right until finally he broke down and placed all the blame at her feet. They parted as friends, well sort of, and since then every time he saw her, he did his best to get her in his bed. Last time they ran into each other he'd ditched his fiancé two days before the wedding to pursue her.

His desperation to get her in his bed had nothing to do with love. It had to do with the fact that she was, according to him, the only woman who had ever said no to him. He'd do just about anything to get her into his bed. She really did not need this tonight. She had enough to deal with.

She was not looking forward to being embarrassed and belittled in front of Jason. Although it wouldn't be on her top ten favorite things to do on a Friday night, Haley would have gladly come tonight to keep her grandmother company. She would have done her best to ignore all their subtle putdowns, but she couldn't stomach the idea of Jason witnessing how little she really meant to her family.

"Mr. Blaine, the rest of your party has arrived," Elizabeth said, smiling politely as she stopped in front of the large round table where Haley's parents, sisters and their husbands sat. Haley frowned when she didn't see her grandmother.

"Thank you," Jason said, ignoring the inviting look the woman was sending him, surprising Haley. His disinterest in all the women who practically threw themselves at him when they were out always surprised her. He wasn't much of a playboy, she thought as she forced a smile for her family.

"Haley, sweetheart," her father said as he stood up. His eyes shifted to Jason before he pulled her into a hug and gave her a quick kiss on the cheek. "It's been too long, sweetheart. I've missed you."

She just barely stopped herself from suggesting that he could pick up the telephone if he missed her so much, but she bit it back. She would not let him know that he'd hurt her when he hadn't called like he promised. It was her fault anyway. She should have known better.

"This is my friend, Jason Bradford," she said, gesturing to Jason who extended his hand to her father.

"It's a pleasure to meet you, sir," Jason said, politely.

Her father shook his hand, giving her a curious look. "It's a pleasure to meet one of Haley's friends."

Haley just barely stopped herself from wincing when she realized Jason was the first friend she'd ever invited to meet her family since she was in school. The fact that Jason was a man was going to be a problem, especially if they thought they were dating.

"Dad?" Haley said, drawing his attention before he sat down.

"Yes, dear?" he asked, throwing Jason another curious look.

"Where's Grandma?"

He frowned down at her. "Didn't she call you?"

"No, why?" she asked, already having a bad feeling where this was going.

"She called earlier to say that you and your friend," he said, giving Jason another one of those curious looks that Haley knew all too well, "were going to join us tonight, but that she remembered she already had plans for this evening."

Haley just bet she did.

Chapter 11

"Jason, this is my sister Rose," Haley said, gesturing to the woman with her hair pulled back into a severely tight bun that looked like it hurt. She daintily offered her hand to him.

He took it gently, not because he was honored or overwhelmed to make her acquaintance, no he was simply afraid of breaking her long thin hand. As discretely as he could, he quickly looked over the other two women in the group and quickly noted that all three of them were tall, skinny, too skinny, and flatter than a ten year old boy. Although they were attractive women in their own right, they didn't have a thing on his little grasshopper.

A few minutes later when he met Haley's other sister Martha, and both women's husbands, John and Edward, he was introduced to Haley's mother who looked upset. It took a minute to realize that she was trying to smile.

Botox.

He should have known, he thought as he reached over and shook the woman's hand just as gently as he had her daughters' hands. He'd come across this expression countless times during parent-teacher conferences.

As he sat down next to Haley, who was fuming adorably, he couldn't help but notice John, Rose's husband's eyes land on the ass of a waitress and stay there as the woman moved around the table next to them. Rose seemed to be oblivious as she frowned in Haley's direction. Jason's eyes shifted to the other two women to find them doing the same thing. Her father was glaring in his direction, which was understandable, and Edward was sipping his wine while he stared at Haley's very generous cleavage. Haley seemed to be oblivious to her brother-in-law's perusal of her breasts as she toyed with a dinner roll.

"Sweetie," her sister, Rose whispered, drawing everyone's attention, "do you really think you should be eating that?" She looked pointedly at the roll Haley was fidgeting with.

At Jason's confused frown she mouthed "Carbs."

Haley muttered something softly as she placed her roll, none-too-gently, on his plate. She thought Haley needed to go on a diet? Jason couldn't help but run his eyes over Haley's small curvy figure, lingering on all his favorite places. Not that he really needed to since he knew for a fact that Haley's stomach was flat. But, damn it if carbs were responsible for those curves then he'd make sure to keep her cabinets stocked with-

"Mr. Bradford," Mr. Blaine said crisply, drawing his attention.

Shit.

Judging by the man's expression he wasn't too happy about Jason's leisurely perusal of his daughter. Not that he could blame him. If he had a daughter, which wasn't happening any time soon, that looked like Haley he'd lock her up and guard her with a shotgun.

"What do you do, Mr. Bradford," Mr. Blaine asked, taking a sip of his wine.

"I teach history at Latin Scribe High School," he answered, noting all the expressions of distaste from the rest of Haley's family at that announcement. Not that he cared, but did they really need to act like he said he picked up horse shit with his hands for a living?

Mr. Blaine gave him an approving nod. "That's a very good school. Several of my clients' children attend." He turned his attention to Haley. "Perhaps you should think about applying for a position there, Haley."

Before Jason could open his mouth and ask the man what the hell he was talking about, Haley smiled tightly and said, "That's a great idea, Dad. I'll send my resume in next week."

"I think that's a smart move," her father said, oblivious to the deep blush spreading over Haley's face as she once again shifted her gaze back to her napkin.

"Doesn't she have to have a special degree to teach high school kids?" Martha demanded in a bored tone that pretty much said she really didn't care. "She teaches preschool, doesn't she? I really don't think they're going to hire her to teach teenagers."

"I'll look into that tomorrow," Haley said, not bothering to look up from her napkin.

What in the hell was going on here?

This had to be a fucking joke, he thought as he leaned back in his seat and discretely looked around the expensively decorated room for hidden cameras. There was just no way his sweet little grasshopper came from such a cold family.

"If you're thinking of going back to college, perhaps you should look into a real career," Mrs. Blaine said, sending him an apologetic smile that really said she didn't care one bit that she'd just insulted him, "I'm sure your father would be more than happy to pay for law school or medical school."

"Of course," her father said absently as he checked his PDA. "Just make sure you send my secretary the tuition bill like you did last time you attended."

Haley's hand stilled halfway to her water glass and Jason had to frown. He knew from her grandmother's bragging that Haley worked three jobs to put herself through college and that she absolutely refused any help from her family. He never understood that until now.

"Perhaps she should apply to wherever Mr. Bradford attended if she wishes to teach high school. What college did you attend, Mr. Bradford?" Mrs. Blaine asked as she sent a small wave to someone at another table.

"Harvard," he said, looking around at the table and noting the bored expressions. This family dinner was like nothing he'd ever experienced. He was used to large meals with warm welcoming expressions and fights over seconds. This dinner was cold and clinical and he couldn't help but think that Haley didn't belong. She was warm, sweet, and full of life.

Mr. Blaine grinned. "A fellow alumnus," he said, holding his drink up in salute. "Your father wouldn't happen to be Richard Bradford, would he? He and I attended law school together. Brilliant man."

Jason took a sip of his water and shook his head. "No, my father's name is Jared. He owns a construction company in Meddletown.

Mr. Blaine frowned slightly. "Well, I suppose your father's company does quite well if he could afford to send you to Harvard."

"Yes, he does well, but I actually attended on a football scholarship," Jason said, not surprised when Mr. Blaine's expression turned back to disapproving.

As a scholarship student he'd been treated little better than the hired help. He'd received gratitude, gifts and slaps on the back when he scored a touchdown. When he wasn't scoring touchdowns he was expected to work his ass off and do what he was told, without complaint.

They hadn't expected much from him academically. He doubted they even expected him to attend class, but he had. He worked his ass off to graduate a year and a half early, pissing the alumni right the hell off. They'd been hell bent on getting four years of football out of him, but he hadn't cared. He made damn sure he got his education as quickly as he could, since he knew if he got fucked up on the football field and couldn't play any longer, that they wouldn't hesitate in throwing his ass out the door.

"I think she should think about settling down," Rose, at least he thought the one next to him was Rose, said, making him sweat. Christ, from the looks they'd been sending him since he sat down, it was obvious that they all thought he was her boyfriend. Did they really think that she brought him because they were serious? Him married with children?

Hell no.

Maybe he should just-

"I'm sure Edward can think of several men who would be interested in our Haley," Rose suggested.

"I think that's an excellent idea," Mr. Blaine agreed wholeheartedly.

Wait, what?

"John probably knows some men that would be interested as well. Don't you, John?" Martha asked.

John looked away from another waitresses' ass and nodded. "I'm sure I can think of several men who would like to meet her." As soon as he answered his eyes were back on another woman's ass.

Was he the only one that realized that he'd been insulted here? This was bullshit. He was a fucking great catch. Plenty of women, much to his horror, wanted to marry him. He was just about to tell them that when something caught his attention.

A little snort of laughter.

He turned his glare on Haley as she shook with silent laughter. They were disrespecting his manliness and she was laughing at him? What the hell?

"Haley dear, are you alright?" Mrs. Blaine asked.

Haley, it seemed, could only nod.

"Oh, I just had a wonderful idea!" Martha, Rose or whatever the hell her name was, said excitedly. "Robert's here. Why don't we invite him to join us? You know how fond he is of Haley."

Who the hell was Robert? Jason wondered as he followed Mr. Blaine's eyes to the table they'd passed earlier and landed on the blond bastard who'd smile at Haley. He had perfect blonde hair, an average face and wore an expensive tailored suit that probably cost more than all Jason's clothes put together. When the man sent a warm smile in Haley's direction he decided he hated the bastard.

"Let me get a server to ask him to join us," Mr. Blaine said, already gesturing for a waiter.

Judging by Robert's suddenly smug smile he knew exactly what was going on.

"No, Dad, that's okay," Haley said, all humor gone, as obvious terror took over. "He looks busy."

"Nonsense," Mrs. Blaine said. "You know Robert always makes time for you. He's such a sweet man. For the life of me I don't understand why you ended things with him."

"If you had listened to me years ago you'd be married and settled and not wasting your time on foolish pursuits," Mrs. Blaine added, making Jason's jaw clench.

"She'll never do better than Robert. That's for certain," Martha said, sending him a bored glance before turning her attention back to Robert.

"I'm not interested in Robert," Haley said quickly, watching as the waiter walked towards her father. "Dad, I-"

Mr. Blaine waved off her concerns. "I think this is the best thing for you, Haley," he said before giving the waiter the message for Robert.

He realized that Haley truly did not want Robert to join them. That knowledge somewhat appeased him. Somewhat. These people were the biggest snobs he'd ever met in his life and not just because they looked down their noses at him, but because they looked down their noses at Haley. She didn't deserve any of this.

"Dad, I wish you hadn't done that," Haley said as the waiter walked away. "I'm not interested in Robert. I've told you that before."

"It wouldn't hurt you to give him another chance, sweetheart," Mrs. Blaine said.

Seriously, did any of them even consider that he was Haley's date? Not that he was, but still it was fucking insulting as hell. If Haley wasn't one of his best friends he'd consider doing something to tell her family right the hell off, but she was and he couldn't or she'd stop cooking for him and he wasn't risking that. What his little grasshopper could do with a chocolate chip cookie.......

He pushed back in his chair. Telling her family off might not be a choice, but that didn't mean he couldn't rescue his little grasshopper. He took her hand into his as he stood up, not missing the dirty looks her family sent their entwined hands, and gently pulled Haley to her feet.

"Dance with me?" he asked softly, nodding towards the small dance floor filled with a half dozen couples.

Her eyes darted back to her family and widened when she spotted Robert heading her way.

"I'd love to," she said, practically dragging him away from the table.

* * * *

When Jason pulled her into his arms she felt herself relax for the first time in an hour.

"You want to tell me about him?" Jason asked, expertly maneuvering them around the other couples on the small dance floor.

Chewing her bottom lip nervously, she watched Robert take Jason's vacated seat. He said something to her father and both men looked over at them.

"He was my high school boyfriend. We broke up senior year."

"And he wants to pick up where you left off?" Jason guessed.

"No," Haley said, absently drumming her fingers against his shoulder, "he wants to perfect his record."

At Jason's frown she shrugged. "I refused to sleep with him."

She felt the muscles in Jason's shoulder go tight as he narrowed his eyes first at her, then to Robert before looking back down at her.

"How can you be sure that's all he wants?"

"He told me," Haley said simply. "He's not interested in anything more than adding another notch to his belt."

"What an asshole," Jason muttered, earning a few gasps from the women around him. She could tell he was just barely holding back an eye roll.

As much as she hated being here tonight, and God did she hate being here tonight, she had to admit that it was nice not being totally alone. Having Jason with her made the night almost tolerable. He'd even managed to make her laugh, not on purpose of course, but she'd been unable to stop herself from laughing at his shocked expression when her family dismissed him so easily. Her family's treatment of him had pissed her off more than the way they'd treated her.

She should just leave. It was obvious that they weren't really wanted here and she wasn't about to have Robert forced on her so she could spend the next two hours discretely removing his hand from her leg or trying to ignore the sexual innuendos he'd whisper in her ear.

Plus, she really didn't want to sit around while they treated Jason horribly for another minute. He was a good friend and deserved better treatment than that, especially since he'd been nothing but kind to them no matter how rude they were to him.

They both looked over in time to see Robert stand up and head in their direction. Great. This night was about to get worse.

Jason grinned that sexy grin of his as he leaned down and whispered, "Let's get the hell out of here."

He really was the best friend *ever*, Haley decided as they made their escape.

Chapter 12

"I'm sorry, Mr. Bradford," Eric, one of his normally best students, mumbled quickly as he averted his eyes away from Jason's murderous glare.

For the past three weeks he'd been biting everyone's head off. His normally easy going façade was completely gone now. It didn't make any sense. He'd been getting the best sleep of his life and Haley had quickly become the most important person in his life. He couldn't imagine living without her. He didn't want to.

No matter what they did during the day, at night they came together. Not in the way he would like, but he was still able to find peace at the end of a long day. Two weeks ago they both gave up on rushing out of the other's bed to go shower and change their clothes in the morning. Now he had toiletries in her bathroom and some closet and bureau space and she had the same in his house.

It was weird, but probably not as weird as two best friends who slept together but didn't so much as kiss. It was like they were living together, but alternating from one house to the other. They spent a lot of time together, but they also spent a lot of time on their own or with friends. When he was away from her, he wondered what she was doing and thinking. A few times he had to stop himself from calling her to find out. The only thing that was saving his sanity, was knowing that she wasn't dating another man. He didn't know how he'd feel about that. Judging by the urge to put his fist into a wall every time he thought about her and another guy it wasn't good.

Another loud cheer went up next door. He clenched his jaw tightly as he focused on the fifteen students of his honors U.S. history class. This was their two hour study block to go over the material for the final exam which was tomorrow. They were only ten minutes into it and he wanted to throttle every last one of his students.

He threw his papers onto his desk in disgust, making his students shift around nervously in their designer school uniforms.

"I don't understand this. We've gone over this material all year and none of you have any idea what the hell I'm talking about!" his voice rose, making the girls look close to crying.

Another roar of applause came from next door, drawing his attention back to the woman who was always on his mind. He speared his fingers through his hair and paced the floor. He was wound so damn tight right now, so close to snapping.

A soft knock came at the door connecting his classroom to Haley's. She popped her head in, smiling. That smile was like a balm to his soul, instantly relaxing him.

"Yes?" he asked her in a much softer tone than the one he'd been using with the kids.

Haley nibbled her lip nervously. "Mr. Bradford, I was wondering if I could ask you and your students a huge favor. I need some help preparing my kids for their test tomorrow and since both classes are studying the same material I was hoping you wouldn't mind coming in here and giving me a hand."

"Yes, of course," he found himself answering immediately. Who in the hell could say no to someone so adorable? She pushed her glasses back up on her nose and smiled again, damn near making his knees buckle.

"Excellent!" she said brightly, pushing the door open all the way. "Why don't you kids come in here?" She turned to face her class. "Alright, you bunch of miscreants, make some room!"

Jason grabbed the review packet he made over the weekend and followed. As he walked past Haley he couldn't stop himself from grabbing her hand and giving it a squeeze. If any of the kids saw they smartly kept their mouths shut.

He watched as his students filled the empty seats in her classroom. They kept shooting him nervous looks. No doubt they were waiting for him to start yelling again. Little did they know his little grasshopper kept him grounded.

Haley hopped up onto her desk and crossed one beautiful leg over the other, drawing every guy's attention. He had to stop himself from killing the little bastards then and there.

His little grasshopper seemed oblivious to the attention she drew as she reached back to grab a large brown paper bag. She winced a little as she picked it up and placed it on her lap. She held onto it, grabbing a large packet with the other hand. He didn't wait for an invite. He sat down on the desk right next to her.

"Alright, guys, for those of you who are just joining us we're having a review. We'll each take a turn asking you a question. If you know the answer you get a prize," she said. He saw his students visibly relax. He didn't think it was over the prize, but over the reprieve from his temper.

Curious about the prize, he leaned over and gasped. How dare she hide these from him! He sent her a glare, earning one of her exasperated eye rolls. He reached into the bag only to have his hand slapped away. How dare she?

"You can have one after five of your students answer a question correctly," she informed him.

He sent a scathing look to his students, letting them know they damn well better answer correctly and quickly if they wanted to live. The woman had a huge bag, probably twenty pounds, of Hershey's Kisses and mini Reese's Peanut Butter cups and he'd be damned if he wasn't getting at least fifteen pounds of that. The hell with the kids. Did they really need an education more than he needed chocolate? They all had trust funds. They could get by with a tenth grade education. He on the other hand needed that damn chocolate. Once his five students answered their questions correctly he was attacking that bag, consequences be damned.

"Alright guys, first question," Haley announced as she looked at her packet. "Who was the first President of the United States?"

Every hand in the room went up.

Jason snorted. "Are you trying to just give away my chocolate? Make them work for it."

Haley randomly picked a student, one of his, and tossed a Kiss. As she asked the questions they got tougher. Nine questions later he was patiently waiting for one of his students, John, to answer one of Haley's questions.

"It was eighteen sixty...." the kid trailed off as he thought it over. Jason was going to fail the kid if he couldn't answer the question. Not because it reflected poorly on his teaching skills, but because this was the fifth question and he wanted chocolate!

While Haley was watching the kid for the answer, Jason discretely raised four fingers.

"Eighteen sixty-four," John answered quickly, trying not to look at Jason.

"Very good," Haley said, tossing John a peanut butter cup.

"Hey, that's not fair!" Cindy, or whatever the hell her name was from the dance, cried. He should have known the little witch would be looking for revenge. "Mr. Bradford told him the answer!"

"Don't be petty. John answered the question correctly," he said, holding out his hand for the chocolate that was due him.

Haley eyed him carefully while he gave her his most innocent expression. "Did you just cheat so you could get chocolate?"

He did his best to look insulted. "Would I do that?" he demanded.

She rolled her eyes and handed him a huge handful of chocolate. "This should keep your cheating ways at bay for a while."

"You would think that, wouldn't you," he said, unwrapping his treats while Cindy scowled at him. He ignored her. He ate his chocolate between asking questions of the class. He only paused to reach back and snag Haley's water bottle to wash down the chocolate.

While they sat there hip to hip asking questions he reached back and casually rubbed a circle on Haley's lower back. He almost groaned when he felt her tremble. Outwardly, she was cool and relaxed. She laughed with the kids and never had any problems carrying on with her questions. He only stopped rubbing her back when she handed him more chocolate, which only happened when she caught him cheating.

The lunch bell rang. Haley held up a hand. "Alright, guys. You've studied hard all year. I want you go home, review and then I want you to relax. This is just a test, guys. Just remember that and you'll do fine. Remember, everyone that earns a passing grade of at least eighty will be joining me next week on the last day of school for a make your own sundae party."

Jason glared at Haley. First chocolate and now ice cream. What else was she withholding from him? He held up his hand to stop everyone from leaving.

"The same deal goes for my class," he said.

"Copycat," Haley mumbled.

"Damn straight," he said as he waved the students out of the classroom.

They got up and left while he reached over and grabbed the bag from Haley. He settled it on his lap and started snacking away. Haley grabbed the bag from him and dropped it in her desk drawer, locking it.

He rolled his eyes. "Yeah, cause that will stop me."

"Behave. If there's any left by the end of the day you can have more," she said as she put her things away. She paused by the door and tried her best to look stern as she said, "That chocolate better be there after lunch, mister."

"Of course," he readily agreed.

She threw him one last look of warning before she headed off towards the cafeteria for lunch duty. He'd be right behind her since they had the same schedule. Only he had one thing to do before that.

After making sure that she was gone he knelt down and picked the lock with two paper clips he found on her desk. Seconds later the lock clicked and he stole the booty and headed for his room, sighing. When would she ever learn?

* * * *

"I still don't understand your problem," Mary said.

Haley scowled across the booth at her friend. "What's not to understand? Somehow, someway I managed to find myself in a serious relationship without the relationship."

"That sounds.......different," Mary said. After a short pause Mary asked, "What the hell do you mean? I thought you and Jason were just friends."

"We are! It's just that......" She sighed heavily as she fiddled with the label on her beer. "He doesn't date anymore. He doesn't even show any interest in another woman. When we're out he sends women away, telling them he's not interested."

"Well, that's sweet-"

"When guys approach me he throws his arm around me and gives them looks that scare the hell out of them. Last night when we were out with Mitch at the movies some guy in line stood too close to me, and Jason got into a shouting match with the guy."

"He's just being protective-"

"He treats me like his girlfriend. He's always touching me and cuddling up with me. We sleep in the same bed every night. We try sleeping positions like they were sexual positions!" she hissed quietly, hoping the loud jukebox music blocked out her voice to the rest of the bar patrons.

"And you don't like any of this?" Mary guessed.

"Like it? I love it! Except I want more. God, I can't stop thinking about him and having him so close but not close enough is killing me. I am so pathetic," she mumbled sadly.

"Does he know?"

"No. If he did he'd step back. He doesn't want a girlfriend. He wants a friend, a sister."

"Doesn't sound that way to me."

"Trust me. There's no chance in hell Jason Bradford is going to change his ways for me."

"Well, not if you don't give him a chance he won't." Mary reached over and took her hand. "You're in love with him, aren't you?'

Haley wiped at her eyes. "Let's talk about something else."

"Fine," Mary sighed. She stirred the tiny red straw in her ginger ale and looked around the bar. "There are a lot of really cute guys here tonight."

Haley followed her friends gaze and nodded her agreement. There were a lot of cute guys here tonight. That brought up another interesting question. If she decided to date and take the guy home would Jason get pissed? If she started dating someone, then she couldn't sleep in the same bed with Jason anymore. It wouldn't be fair and it would make everything weirder. The fact that she didn't want any other man but Jason holding her didn't help.

She inwardly groaned. Tonight was about relaxing after a long day of review. She wasn't here to moon over Jason Bradford. Tonight she was here to have a few drinks, play a game of pool, and relax.

"Ah, Haley, maybe we should go somewhere else. How about we rent a movie and get some pizza and head to my place?" Mary asked, sounding nervous.

Haley frowned at her. "We've been waiting an hour for the pool table and we're up next. Besides, I'm not done with my beer. What's wrong?"

Mary looked down at her drink and nibbled her lip for a moment. She looked close to tears.

"Mary?" Haley said softly.

Mary shook her head and sobbed lightly, but didn't look up.

Loud laughter drew Haley's attention to the door. Her eyes narrowed dangerously.

"That son of a bitch," she snapped.

"Haley, please don't make a big deal out of this. Let's just go-"

Haley was already on her feet and heading towards the small group near the bar. She pushed her way through the group until she was face to face with Mary's ex-fiancé and the voluptuous blonde snuggling up to him. She snorted. It wasn't even the same one he left Mary for. He was pathetic. She really wished she had spoken up years ago about how much of a loser he was.

"What the hell do you want?" Ted practically sneered.

She shrugged. "Nothing much. Just wondering if you're going to grow some balls and help Mary. You remember Mary, don't you? The woman you dated for four years, cheated on constantly, asked to marry, and then knocked up, all before you dumped her for a stripper? Well, I was just wondering if you were planning on manning up anytime soon and helping Mary with the medical bills for this pregnancy. Just thinking it might be nice if she could afford to keep your kid in diapers and formula. I'm kind of funny like that."

The woman under his arm looked startled and pushed away from him with open disgust.

"You got a woman pregnant and left her? What an asshole!" she said before stalking off and giving him the finger. His buddies laughed at him. Ted glared at her.

Ted groaned. "You stupid bitch! I am so sick of you fucking up my life! Mary's accepted our break up so when the hell are you going to? I don't want anything to do with that flat chested ugly bitch or her brat so fuck off and leave me alone! And if you're so concerned about the baby's shitty diapers then you buy them for her, bitch!"

"Listen you-"

"Haley, please!" Mary, suddenly by her side, pleaded as she tried to pull Haley away. "Let's just go!"

"There you are! You need to tell her to mind her own fucking business!" Ted said, pushing Mary in the shoulder hard to make his point.

"Oh, no you didn't, you son of a bitch!" Haley said just before she released her fists of fury on the bastard.

Chapter 13

"Would you two cut the shit? We're here to have a guy's night out, not a pissing contest," Brad said to the two men glaring at each other. He looked heavenward and sighed, "This is fucking ridiculous."

"He's the one being an asshole," Mitch said, shoving Jason.

Jason shoved him back, harder, sending his friend into a parked pickup truck. He pointed a finger at Mitch. "Stay the fuck away from her."

"Oh, fuck off, you sanctimonious asshole. You don't want her, but you don't want anyone else to have her. She's not your property!"

Jason felt his jaw clench tighter.

"What are you going to do when she starts dating some other guy? Huh, tough guy?" Mitch pushed him. "Someday soon this little friendship of yours won't be enough for her and she'll go to another guy and you won't have her anymore. Have you thought of that, yet?" Mitch snorted. "She's a beautiful, funny, sweet woman. A lot of guys would give their right nut for a girl like her!"

Jason felt all the blood drain out of his face. He stood there as the reality of Mitch's words hit him hard. One day it would be another man Haley would talk to, watch games with, or just sit in absolute peaceful silence while they worked or ate, and worst of all, it would be another man holding Haley in his arms at night.

"Fuck….," he gasped.

"Oh great, you broke him! Are you happy now?" Brad demanded. "Come on, buddy, we'll get you fixed up with a cold beer and a plate of hot wings. How does that sound? Does that sound good?"

Numbly, Jason nodded.

Brad scowled at Mitch who looked profoundly shocked by Jason's reaction. No doubt the man probably expected a good shoving match and a few outbursts. Jason going suddenly quiet was absolutely frightening.

"I hope you're happy!" Brad yelled at Mitch. "You broke him!"

"I was just pissed….I didn't know….I…" He shrugged helplessly as he helped Brad steer a very numb Jason into the bar. "Look, I'm sorry. I just thought you didn't think I was good enough for her. Shit. I didn't realize that-"

His words were cut off when Brad shook his head. Mitch looked at Jason and nodded. The man clearly wasn't ready to hear any of this. Jason wasn't aware his friends were talking. He couldn't focus past the idea of another man touching Haley.

His Haley.

"Please stop!" a woman screamed as they pushed a still frighteningly quiet Jason inside.

They spotted a familiar looking tall woman, being held back by two women who were trying to calm her down while they looked nervously at a small group of men. Suddenly the group parted.

All three men stood in shock as Haley hit, well sort of slapped with her fists in a windmill type fashion, a large man who looked more pissed with her assault than actually hurt.

"You don't ever touch her again!" Haley yelled, as she continued her weird ass assault.

"Shut up, bitch!" the man said, shoving Haley away. She stumbled backwards and hit the floor, hard.

Jason saw red as everything around him blurred into a haze. He focused on the man that just put his hands on Haley. Without a word he stalked over to the son of a bitch and punched him in the face, sending him slamming back into the bar.

The man bent over in agony, cupping his nose. "You broke my nose, asshole!"

"If you ever lay another finger on her again I will kill you. Do you understand me?" he promised with barely restrained fury.

The man tried to glare, and winced. Finally he nodded.

"Good," he said slowly, turning around. "Whoa!" he gasped as his little grasshopper ran into him as she attempted to renew her cute attack.

"Haley!" he said, trying to snap her out of it. She ignored him, trying to swing at the guy or whatever the hell she was doing. With an exasperated sigh, he threw her over his shoulder and headed for the door.

"You're lucky, Ted! Next time I will kick. Your. Ass!" she yelled.

Jason gave her bottom a patronizing pat. "I'm sure you have him quaking in his drawers, my little grasshopper. No need to scare him."

She grabbed the waist of his jeans to help push herself up so that she could glare at the bastard. "Ass whooping! Next time I'm not holding back!"

"Tell him to watch his back!" Mitch suggested, laughing.

Jason nearly rolled his eyes when Haley did just that. He released a weary breath. "Let's get you home before you have the man wetting himself."

"You're lucky, punk!" she yelled, making him grin. She was so damn cute.

* * * *

Haley grunted and kicked the covers off of them.

"Are you going to whoop the sheet's ass as well? Should I run to safety?" Jason asked, biting back a huge smile that was threatening to take over.

"It's hot!" she said in a cute little whiny voice. "And stop making fun of me. I totally kicked ass tonight," she said with a sniff. "They might even ban me from the bar after tonight."

He blinked. "For what?"

She rolled over onto her back away from him. "What do you mean for what? I started a brawl!"

"Really? When?"

"What do you mean when? You were there. You saw me kicking some ass!"

"That thing you were doing with your hands?" She nodded. "I thought you were having a seizure of some kind."

She gasped and gave him a playful shove. "Jerk! I totally kicked his ass and I could kick *your* ass."

He looked at her for a moment before he burst out laughing. The entire bed shook as he laughed, probably harder than he'd ever laughed in his entire life. Tears streamed down his face as he gripped his side, as a cramp started.

"Hey! Stop laughing at me! I'm a major threat damn it!" her serious tone had him laughing harder. Damn, she was really killing him here. "Keep it up and I'm going to kick your ass with my fists of fury!"

Somehow he managed to laugh harder. He really didn't think it was possible, but he did.

"That's it!" Haley snapped. She sat up, quickly straddled his hips and grabbed his arms. She tried to pin his arms by his side of his head. His laughter became more controlled as he quickly turned the tables on her and rolled over, pinning her beneath him. He didn't bother pinning down her hands. Really, what was the point? He'd seen her in action after all.

"Alright, my little grasshopper, kick my ass. I'm ready," he said, grinning. He made sure to keep his hips raised. No point in torturing himself, especially since she was only wearing a tiny camisole and pink cotton panties.

She began pushing at his chest, trying to shove him off. When that didn't work she tried to kick him and he thought she may have tried to give him a good old fashion Indian sunburn on his arm.

It was just sad.

"Come on, my little grasshopper, I'm ready any time you are. Show me some of that fury."

Haley shoved and pulled harder, but still he didn't move.

"Seriously, I'm ready whenever you are," he said, smiling down at her.

She groaned loudly as she increased her attempts. Still she couldn't budge him.

He couldn't stop himself from taunting her. She was just so damn cute. "Aw, is my little grasshopper getting tired? Where's all that fury gone? Come on let's see those moves-"

She cut his words off with a kiss, surprising the hell out of him. It was a quick gentle brush of her lips over his, but it knocked him on his ass. Haley dropped her head back on the pillow staring at him while she worried her bottom lip nervously.

Jason hovered over her, panting for breath that had nothing to do with laughter. That kiss..... That innocent, sweet kiss hit him harder than every make out session he'd ever had in his life.

"Jason?" Haley's broken whisper brought his attention back to her lips.

This was over. He was going to climb out of bed, apologize to her, walk her back to her house and put some distance between them. He was no good for her. He treated women like shit and had no clue how to treat someone as special as Haley. She deserved a man who would make her his entire world. A man who would take care of her, hold her and love her. And he was not that man.

"Haley, I-"

His words broke off in a groan as Haley's mouth covered his again. She brushed her lips against his enticingly. His entire body went rigid as he forced himself not to respond. He couldn't do this to her. As much as it would hurt both of them he couldn't give in to her. His body shook with the need to kiss her back and lower his body onto hers, but somehow he found the strength to fight it.

* * * *

He wasn't kissing her back.

There, she had her answer. She just had to go and kiss him to find out. She couldn't just ask him like a normal person. Now, she not only probably just wrecked everything between them, but she was also horribly embarrassed. Peachy. Just freakin' peachy.

She felt tears burn her eyes. He was not going to see her cry. She absolutely refused to let him see how much this hurt her.

"Excuse me," she mumbled softly, breaking away and pushing at his chest. He didn't fight her this time. He moved off her. She was so close to breaking down. She jumped off the bed and headed for the bedroom door. She didn't care about her clothes or anything else at the moment. She just needed to get out of there.

"Haley!" Jason called after her. "Let's talk about this!"

The last thing she wanted to do was talk about this. She ran out his front door and across the yard to her door. Barely able to see through the tears that were now flowing freely down her face as she searched for her hidden key beneath the front step and went into her house.

She locked the front door and ran to her room to lock her window and pull her curtains shut, knowing Jason would just come through the window for her and try to joke his way out of this. She didn't want to joke about this. This hurt! Her heart was broken and she just lost the best friend she ever had over her own stupidity.

A sob broke free and then another until she was sobbing uncontrollably. She dropped onto the edge of her bed and buried her face in her hands as she let it out. She was too tired to fight it anymore.

Warm breath tickled her hands the same time strong fingers gently pulled her hands down. She averted her face so she wouldn't have to face him kneeling in front of her. She just couldn't.

"Will you look at me?" he asked softly.

She bit her lip and shook her head.

"I'm not......Haley, I'm just not good enough for you. Do you understand what I'm saying?"

Haley shrugged, wanting him to get to the point quickly and leave. At the moment, she didn't trust herself to open her mouth, afraid she'd just embarrass herself more.

"You're too good for me, my little grasshopper," he said softly as he laid his forehead in the crook of her neck. "You could do so much better than me without even trying, Haley. So much better."

His voice dropped as he continued and he sounded like he was in pain, but still she said nothing. "You're kind, smart, funny, you have the biggest heart of anyone I've ever met and you're sweet. God, are you sweet." His hands slid up her sides and gently rubbed up and down.

His breath came quicker against her skin and Haley wanted nothing more than to wrap her arms around him and hold him one more time, but she couldn't do it. She couldn't stand for him to push her away again.

"Do you know how sweet you are, my little grasshopper?" his voice was hoarse as his hands moved lower to her hips and slid back up until his thumbs brushed beneath her breasts and then down again. He pressed a kiss to her neck almost as if he couldn't help himself. A pained groan escaped him when he did it.

"I should walk out of here and never come back and let you go meet some nice guy who will give you everything in life that you deserve." He pressed another kiss to her neck and she barely bit back a moan. His hands slid down her sides and this time when they moved back up they were beneath her shirt.

Large warm hands slid up her sides only to stop right beneath her breasts. They hesitated there for a second before continuing their journey downward. He continued to kiss her neck almost desperately. The next time his hands moved up he ran his thumbs along the underside of her breasts and groaned.

Haley's head dropped back while her hands fisted in the comforter. She still hadn't spoken, but for other reasons now. She was afraid if she spoke, she would break through to him and he would realize what he was doing and leave her. Heaven help her, but he had her too desperate to chance it.

"I need to leave." He pressed an open mouthed kiss to her neck and gently sucked while his hands moved further up only to teasingly brush over her hard nipples. They moaned in unison. "It's the right thing to do......the um,....the um......" His hands made another swipe this time gently squeezing before moving back down.

"I um, I shouldn't want you.....I shouldn't.....I care for you so much, my little grasshopper. That's why I should.....I should," he groaned loud and low, "*you're so sweet.*"

She decided enough was enough. He obviously wanted her as much as she wanted him, well she hoped he did at least. Taking a deep fortifying breath, she leaned back, dislodging his mouth from her neck. He looked dazed as he tried to figure out what just happened.

Haley held his eyes as she reached down and grabbed the hem of her shirt. Hoping she wasn't wrong about him, she pulled it up and off and tossed it to the floor.

Jason froze. His hands stilled on her hips as his jaw clenched tightly. He locked eyes with her and she had to bite back a smile as he struggled not to look down. He lost that battle several times.

He sucked in a reverent breath as he allowed his eyes to linger on her breasts. He mumbled something about not being a saint before looking back up. He studied her face for a long moment.

"You know you could do better than me, right?"

She rolled her eyes and gave him a watery smile. "Well, duh."

"As long as we're on the same page," he mumbled before his mouth came down on hers.

Chapter 14

None of the fantasies he had about his little grasshopper came close to the real thing. Her lips were full and warm against his as he moved over them in a hungry kiss.

He gave her a chance. Hell, he'd let her run out of his house in nothing more than her panties and a skimpy shirt. He'd have to talk to her about her flashing ways, but later…much later. Right now he was busy running his hands over the most perfect breasts in creation. They were big, but not too big. They were just perfect for his hands.

She moaned and he attacked, sliding his tongue into that warm heaven she called a mouth. Her tongue came out to play and slid against his, making him growl into her mouth.

Her hands slid up his chest, sending ripples of pleasure throughout his body. He'd dreamed of her touching him. He loved the way she ran her fingers through his hair at night when they held each other. He'd fantasized about her running her fingers over the rest of his body.

With one last deep kiss he moved his mouth down along her jaw and ran his tongue down her neck between her breasts. His hands never stopped their ministrations. He gripped one breast and held it for his mouth as an offering. He ran his tongue around one large hard nipple, earning the most erotic moan he'd ever heard from a woman before he sucked it between his lips. He released the nipple with a loud *pop* and turned his attention to the next one.

After a moment his hands slid back down her stomach where he gripped her panties. She didn't hesitate in lifting her hips. His little grasshopper was a good girl. He pulled the panties off while he kissed his way down. When they were gone he gently pushed her back onto the bed and moved his mouth to one inner thigh and then to the next.

"I wonder if you're as sweet as I imagined, Haley," he said, kissing her thigh before pushing her legs further apart. Even in the dimly lit room he could see her sex clearly. The pink lips were puffy with arousal and her short trimmed curls were soaked, making him lick his lips in anticipation.

He pressed a teasing kiss close to her juncture. "Are you sweet, Haley? Hmmm?"

Her answer was a whimper.

"I bet you're sweeter than honey," he murmured as he leaned in and ran his tongue between the swollen pink lips in one long lick. His eyes closed as he moaned deeply. Sweeter. Much sweeter than he imagined. Haley's hips shot off the edge of the bed, but he was ready for that. He grabbed her feet and placed them on his shoulders.

Using his thumbs, he spread her open and nearly came from the sight. Using his thumb he spread the warm clear liquid over the tiny nub.

Haley moaned.

"You like that?" he asked in a husky voice. "Then you'll love this."

He ran the tip of his tongue around the little nub, careful not to touch it. Haley squirmed beneath his hands, trying to find relief. He slid two fingers inside of her, but switched to one when he realized how tight she was. He was glad he wasn't the only one who hadn't had sex in a while. He wanted her desperate for him.

Finally he ran his tongue over her sensitive little nub, earning a moan so he did it again and again while slowly sliding his finger in and out of her. He had to close his eyes. He was so close to coming and she hadn't even touched him yet. He prayed he wouldn't embarrass himself tonight. He planned on being inside of her most of the night.

Her sheath tightened around his fingers like a vice. He sucked her clit between his lips while flicking his tongue over it.

"Jason....Jason....," she moaned his name softly. *"Jason!"* she screamed his name as her body throbbed hard around his finger.

He waited until she lay boneless on the bed, panting before pulling away and slowly licking his lips and fingers clean. He leaned over and kissed her.

"Condom," he said through clenched teeth. He was on the edge of coming. He'd never been more turned on in his life. He wanted to fuck her in every imaginable position and in some he was sure were physically impossible, but he was willing to give them all a try.

He felt Haley still beneath him. It was so quick that he almost didn't notice it. Before he could ask what was wrong, she pushed him off. Shit. She was still pissed about earlier.

"Haley, I- *fuck*" he groaned loudly, well yelled really, as Haley in one swift move yanked his boxers down and took him in her hot wet mouth. He braced his hands on her shoulders while she worked him. She took the tip of his cock into her mouth with a well practiced move that nearly had his eyes crossing.

She cupped his sack with one hand, rolling it in her palm, making him groan and buck. He forced himself to be still so he wouldn't hurt her. She met his eyes when she slowly took him in and went past the point any other woman had ever managed.

He whimpered.

His head dropped back as Haley deep throated him. Never had it felt like this, so good, so complete. His little grasshopper had a secret side to her. A side he very much planned on exploring. He wondered what else she could do and who had taught her. Anger surged through him just thinking about her doing this with any other man and he quickly pushed those thoughts away with Haley's help.

For several minutes, panting and suckling sounds echoed throughout the small bedroom, making it harder for Jason to hold back. He was so damn close. Hell, he could have easily come a hundred times over by now, but he was desperate to keep this going. It felt so good....so fucking good.

Finally, he couldn't hold back any longer. He tapped her on the shoulder, the universal sign of warning, and started to pull back when Haley gripped his hip with her free hand and held him in place as she doubled her efforts.

"Haley baby, I'm gonna *come*!" he moaned the last word loudly. His entire body spasmed as his cock hardened beyond belief and erupted in her sweet little mouth. Haley didn't miss a beat sucking him dry. She was truly wonderful.

Gasping for air, he pulled back, sucking in a deep breath as he slid out over her tongue. Lazily he shoved down his underwear and climbed onto the bed over Haley.

She licked her lips, making him groan. He leaned in and kissed her, mixing their flavors. As they kissed they slowly moved up the bed. Once Haley's head hit the pillow Jason laid on his side and gathered her close.

As good as it felt to simply hold her in his arms over these past weeks it felt better to have her in his arms naked. Surprisingly it had nothing to do with sex. He loved feeling her warm skin against his and feeling her heartbeat as it lulled him into a deep sleep.

* * * *

"Shit!" Haley heard Jason yell as something crashed in the other room. From the sounds of it he just knocked over her stack of books on the hallway table, again.

She leaned against the kitchen counter, nibbling on a piece toast as she watched Jason stumble in. His hair was still wet and he was still fumbling with his clothes. His shoes were untied, his pants undone, his shirt was only halfway buttoned up and he was having a hell of a time with his tie.

He glared accusingly at her while he made short work of his clothes. "You didn't wake me up."

She rolled her eyes as she speared a piece of sausage with her fork. "I did wake you up. Three times in fact. Each time you threw something at me and went back to sleep."

Jason gaped at her. "And you gave up? You know our routine, woman. You have to keep at it until I'm forced to get off the bed to find something to throw at you." His eyes narrowed dangerously on the large breakfast in front of her.

"And you've eaten without me?" he asked in shocked outrage. Eating to Jason was sacred, probably because he liked stealing food from her plate when it was still hot.

Any other morning and she would have made sure he got right up. She enjoyed their quiet mornings together before they faced their hormonal charges. This morning she didn't want to give him a chance to finish what they started last night.

As much as she wanted to, needed to, take that next step with him she was frightened. He was a man with experience and expectations and she was.....well, for the lack of a better word, a chicken.

She was fortunate to be the youngest child in the family not only because her grandparents took her in, but because she was able to see from a very young age how her sisters and older cousins were treated by so-called friends and men. Men came and went out of their lives, turning them into slobbering idiots. She'd known more than one woman over the years that thought sex meant love to men, only to have their heart broken in the end.

It might seem old fashioned, but she only planned on sleeping with one man in her life, the man she would spend the rest of her life with. She dated over the years and handled her "needs" in other ways but never took the chance on any man she'd dated. Since she never fell in love with them it had been easy, but with Jason it was going to be difficult.

She knew without a doubt that she was in love with him and that he at least cared for her deeply, as deeply as a man like him could. Haley had no delusions about what kind of man Jason had been in the past. He'd never had a serious relationship and never cared for any woman he'd been with. Although he had changed a great deal and even matured over the past couple of months she wasn't one of those delusional women who thought she could change a man.

Jason could very well be the person to get her to break the rule of only one man for life, because she knew without a doubt, that he would never marry her. He might be able to handle an exclusive relationship with her, but for how long? She knew, sooner or later, he'd get bored and moved onto the next girl. It would hurt like hell, but she knew it was coming.

So, that left her with a very important decision to make. Did she take a chance and give herself to him, hoping her heart wouldn't completely shatter when he moved on, or keep it at the physical level that she was comfortable with?

The only thing stopping her was the regret she knew she would feel a year from now when yet another woman came screaming and banging on his door in the middle of the night.

She watched as Jason finished dressing. The entire time he scowled at her or looked longingly towards the stack of waffles, toast, eggs, bacon and sausage. Of course she cooked this for him, and he knew it on some level, but it was Jason and he took his food seriously. Too seriously, but that was a job for Dr. Phil to work through, not her.

When he finished dressing he threw his bag over his shoulder, grabbed the bottle of syrup and soaked the waffles. He grabbed a fork and the plate and headed for the door, leaving her to roll her eyes and follow him.

While she drove they ate. For every two bites he took he gave her one, which worked for her since it didn't take much to fill her up. Secretly, she loved it when they did things like this, especially when he took care of her. It was so sweet. He made sure that she was given the best piece of bacon or bite of sausage and always made sure to double dip her bite of waffle into the syrup, knowing how much she liked it.

By the time they pulled into the staff parking lot, they had finished and the plate was on the backseat, sitting on the large beach towel she put back there for times like this.

They sat there for a moment and watched as buses and cars drove up in front of the building. It occurred to her that she was suddenly nervous. After last night, she thought it would be awkward first thing this morning, another reason she left the bed early. Instead, they jumped right into their normal relaxed routine. Now that the food was gone and they were sitting here she was really nervous.

Did he regret what they did? Was she about to get the speech that he didn't want anything serious? Would he get pissed when he found out she wouldn't sleep with him like several men before him had? Damn it! What earth shattering thing would he say?

"You've got syrup on your lip."

Okay, not exactly life altering.

She licked her lip. "Is it gone?"

"No."

She wiped her mouth with her fingers. "How about now?"

He sighed. "I see I'm going to have to handle this." He leaned in quickly and brushed his lips against hers. She sucked in a breath as he ran his tongue over her bottom lip.

"So sweet, my little grasshopper," he whispered against her lips. He brushed his lips against hers again. "I know why you left the bed early this morning and why you made sure that I had very little time to do anything else but get ready for work."

He pressed another kiss to her lips as he took her hand into his. "I'm sorry for being a jerk last night and almost making the biggest mistake of my life. I was afraid of hurting you. I know what I am and I also know you deserve a guy that can spoil you rotten and take you to all the nice places that you deserve. I-"

"Jason, I don't care about those things," she said softly.

He shook his head stubbornly. "It doesn't mean that you don't deserve them, but if you give me a chance to make up for my past stupidity, and I'm not just talking about with you, I promise that I will do my best to make you happy."

"Jason-"

"I want to try this. You and me, I mean. I know I'll most likely fuck up along the way and you'll want to wring my neck, but I want to try. I'll do my best not to hurt you."

Haley smiled, knowing that was the best she could hope for, from him. She appreciated his honesty and knew that if they were going to try to make this work then she had to be honest with him, at least about the extent of their relationship. He might not like being with a woman where sex, well, intercourse wasn't involved.

She gave his hand a small squeeze. "Jason, if we're going to try this then I'd like to take things slow." He frowned. "What I mean is nothing beyond the level we were at last night." She worried her lip between her teeth. "What I mean is no actual sex."

He narrowed his eyes on her. "But, you'll still sleep with me naked and let me do a hundred other naughty things to you?" he asked in a serious tone.

"Yes."

He brushed his lips against hers again and moved back a few inches to look into her eyes. "And you'll still cook for me and call me Master?"

Her lips twitched. "Yes to the cooking and not a chance in hell for the other."

He sighed wearily. "Fine, how about Lord and Master?"

"Uh...no."

"God?"

"Nope."

"My liege?"

"Wait.....no."

He gave her one of his lopsided smiles. "I'll wear you down, eventually."

She wasn't so sure he would stick around long enough to make good on that promise, but for the chance to be with him even for a short time, she was willing to risk it.

Chapter 15

"I hate this. Why did we have to come here?" she said in a snooty tone as she looked around the large carnival with clear distaste. "If I had known we were coming here, I would have stayed home. God, have you ever heard of a restaurant? That's where I should be eating, not something on a stick like some slob." She flipped her long hair over her shoulder.

Jason glanced at Mitch whose jaw was clenched. The man did not look happy and Jason didn't blame him one bit. If Jason had known that she was going to react this way to going to a carnival he never would have suggested it or at the very least, not brought her.

Personally, he loved carnivals and theme parks. He couldn't pass one by without stopping in for a fried treat and a few rides. Mitch was the same way, which was why they were here. They came to have a good time. Instead they were stuck listening to this woman bitch and whine. She started as soon as she heard the plans for the evening.

As soon as she found out she put her foot down and demanded a nice restaurant and drinks. She'd been outvoted and offered a ride home. She refused. Jason knew that she decided to come along to make their lives a living hell for not jumping to meet her demands.

"We can go on the bumper cars or the Ferris wheel," Mitch started to suggest.

She folded her arms over her chest and glared, just glared at the man. Mitch cursed under his breath. She turned her cold glare on Jason and he didn't bother hiding his eye roll. This was ridiculous. No way was he letting her wreck his good time.

"Jason!"

He turned around and his frown was instantly gone, replaced by a huge pleased smile. He watched as his little grasshopper quickly walked towards him, grinning from ear to ear. She had a stuffed animal, a snake, from the looks of it, around her neck, a large soda in one hand and her other arm wrapped around a fake sword, a teddy bear and she held the largest piece of fried dough he'd ever seen that was generously covered in powdered sugar.

"Look what I won!" she said, practically beaming with excitement. It was hard to believe someone loved these places more than him and Mitch, but apparently Haley was that person.

When he told her where they were going today she squealed excitedly and threw herself into his arms. He laughed so hard that he almost dropped her. This was their first date since they came together a week ago and thankfully he'd chosen well. He would have liked to have been able to take her out sooner, but they'd both been swamped with giving final exams, correcting them, and going over final grades. School was over and now they had a whole summer together.

"This is so much fun!" Haley said, seeming oblivious to Mitch's date's attitude or she simply didn't give a damn, he suspected the latter. His little grasshopper didn't let things bother her.

"Where did you get all of this?" he asked as he leaned in for a kiss and a bite of that dough.

"Oh, um," she gestured with her drink towards the direction in which she came from, "after I hit the bumper cars I couldn't resist the basketball game or the darts and then I smelled the fried dough and," she shrugged. "I guess I got distracted."

"I thought you were just going to find the bathroom. We've been standing here waiting for you for over a half an hour!" Mitch's date, Sue or Jude or whatever the hell her name was, pointed out.

Judging by Haley's expression she'd forgotten all about the bathroom and just remembered that she had to go. That was confirmed a few seconds later when she shoved her drink, food, and winnings in his and Mitch's arms and took off running.

Jason took a huge bite out of the dough and sighed happily. No doubt he was going to have to hunt his little grasshopper down in a few minutes near some game or ride and carry her to the bathroom.

Mitch looked down at his arms, frowned and looked at the things Jason was now holding. "How come you got the sword? I want the sword." He reached out to snag the sword. Jason bitch slapped his hand away with the dough.

"My sword!"

"Jerk," Mitch mumbled as he eyed the sword.

Jason looked at his sword too and took another bite. "We could always go win another one and have a sword fight."

"Sweet!" Mitch said. Yeah, they were big kids when it came to carnivals, but who cared?

"I'm not going anywhere," Mitch's date said, intent on wrecking their good time.

Mitch shrugged. "Well, then have a good night."

* * * *

Haley increased her pout.

Jason chuckled. "I don't care. You're not getting it back."

"That's not fair! You're just mad because I kicked ass!"

Mitch rubbed his shoulder while he glared at Haley. She bit her lip and took a step back, ducking beneath Jason's arm. He pulled her closer and kissed the top of her head.

"Fine, keep the sword. I don't care," she said in a sulky voice. Mitch muttered something and sighed heavily.

"You want to go on the bumper cars again?" Mitch asked with an easy smile. He'd never seen his friend forgive anyone so fast before, but of course Haley had that affect on everyone. It was just so hard to stay mad at her. She was too damn cute for her own good.

"I suppose we could do that," she said, already tugging Jason towards the bumper cards. "If you insist that is."

Jason looked back in time to catch Mitch leering at Haley's ass.

* * * *

"That was so much fun," Haley said dreamily as she pulled her shoes off.

"It was okay," Jason mumbled.

For the past four hours Jason had been uncharacteristically quiet. He didn't seem to do much more than glare at Mitch. A few times there she thought he was going to kill the man. She wasn't sure what she missed or if she should even get involved.

A few minutes later they were naked and crawling beneath Jason's sheets. That's when he really frightened her. He didn't initiate any kissing or touching. In fact, he didn't even glance at her breasts and Jason always looked. Always. They were like magnets for his eyes.

Now he was lying on his back with his arms behind his head. He made no moves to get closer to her or to pull her against him. He was truly starting to scare her now. She rolled over onto her stomach and watched him for a moment.

"Are you okay?" she finally asked.

He shrugged. "Why wouldn't I be okay?"

"You're quiet."

"I just don't feel like talking."

"Do you want me to go home?"

He hesitated before answering, "No."

"Then what do you want?"

"Nothing. I just want to lay here."

"So, you just want to lay there and nothing is wrong," she said, summing it up.

"Yeah."

She rolled her eyes. Seemed she didn't have much choice about getting involved now. It was either that or get up and leave, because she wasn't about to stay here for another moment of this.

Before he could stop her, she was up and straddling his hips. She made another shocking discovery. Jason wasn't hard. Jason was always hard when they were in bed, the shower, or making out on the couch and all those times in between. She was pretty sure the man would never have to worry about needing Viagra.

He made no attempts to push her off, but neither did he look at her.

"I'm not going anywhere until you tell me what's wrong," she said softly.

"Nothing's wrong."

"Don't make me use my fists of fury to get an answer out of you," she threatened.

His lips twitched, but still he said nothing.

"Okay, you just lay there and sulk then. I'm going home," she said, moving to climb off him.

Jason's hands shot out, stopping her by gripping her hips.

She raised an expectant brow.

He sighed heavily. "You pissed me off."

Well, that was totally unexpected....sort of.

"Hey, I said I was sorry about hitting Mitch with that sword. How was I supposed to know the thing would leave a welt?" she said defensively.

"That's not what I'm talking about. That didn't bother me."

"Is it because I kicked your ass at skee ball?"

"No! And that game is rigged anyway, so it doesn't count."

"*Riigghhht*," she said, drawing out the word. She thought over the rest of the night and couldn't figure out what she'd done. "Okay, you're gonna have to help me out here because I'm drawing a blank."

"I'm pissed because all those men hit on you and not once did you tell any of them to fuck off because you had a boyfriend!" he yelled.

Her face went expressionless. She blinked once and then again. Then she burst into uncontrollable laughter.

* * * *

"It's not funny," he snapped. That only seemed to make her laugh harder.

All day at the carnival, he'd been forced to watch men notice Haley. Every time she smiled or laughed they smiled as if they couldn't help themselves. Every time she jumped up and down excitedly their eyes zeroed in on her bouncing assets. He caught them checking her out and sending her appreciative looks. Mitch, the rat bastard as he was now known, completely ditched his date and focused entirely on Haley.

It only got worse when they went to Joe's Tavern. The place was large, homey and clean and today Joe put out a huge buffet. So with an all you can eat barbeque and several flat screens and five pool tables the place had been filled to the rim with men.

When Haley went up to get food, they crowded her, offered to carry her plate, get her a drink, sit with her, scoop her food. When she played pool, and she really sucked at pool, but clearly loved it, they offered to "show" her how to play. Two guys had the balls to send drinks over to their table while she was with him. Several actually had the balls to come over and flirt with her in front of him!

Mitch was no help. When he wasn't trying to pick up some bar tramp, he was watching Haley and hitting on her like there was no tomorrow. The bastard didn't even try to hide his leers from Jason. What the hell kind of friendship was that?

Okay, granted in the past, before Haley, he'd been a complete jerk. He openly checked out and hit on his buddies' girlfriends. If he was out and he liked what he saw he never let a boyfriend worry him. But that was no excuse for what Mitch was doing. This was Haley! *His* Haley!

"Sweetie, I think you had too much sun today," Haley said once she calmed down.

"You should have said something!"

She rolled her eyes. "First off, I have absolutely no idea what the hell you are talking about. I don't think anyone was looking my way any differently or flirting. They were just really friendly."

He snorted.

"Secondly, even if they were, and they weren't, I don't know why you're complaining. I didn't exactly hear you tell every woman that was drooling over you today, that you had a girlfriend."

Another snort.

"I don't give a damn about those women. I've got what I want," he said, gently massaging her hips.

Haley leaned over and pressed a quick kiss to his lips before sitting back up. "Exactly. I didn't notice any other man but you," she said softly as she ran her hands over his chest and stomach.

He rolled his eyes. "Of course you didn't. I'm awesome."

"I'm glad to see you're humble."

"Hey, I could have said I was the epitome of manliness, but I didn't." He pursed his lips up thoughtfully. "Even though we both know that it's true."

"We do?" She arched a brow.

"Yes, I believe we both do."

"Fine, whatever, as long as you stop paying attention to your hallucinations then I don't care."

He watched her for a moment. The expression on her face was shy and sweet as she traced shapes on his stomach. She truly did not know how desirable she was. He would bet money that she didn't think men noticed her and she'd probably broken a hundred hearts unintentionally up to this point. She was just so damn sweet and innocent, well except for in bed of course. There she was eager, insatiable and thrilling. He never thought foreplay could be so pleasurable before. He had no doubt sex with her would be life altering.

"You are so beautiful, Haley," he said softly. He'd said that to other women before, but he'd never meant it more. She was beautiful inside and out.

Even in the dim light he could see her blush and shyly avert her eyes. "Thank you," she mumbled, sounding unsure.

She truly didn't realize how beautiful she was. That made her even more beautiful to him. He skimmed his hands over her belly and up until he was palming her breasts. He brushed his thumbs over her nipples, loving the way she licked her lips and arched her back into his hold.

Haley began squirming on him, letting him know she could feel his body harden. He loved the way she looked, the way she reacted, he loved everything about her. She was the most precious thing in the world to him. So beautiful, so sweet, so giving and too damn good for him, but he was a selfish bastard and wouldn't let her go.

Ever.

He slowly massaged her breasts while playing with her nipples, just enjoying the way she licked her lips, moaned and whimpered. His erection was pressed firmly against her. Her bottom nestled it very nicely and he loved the way it caressed him as she squirmed on him. He could feel her getting wet against his stomach.

"You want to try something different?" he asked in a husky voice.

She licked her lips slowly, nodding as she looked down at him with an expression of pure trust. It humbled him.

"Hold on," he said as he pulled her down to him, kissing her slowly as he rolled them over until he was on top of her. He deepened the kiss as he pulled her knees up and over his shoulders, angling her where he needed her, giving him better access to her hot wet core.

"Jason....," she said nervously.

"Shhh, don't worry. No penetration," he said against her mouth. "I just want you to feel how much I want you." He settled himself more firmly between her legs, making sure his hard shaft was nestled between her warm wet folds.

He deepened the kiss as he pulled back and then slid forward rubbing the underside of his cock against her hot wet core and clit. They moaned into each other's mouths as he continued to grind against her.

Haley's moans echoed off the walls as Jason fought for control. His body screamed for him to arch back and slam into her, but Haley wanted to go slow. He would do anything for her, even torture himself with being so close to the prize and not going for it.

She fisted her hands in his hair as she licked and sucked his neck. He groaned loudly as he pressed himself more firmly against her and thrust harder. Haley's grip in his hair tightened seconds before she started screaming his name. It triggered his own violent release.

"Haley......oh, Haley.....I..oh, God, Haley!" he yelled while his mind shouted "I love you" over and over until he released her legs and lay bonelessly on top of her.

As he was gasping for air he realized something. He was in deep shit. Haley was his life now. His woman. His heart.

He was so screwed.

Chapter 16

"Oh my God, stop eating that!" Haley said, trying not to laugh and failing miserably.

Jason popped the fudge brownie in his mouth and winked at her. With an exasperated sigh, she reached back into the backseat to fix the plastic wrap on the plates of brownies, cookies, and cupcakes.

"If you keep stealing food there won't be any left for your family's cookout," she said, knowing that wasn't a good enough reason to stop him from eating. She was willing to bet there wasn't much that would come between him and food.

He turned his attention from the road to pout. "But I love your cooking."

She rolled her eyes at his lame attempt. "Uh huh."

"Well, at least I'm not touching the potato salad. You really should appreciate the little things in life, my little grasshopper."

Haley scoffed in disbelief. "The only reason you're not scarfing that down is because I have that and the pasta salad in a cooler safely locked away in the trunk."

His brows shot up. "There's macaroni salad? Why was I not informed of this?"

"Probably because I wanted it to at least make it to your parent's house before you devoured it."

He shook his head, sighing, "So little trust."

"You ate an entire bowl of cookie dough yesterday when I made the mistake of running out to the market without hiding it first. Seriously, I thought it would be safe."

"You were wrong."

"Your obsession with food is starting to scare me," she said wryly.

"It's not an obsession. I'm a growing boy, damn it."

She raised one brow in disbelief.

"Thank God we're here. I'm starving," he grumbled as he parked in the only empty spot on the street, which just happened to be in front of a large white Victorian house with black trim where a party was clearly being held, judging by the amount of people walking around the property.

They loaded their arms up with all the plates Haley made and headed for the front door. Jason kicked the door lightly since his hands were full. The door was opened by an older woman with salt and pepper hair. She took one look at Jason and smiled.

"It's my baby boy!" she announced loudly to the crowd in the house as she cupped his face and pulled him down to give him a sound kiss on the cheek. She stepped back and noticed Haley. Her expression went from excited to stunned in a matter of seconds.

Jason smiled sheepishly. "Mom, this is my girlfriend, Haley Blaine." He gestured with the plate of brownies. "Haley, this is my mother Megan Bradford."

"It's very nice to meet you, Mrs. Bradford," Haley said, feeling a little awkward with his mother standing there gaping at her and her hands too full to offer to shake the woman's hand. Not that his mother seemed to be able to respond or anything at the moment. Actually, Haley was starting to become a little worried.

"Girlfriend?" Megan finally choked out.

"Yeah, why do you sound so-" Jason started to say only to be cut off by his mother.

His mother turned her head and yelled into the house. "Jared!"

Haley shot a nervous look at Jason who was muttering something about putting his mother into a nursing home that only served green Jell-O. She looked back at the door in time to see an older man, who was clearly Jason's father judging by the almost identical features, step into the doorway. He smiled when he saw Jason.

"What's going on?"

"Mom's freaking out," Jason said. "Any chance we can get in there before my girlfriend's arms fall off?"

The man noticeably started as he looked at Haley and then did a double take.

"Girlfriend?" he asked in clear disbelief.

"Yes! Girlfriend!" Jason snapped, but his parents didn't seem to notice because they were staring at her like they couldn't believe such a person existed. On top of that her arms were starting to feel like they were about to drop off.

"Ah, about to drop the cupcakes," she mumbled as she tried to readjust the three plates in her arms.

"Oh, sorry," Jared said, reaching out and relieving her of the cupcakes while his wife grabbed the plate of peanut butter chocolate chunk cookies from her.

Jared looked from her to the plate in his hands. "Where did you buy these? They look good," he said as his hand expertly snuck beneath the plastic wrap. Ah, like father like son, Haley thought. She looked him over quickly. The man was clearly in great shape, a good sign for Jason since the man couldn't stop eating.

"I made them," Haley said, feeling a little embarrassed by the attention.

"You made these?" Jared asked with a cupcake in his hand.

She nodded.

"She's a great cook," Jason announced proudly.

Jared took a big bite, closed his eyes and made a yummy moan sound. In seconds, he had the entire cupcake devoured. He reached out and snagged the second plate of cupcakes from Haley and headed back into the house without a word.

"My cupcakes!" they heard him snap at someone. Haley just barely stopped an eye roll. Definitely like father, like son.

"Hey, old man, she made those for me!" Jason yelled, charging past his mother to go after the cupcakes, leaving Haley with Megan, who was still staring at her.

"Um," she gestured to the car. "I have two more plates of cupcakes. I didn't think those two would survive the trip over here," she said, feeling foolish. Perhaps she should go hang out in the car until after the party was over. Seven hours in a car with nothing to do sounded better than being gawked at.

Megan's eyes narrowed on her. "You're really his girlfriend?"

"Yes."

"This isn't just some sick game he's playing?"

"Uh, no...is there something wrong?" She was really starting to feel self-conscious.

"Nothing other than you are the first woman he's ever brought home and you'll have to forgive me if I seem a little surprised. For a moment there I thought hell had frozen over." She put her arm around Haley's shoulders as if they were old friends. "Now, let's go in there and give a few dozen people the shock of a lifetime."

* * * *

"Mom," Jason growled in warning.

She ignored him. Again. He leaned forward and tried to grab the photo album off Haley's lap only to have his hand slapped away by two women.

"Damn it, mom! This is supposed to be a barbeque. Shouldn't you be mingling and being a good hostess or something, instead of sitting here and embarrassing me?"

"The hell with the barbeque! I've waited over thirty years for my only child to bring home a woman and I'll not be denied!" Several people around his mother smartly moved back while he just glared.

"Ah, you look so cute-"

"Naturally," he said with a sniff.

"-playing dress up in your mother's clothes," Haley said with an evil little smile. He turned his glare on her. She simply smiled sweetly and returned to the pictures from hell.

"Haley?"

She ignored him pointedly and laughed along with his mother.

"Haley? Do you want to go get something to eat?"

"Huh? Oh, yeah, I could go for a burger and potato salad, thank you," she said dismissively before laughing at something his mother pointed out.

"Oh, that sounds good. I'll take the same. Thank you sweetie, oh, and get us each another soda since we seem to have run out," Megan said, gesturing to their empty cups without looking away from that damn album he was going to have to torch.

Where the hell was the adoration and love? His mother normally babied him. Hell, at this point she normally was getting *him* a third plate of food and a drink. Let's not forget Haley who should be loading up a plate for herself with food for him to steal. What was wrong with his women?

He walked into the kitchen where food covered every surface. As he made up their plates, his father, who was licking icing off his fingers, walked into the room with two of Jason's uncles and three of his cousins. The bastard hid the cupcakes and wouldn't share. When Haley made the mistake of mentioning the two plates of cupcakes still in her trunk he ran for them with his father close behind. The man actually tackled him to the ground, stole his keys and his beloved cupcakes.

"Those were without a doubt the best cupcakes I've ever had," his father announced happily.

"We wouldn't know since you wouldn't share any of them, you greedy bastard," Uncle Chuck said.

"I don't share," Jared said simply.

The men rolled their eyes.

"So," his cousin Trevor said as he leaned against the wall with his arms crossed over his massive chest, "how much did you pay her?"

"What the hell are you talking about?" he asked, placing the ketchup back on the counter.

His other cousin Nate answered, "What he means is, why is she here? Did you pay her? Did she owe you a favor? We're just wondering how you managed to get her here."

Aggravated, he snatched the ketchup bottle with more force than necessary and squeezed an insane amount on both burgers.

"She's my girlfriend, plain and simple," he said.

"Uh huh," his father said in clear disbelief.

Jason slammed the bun on top of the burger, forcing ketchup out the sides. "What the hell is that supposed to mean? Why is it so hard for you bastards to believe that she's my girlfriend?"

They took that as their cue to tell him exactly why they didn't think she was his girlfriend.

"She's too nice."

"Too sweet."

"Nothing at all like the skanks you normally date."

"She doesn't come off as a brainless bitch like the girls you took to the clubs."

"She doesn't annoy the shit out of us."

"Plus, there is that whole thing where you've never claimed to have a girlfriend before, never told us about her, and gave your mother and me the surprise of a lifetime when you announced her earlier. So, you can see why we're curious," his father finished with a shrug.

"Plus, she's clearly too good for you," Uncle Mark added for good measure. "That's my main reason for not believing this bullshit story."

Well, that.......hurt. Not that he could or would argue that she was too good for him. She was. There was no question about that. What really hurt was that they didn't believe him. He was known for being an asshole, not a liar. There was a big difference as far as he was concerned.

His mother chose that moment to come in, smiling. Thank God. She'd put an end to all this nonsense.

"Do you need help with those burgers, sweetie?" she asked, frowning down at the hamburger he squished into a pancake. She lightly tsked him as she threw away the burgers and started over.

"I'm glad you're here, Mom."

She smiled warmly up at him.

While looking at the men of his family he asked her, "What do you think of Haley?"

Her smile grew. "Oh, she's such a sweet girl. I'm so glad you brought her." Her smiled turned wistful. "I just wished you would date a girl like her instead of the girls you find at bars, sweetie. A woman like that is just what you need. I'm sure if you straighten out your act a bit, you'll get a woman like Haley one-"

The men laughed.

Jason held up a hand. "Whoa, whoa, whoa, woman, back up there a second. I bring a woman home and introduce her as my girlfriend and you're giving me a lecture on how to get her to go out with me? Are you serious?"

She blinked up at him. "Well, yes. I've heard about some of those girls you date, sweetie, and while I appreciate the fact that you've never brought them home to me, I would really like to see you with someone. It would be nice if you considered dating Haley. She's such a nice woman."

He thrust his hands into his hair. This was crazy. Was this what normally took place when a man brought a woman home to meet his family? He was pretty sure it wasn't. This was worse than when he met Haley's family.

"Shouldn't you be getting all excited and trying to push for marriage and grandbabies at this point?" he asked, not really wanting to encourage his mother to do that, but that's what happened when Brad brought Jill home six years ago to meet his family.

Megan looked thoughtful for a moment. "You know, I probably would if you were dating her. She's a very nice woman and I think she would do you a world of good." She smiled excitedly. "Are you thinking of asking her out?"

"Why the hell would I have to ask my girlfriend out? She's already going out with me? What is wrong with you people?"

She rolled her eyes and playfully slapped his shoulder. "Oh, honey, you don't have to keep pretending. I'm glad you have a friend like Haley. Everyone thinks she's great." She tapped a finger to her chin. "Of course, your Aunt Ruth has been pushing her towards Jeff for the past ten minutes and Chris and David have been trying to ask her out for the past hour. I mean clearly she's a catch. What I don't understand is-"

Jason cut her off. "Men from my own family are hitting on my girlfriend?"

"They've been hitting on your *friend*," his mother clarified in an annoyed tone as if he was the one messing with her mind. Seriously, what was wrong with his family? Why was it so hard for them to believe Haley was his girlfriend?

"Actually," Trevor said a bit sheepishly, "I was going to ask her if she wanted to catch a movie and dinner after the party."

Jason's jaw dropped so fast that he was surprised the damn thing didn't unhinge. He quickly recovered so he could threaten his cousin. "You stay the hell away from my girlfriend!" he said, pointing. He turned his finger on the rest of his family. "Just know that at this moment I hate you all." They rolled their eyes. His finger stopped in front of his father. He narrowed his eyes on his old man. "And I'm *never* sharing any more of Haley's baked goods with you!"

Jared gasped. "But...but....but...."

With that he stormed out of the kitchen. He just thanked God his friends were there for him, because clearly his family wasn't. Was it really so hard to believe that he could land a woman like Haley?

Chapter 17

"Let me get this straight," Brad said, putting his beer on the ground between his feet. "You took Haley to meet your family without any type of warning and you were surprised that they didn't believe the two of you were dating?"

"Yes!"

"Well, I can see why they didn't believe you," Mitch said as he snagged another beer out of the ice bucket.

"Oh, and why is that?" Jason asked as he stole the beer out of Mitch's hands.

Mitch grumbled something, but smartly let it go. He grabbed another beer and popped the top.

"Well, wasn't your mother getting on your case about settling down?" Brad asked.

"Yes, and you would think she'd be happy when I brought Haley home."

Brad nodded. "And for the past year hasn't she been threatening you with finding someone for you?"

"Yes, but-"

"And every time you went over there for dinner, party or cookout hasn't your mother had several women on hand to meet you?" Brad continued.

"Yes, but-"

"Did she have any women at the BBQ for you to meet?" Mitch asked.

"Five or six I guess," Jason said with a shrug of his shoulders. He hadn't really paid attention to any of them other than to duck the hell out of the way when they were looking for him. Just like every other time his mother tried to play matchmaker she'd chosen needy, well more like clingy, women who had no other interests other than themselves and finding a boyfriend.

Both of his friends sucked in a breath. "Shit."

"That must have pissed Haley off," Brad said.

"I don't think she had time to notice. Not with half the men in my family hitting on her," Jason bit out angrily.

"That's fucked up," Mitch said.

It was pretty fucked up. No one listened to him. It was one of the most annoying parties he'd ever been to. When he wasn't trying to get away from some really annoying, clingy woman his mother had invited with the sole purpose of marrying him, he was busy getting into arguments with whatever bastard in his family was asking for Haley's phone number.

Like every single other time Haley was completely oblivious to it. Every time he pulled her aside to talk to her about it, she just laughed until tears were rolling down her cheeks. When they returned to the room it was obvious that she had cried and every man would glare at him. They acted like Haley needed protection from *him*.

It should have been painfully obvious to everyone in the room how he felt about Haley. He made no secret that she was his world, not that anyone believed him. Why was it so hard to believe that he'd straightened out for Haley? He didn't think there was anything difficult about it. Even if he wasn't constantly hugging her, putting his arm around her, holding her hand or trying to kiss her, he told them, but had that stopped any of those bastards from trying to make a move on her?

"Your family probably thought you brought Haley there as a decoy to get your mother to stop harassing the hell out of you about settling down and to use her as an excuse to avoid those women," Mitch pointed out.

Jason crushed his empty beer can and tossed it into the bucket in the corner of his deck. It should be obvious to everyone that he'd changed. Hell, a year ago he would have had Mitch toss that beer can up in the air so he could shoot it with his paintball gun. Didn't it strike any of his friends as odd that not only did he toss it into a bucket, but his deck and patio furniture were also cleaned and repaired, his lawn freshly mowed and the inside of his house was clean? Those were big goddamn changes in his book.

"That's what I was thinking," Brad said, tossing his can at the bucket and missing. It landed on Jason's freshly cut lawn. Jason gestured angrily for him to pick it up. With an eye roll Brad did just that.

"Whatever. This is really boring sitting around here talking about relationships like we're a bunch of women," Mitch said. "Let's get the hell out of here." He stood up, waiting for the other two men to follow.

Brad and Jason shared a look, shrugged and got to their feet. What the hell, it wasn't like they had anything better to do since Jill was off with a client and Haley was off hitting yard sales.

"Great, let's go hit the strip clubs," Mitch said merrily.

"Whoa there, Skippy," Jason said, coming to a sudden halt. "That shit isn't happening."

"What the hell do you mean?" Mitch asked, sounding like a petulant child. "I want to go stare at hot chicks getting naked."

"I'm out as well," Brad announced, not that it was really necessary. The man hadn't been to a strip club since he met Jill.

"Come on, it's Tuesday. It's all you can eat hot wings at the Hot Bunny Club. We can go there, fill up, and get a few lap dances. We can hook up with Candy and Mandy afterwards. What's more fun than stripper sex?"

Jason could only look at his friend dumbly for a moment. Mitch was serious, really serious.

"Have you forgotten about something?" Jason asked calmly, more calmly than he felt.

Mitch looked truly confused when he asked, "What?"

"I have a girlfriend!" Jason snapped, quickly losing patience. "Why in the hell would I want to pay some woman to show me something I'm not interested in when I'm dating Haley? And why in the hell would you think I wanted to cheat on my girlfriend?"

If humanly possible Mitch looked even more confused. "How is it cheating if you're not married?"

Brad and Jason just stared at Mitch. What the hell was he supposed to say to that? Actually, it worried him that not even a year ago he would have been on Mitch's side of this argument. That was truly frightening.

Hell, he would have been the one starting that argument before Haley. Wow....wow..... It wasn't exactly the best feeling in the world to discover how big an asshole he once was. He'd really changed since getting to know Haley and shockingly for the better. Surprisingly, he didn't feel pissed off or scared that she'd been able to bring out these changes in him.

"Come on, man! Come with me. It'll be fun," Mitch pleaded.

Jason grabbed a fresh beer and dropped back into his chair.

"What the hell, Jason?" Mitch whined.

Shrugging, Jason took a long sip of his beer.

Mitch folded his arms stubbornly over his chest while he scowled at Jason. "I never thought this day would come," Mitch said with obvious disgust.

"Oh, what day is that exactly?" Jason asked as he leaned his head back to catch some sun. Anything was better than watching a grown man pout.

"The day Jason Bradford became pussy whipped," Mitch announced, earning a chuckle from Brad.

Jason threw Brad a killing glare, but the man ignored him. He focused his attention on the little bastard who was obviously drunk or possibly high, probably both.

He snorted. "I'm not pussy whipped," he said. Since he'd done everything *but* slide into that little piece of heaven he didn't think the term applied to him. The things they'd done together made him stifle back a groan. He loved what they did and at the same time he absolutely hated it.

Having Haley but not having her was difficult as hell. For any other woman, he would have simply shrugged at the "no actual sex" rule and walked away. But for Haley, there wasn't anything he wouldn't do. She was the love of his life, his future and the woman he planned on spending the rest of his life with.

So for now, he'd grit his teeth and fight against the urge to jump her every time he saw her. His little grasshopper wanted to stick with foreplay, so that's exactly what he was going to do. As long as she kept doing that unbelieving erotic thing with her tongue and teeth along the ridge of his-

"I'm surprised he's not panting after her right now," Mitch said, yanking Jason away from his thoughts of Haley, naked, bending over.... He shifted uncomfortably in his seat as discretely as possible.

"We don't spend every minute of the day together," Jason shot back.

Mitch shrugged. "Pretty much."

"Well, I'm not with her right now, am I?" Jason snapped back.

"Probably because she didn't want you with her," Mitch said, snagging another beer. "She's probably getting sick of you."

Jason snorted. Then for good measure he snorted again. His little grasshopper wasn't getting sick of him. He was damn sure of that. She absolutely adored him, loved him. He knew it, even if the stubborn woman hadn't said it yet, but she would. Then he'd tell her how much he loved her, but only after she told him because he really didn't want to feel like an idiot saying it first. He'd never said it before and had absolutely no idea how to go about doing it now. So, the safe plan was to wait until Haley said it. He knew that she'd say it soon since there was no doubt in his mind that she loved him.

No, the reason he was hanging out with the guys today wasn't because she was getting sick of him. It was quite simple. He was banned from going yard sale hopping with her for one year. Not that he cared, he didn't. It did seem a little unfair to him that's all. It's not like he intentionally went out of his way to embarrass Haley. Those things just seemed to happen to those around him. Most accepted that little fact of life, but that hadn't stopped Haley from banning him.

He may have told one or six people that the stuff they were trying to hawk on their front lawns was crap and all of a sudden he's banned. Well, that and the box of antique dishes that he broke might have had something to do with it. He didn't know why the guy was pissed. He gave him the fifty bucks for the broken dishes. He should be the one that was mad after all he was the one who was out fifty bucks for a set of broken girly dishes.

"I bet Haley's off with another guy right now-*Ow! What the hell*?" Mitch whined as he rubbed the nasty looking red spot on his forehead that would no doubt be a noticeable bump by morning.

Brad sighed as he picked up Jason's half empty can of beer that rolled to a stop by his feet. He poured the rest of the beer onto the lawn as he shook his head in disbelief. "You knew better," he told a sulking Mitch.

"I was just kidding!"

Brad shrugged.

"That's fucked up!"

"Don't talk about my little grasshopper," Jason simply said. The man should be happy that all he did was throw his beer at him.

Mitch grabbed a handful of ice from the bucket and pressed it against his forehead. "She's not even that beautiful," he muttered quietly to himself.

Jason was out of his chair and lunging for the little bastard before the last syllable left his mouth. Brad being Brad, dropped his beer and jumped between the two men seconds before Jason would have slammed into him. All three men went tumbling off the deck to the ground with Brad doing his best to keep a very pissed off Jason from killing Mitch.

"Get him off me!" Mitch screamed like a girl as he tried frantically to crawl away. With Brad on his back trying his best to hold him back, Jason lunged and managed to grab Mitch's leg and proceeded to drag the man to him so he could beat the shit out of him.

"For fuck's sake, take it back!" Brad yelled as he struggled to restrain Jason.

"Aaah!" Mitch screamed as he was dragged inch by inch towards a future in a body cast. He tried to dig his nails into the lawn to no avail.

"I didn't mean it like that! She's hot! Insanely beautiful! I just meant that you've dated really beautiful women before and you've never acted like this before! Oh my God, don't kill me!" The words rushed out of Mitch's mouth, ending on a squeal as Jason dragged him beneath him and flipped him over and raised a fist, ready to beat the crap out of the man.

Mitch held his hands out, palms out, trying to get Jason to stop. "I swear to God I didn't mean it! I love her!" At Jason's growl of anger Mitch rushed to continue. "Not like that! I love her like a friend! I think she's great! I swear I didn't mean it!"

"I told you not to tease him about her," Brad groaned as he tried to pull Jason off the man, but Jason outweighed him by a good thirty pounds of muscle. Jason watched his friend through narrowed slits as he fought back the urge to beat the shit out of him. This was one of his oldest friends and part of him knew the man was only giving him shit, but he didn't allow anyone to talk about or treat his little grasshopper with anything but respect.

With barely controlled rage, Jason took a deep breath before he spoke. "Let's clear this up once and for all." At Mitch's enthusiastic nod, probably because if Jason was talking it meant he wasn't beating the crap out of him, he continued. "Haley is my world," he said, ignoring Mitch's eyes bugging out at that announcement. "Because we've been friends since we were five, I'm going to overlook this little act of stupidity." Mitch noticeably relaxed at that announcement. "As long as you stop ogling my girlfriend's ass."

Mitch pursed his lips, thinking over the ultimatum. After a minute he dropped his arms to his side and sighed, "I'd rather get my ass kicked."

Chapter 18

"Baby, stop!" Haley said, giggling.

Jason hugged her waist tighter, keeping her from walking away. "Stay home with me. I missed you," he said, giving her his best pout.

She gently ran her fingers through his hair the way he liked it. "I'm sorry, sweetie, but I can't back out again. I promised Amy and the girls that I was definitely coming tonight."

There was no way she was allowing herself to stay home tonight. Over the past week, she'd come so close to wrecking the surprise by telling him. She knew that if she stayed home tonight, that the excitement would get to her, she'd blurt it out and everything she'd gone through over the past month to plan this would be wrecked.

Of course none of this would have been possible without her grandmother's help. A few times Haley considered giving up when money and location became an issue, but then Grandma offered to help her out. Grandma found her the perfect place at less than half the cost of every place Haley had looked into.

It was the first time Haley had ever accepted her grandmother's help. It had always been important for her to make it on her own without her family's money and influence. For Jason, she'd sucked up her pride and asked Grandma to help her find the perfect cabin to rent. Everything was going to be perfect.

"Does it not matter that I'm on my knees begging you? You're really going to be able to leave someone this pathetic?" he demanded in a sulky tone.

Haley rolled her eyes as she gently pried his arms from around her waist. "It's just for a couple of hours. You won't even know I'm gone," she promised him.

He sat back on his haunches, doing his best to look pathetic.

She did her best not to roll her eyes, again. It was just so damn cute and sweet that he didn't want to spend even one night without her. This was something she never expected from Jason Bradford, one of many things actually. He was so sweet and attentive.

"What if I promise to make you a batch of brownies tomorrow?" she asked, deciding to use his love of baked goods against him.

He snorted in disbelief as he got to his feet. "I'm not some whore you can buy with a pan of yummy baked goods, woman. How dare you insult me?" he said on a sniff as he folded his arms over his chest and did his best to look put out.

"Fine," Haley said with a sigh. "What if I promise to make a big bowl of frosting tomorrow and let you lick it off me?"

She had to bite back a smile as Jason shifted anxiously while he licked his lips and ran his eyes hungrily down her body. "Buttercream?" he croaked out.

"Mmmmhmm," she said, walking over to him. She cupped the back of his head and gently tugged him down for a quick kiss. "And if you're good I might lick some off you," she said, loving the idea.

"Get your own bowl of frosting. I don't share," he simply said, giving her one last kiss before walking out the door, whistling happily, no doubt thinking about the large bowl of frosting he was going to devour tomorrow.

With a smile, she grabbed her small black purse and headed out the door. She wasn't too surprised to find Jason playing basketball with Mitch and Brad. Not that she would ever really expect it, but it was nice to know that he'd pick her over his friends. She wasn't the type of woman that expected a guy's attention twenty-four seven, but it was nice to know that it was hers if she wanted it.

She blew a kiss in his direction and couldn't help but laugh when Mitch jumped in front of Jason to snag it.

"That was my kiss, you bastard!" Jason yelled, placing a choke hold on Mitch and taking him down to the ground while Brad stood by sighing.

He really was a sweetheart. Maybe she'd make him a big batch of fudge brownies to go along with that bowl of frosting.

"And stop looking at her ass!" Jason snapped.

* * * *

"Oh my God, I can't believe you came," Amy said, leaning back in her chair as she watched Haley approach the table.

"He's probably following right behind her," Sarah pointed out with a laugh.

"Ha, ha, very funny," Haley said, taking the only empty seat at the table as her four friends and a woman she had never met before, gave her knowing looks.

Amy gestured to the new woman. "This is my friend, Kate. Kate this is Haley, the woman I told you about."

Frowning, Haley reached over to shake the woman's manicured hand. She couldn't help but wonder what Amy said about her. Thankfully, she didn't have to wonder for long.

"So, this is the woman that brought Jason Bradford to his knees?" Kate asked, cocking her head to the side as she ran an assessing eye over Haley. Haley didn't miss the woman's lips twitching when she came to her glasses. Obviously the woman thought she came up short.

Haley didn't care what this woman thought. It wasn't the first time someone had a hard time believing that she was with Jason and probably wouldn't be the last. There was no denying that she wasn't Jason's usual type. She hadn't lived next door to the man for five years without learning a thing or two. Granted, she never saw the women until after he dumped them and they were drunk screaming messes, but it was pretty easy to guess his type.

The old Jason, as she liked to think of the not so sweet Jason, used to drive her insane and liked women who were a walking breathing advertisement for sex. Kind of like Kate, Haley thought with an inward groan. With her perfect silky long raven hair, makeup that made her look sultry, clothes that were a little too tight and showed off way too much, Kate could be a walking advertisement for Jason's type.

Judging by the smug smirk on the woman's face, she'd guessed what Haley was thinking.

"How long have the two of you been together?" Kate asked casually, but Haley hadn't missed the calculating gleam in her eyes.

Before she could tell her it was none of her business, Amy answered for her, "About two months."

The surprised look on Kate's face was rewarding. She knew she'd lasted longer with Jason than any other woman, surprisingly, since she never put out. Well, she did do a thousand and one naughty things with him and kept his interest with baked goods, but that was neither here nor there. She was pretty sure he really cared about her, maybe even loved her.

Okay, love might be pushing it for a man like Jason, but she was damn sure that he cared about her. He was always sweet to her and seemed genuinely happy to see her. Not to mention that he went out of his way to spend time with her. She wasn't entirely sure, but she didn't think he'd done that with anyone before her.

"That's pretty impressive," Kate mumbled distractedly.

Amy waved off her comment, leaning closer towards Haley with an unholy gleam of interest in her eyes. "Well?" she said expectantly.

Haley could only frown as she looked past her friend for the waitress. Suddenly she had the feeling that the only way she was going to survive this girl's night out was with a lot of alcohol.

She looked back and was startled to find Beth, Alice, and Jen leaning towards her as well with similar expressions.

"Well what?" Haley asked, wondering if she needed to start drug testing her friends. They were seriously freaking her out.

As one they rolled their eyes. It was seriously creepy. She barely fought back the urge to flee.

"Have you slept with him yet?" Amy hissed excitedly.

"Oh.....that," she said, squirming and feeling a little self-conscious. "We sleep together every night," she said, hoping against hope that they'd drop the subject, especially with the way Kate was glaring at her.

Beth snorted. "We know you sleep together every night. What we're wondering is if you finally had sex with the man!"

Her cheeks began to burn with that little announcement.

Kate looked confused. "She just said she's sleeping with him."

Amy leaned back in her chair, taking a sip of her martini. "Haley here doesn't sleep with a man unless she's in love with him. Right?" she said, giving Haley a pointed look.

Why oh why had she shared that little tidbit of information all those years ago in college? Oh, that's right, she'd been drunk.

She squirmed uncomfortably in her seat. "I just want to be sure," she mumbled pathetically.

Kate sat up straighter, holding her hand up to stop Haley's friends as they opened their mouths to no doubt give her another lecture on sex in the twenty-first century. None of them understood why she wanted to wait.

"You've kept Jason Bradford interested for two months and you haven't even had sex with him?" she asked, clearly as surprised as her friends were.

"Yes," she said somewhat defensively. "Our relationship isn't about sex."

Kate sat back, back to giving her a condescending look. "Clearly."

Haley opened her mouth to give the woman a piece of her mind when Beth cut her off.

"Oh, look at that," Beth said, gesturing with her frilly pink drink towards the entrance of the bar. Everyone looked and chuckled and for once Haley was glad that they lived in a small town.

Jason spotted her and waved and then of course slapped Mitch upside his head when the man blew a kiss to her. Rolling her eyes, Haley stood up and grabbed her purse.

"I'll be right back," she said, not really sure if she would. She really didn't feel like spending a night getting hounded over her virginity again.

"Uh huh," Beth said.

"Sure," Amy said.

Haley didn't bother arguing with them. She was in no mood. All she wanted to do was cuddle up with Jason while he fed her hot wings. Was that too much to ask for?

She walked over to their table. He paused mid-order when he saw her. Frowning, he asked the waitress to come back in a few minutes.

"What's wrong, my little grasshopper?" he asked, pulling her against his side.

"Girl's night sucks," she mumbled pathetically against his shoulder.

He chuckled, pressing a kiss to the top of her head.

"Do you want to join guy's night?" he asked, sounding amused.

After a short pause she asked, "Do I have to have a penis?"

"I think we can ignore that requirement tonight," he said, chuckling.

"Will you buy me hot wings?" she mumbled, tracing circles on his knee.

He sighed heavily. "If I must."

"You must," she said solemnly.

"Alright. Anything else?"

She shook her head standing. "No, that will do," she announced, leaning over to press a kiss to his cheek.

"I'll order you hot wings if you kiss me," Mitch offered. "In fact if you kiss my--Ow! Damn it!" he snapped, glaring at Brad.

Brad gestured towards Jason with his beer. "It saves time this way."

Laughing and feeling better already, she gave Jason one last kiss before heading to the bathroom where she would no doubt spend half the night just waiting in line.

Chapter 19

"Did you just growl?" Mitch asked, laughing.

Jason tore his eyes off his little grasshopper's retreating ass and sent a scowl towards the man. "No." But he had. Oh goddamn, he had. He'd been imagining licking frosting off of Haley in a hundred different ways since she'd offered.

Licking frosting off a woman was a simple fantasy, one he'd dreamed of doing for years, but hadn't found the right woman to share it with. There was no doubt that he could have asked any one of the countless women he'd slept with in the past to live out this little kinky fantasy with him before, but he never felt comfortable enough with any of them.

With Haley.......

There wasn't anything he couldn't talk to the woman about. In fact, he'd mentioned this fantasy to her only last week. After she playfully teased him for a good hour about it, she swore she'd let him lick anything he wanted off her body. Anytime. Thirty seconds later he was struggling to get his damn legs in his pants and mentally making a shopping list when she walked back into his bedroom wearing a smile and a whip cream bikini.

He may have tackled her to the ground and licked every damn creamy morsel off of her before he threw his giggling grasshopper over his shoulder and carried her to the refrigerator where he proceeded to put all the sundae toppings he had to good use.

God, he loved that woman.

"Excuse me? Do you remember me?" a beautiful woman with silky black hair asked, tearing him from his thoughts.

Jason looked at her and frowned. He didn't have a clue who the hell she was and judging by the appreciative look Mitch was sending her way, his friend wouldn't mind getting to know her better.

"No, I'm sorry," he said, taking a sip of his beer.

Her coy smile faltered for a second, and then was back in full force. Without asking, she pulled out the chair to his left and sat down, making sure to lean forward enough to give him a view of her generous cleavage. She reached forward to run her fingers down his arm only to find his arm pulled back.

"Can I help you?" he asked, feeling all his good humor fade away. There was no doubt this woman had seen Haley with him only a few minutes ago. It's funny how once upon a time he would have found this woman's assertive behavior flattering and probably would have ditched his date for her, but now he was with Haley. It pissed him off to no end that women took one look at his little grasshopper and dismissed her as if she was nothing.

"Well," she said, drawing out the word as she shifted in her chair, giving him a better glimpse of her breasts, "I was over there with my friends and funny enough you were the subject of conversation. Then suddenly you were here and I couldn't help but feel that fate was telling me that you and I should be spending a long sleepless night in my bed tonight," she said in husky voice.

"Holy shit," Mitch muttered, taking a much needed sip of beer.

"Weren't you sitting with Haley's friends?" Brad pointed out, sounding as pissed as Jason felt.

She shrugged Brad's comment off. "I'm sitting with *my* friend," she stressed. "I would never be friends with someone as cold as Haley."

With that announcement all three men broke out laughing. Haley was many things, but cold? Hell no.

She may still be a bit of a pushover, but only because she truly cared about not hurting other people's feelings. That was something they needed to work on, but he was willing to overlook it for now.

The woman glared at him as she crossed her arms over her ample chest, giving him what was probably her best bitch look.

"I wonder how you would feel if you found out you were being played," she snapped.

"Oh, and who's playing me?" Jason asked, still chuckling.

"Haley," she said.

"You can go now," he said, gesturing with his beer for her to leave. Damn, women truly could be cold hearted bitches. Putting down his little grasshopper for a chance at him was low. It was understandable, but low.

She cocked her head to the side, studying him. "Oh, really? Don't think she's playing with you?"

"Would never happen," he said, gesturing again for her to leave. Even Mitch looked like he wanted her to leave and that was saying something. The man usually wasn't so selective about his bed partners and for him to want an easy woman to leave, said a great deal about how he felt about Haley. Jason knew the man was starting to see Haley as a sister otherwise he'd have to bitch slap him.

"Then why hasn't she slept with you yet?" she asked, grinning smugly.

Everything in him froze with that question. His eyes darted over to his two friends to see that both men were staring at him, clearly shocked.

"You have absolutely no idea what the hell you're talking about," Jason snapped, trying to ignore the dread that was starting to rise.

They'd been together for two months and never once had he pushed or questioned her about her refusal to sleep with him. Even during those times when he'd thought he'd die if he didn't slide inside her, he held back. He'd assumed she just wanted to take it slow, make sure that he wasn't going to be an asshole and drop her ass when he got bored with her. Suddenly he wished he'd asked her why she wouldn't sleep with him the first and only time she'd brought it up, instead of just being happy that she was giving him a chance.

"Oh? I happen to know that she hasn't slept with you and has no plans to. She's playing you right now. According to her, you just don't measure up to her standards."

Mitch laughed it off. "Sweetheart, go try and play someone else. You don't know shit about what you're talking about."

She cocked a perfectly trimmed eyebrow at him as she stood up. "Don't I? I know she won't sleep with him because she's not in love with him," she announced triumphantly, causing the air in his lungs to rush out of him.

"When you get tired of being played with, give me a call," she said, pushing a folded napkin towards him.

He was barely aware of what Mitch and Brad said to her or Mitch grabbing the napkin and tearing it up.

Haley didn't love him.

"Jason, you don't look so good, man," Mitch said, getting up and taking the seat the cold hearted bitch just vacated. He grabbed the pitcher of beer and filled Jason's glass. "Take a drink," he said, shoving the glass at him until he had little choice but to do exactly that.

"Look, I don't know what bullshit she was spewing, but I do know that Haley absolutely adores you," Mitch said in a reassuring voice, scaring the hell out of him. Mitch wouldn't try comforting him unless it was bad.

"He's right," Brad easily agreed. "She's obviously trying to start some shit for Haley. Just ignore her bullshit. She doesn't know what she's talking about."

Jason forced a smile. "Maybe you're right."

Mitch snorted. "Of course we're right. Anyone who's been around the two of you the last two months knows that-you two can't keep your hands off each other."

But they hadn't made love, Jason thought bitterly. She'd done everything with him but that and now Jason had a sneaking suspicion the reason behind it was no longer so simple.

"Did you order hot wings?" Haley asked, wrapping her arms around his neck and pressing a sweet kiss to his cheek.

Brad sent him an "I told you so" look over his beer.

"No, not yet," he said, putting his beer down so he could take her hand into his. His eyes shot past Haley to the table of women who were looking this way and laughing. His jaw clenched almost painfully at the idea of Haley playing him.

Haley, of course, was oblivious to everything including the change in his mood. "Well, I'm going to go place an order at the bar then. I'll be right back."

"Okay," Jason said, unable to take his eyes off the women laughing at him.

Mitch and Jason must have followed his gaze.

"Don't tell Haley this, but most of her friends are bitches," Mitch said, pouring the last of the beer into his cup.

Normally he'd agree with that, but right now he had a sinking feeling that he was the brunt of a joke. He really couldn't help but feel that Haley might have been playing him this whole time.

There was only one way to find out and tonight he was afraid he'd get his answers one way or another.

"Don't fuck this up," Brad said, no doubt reading the determined expression on his face correctly. "I don't know what's going on between you and Haley, but those women are clearly out to fuck her over. Please don't screw yourself over in the process."

Jason didn't answer right away. He drained the rest of his glass, slowly. Finally he put the glass back on the table and sat back, allowing his eyes to search out his little grasshopper. She was at the bar laughing at something Becky, the bartender, said.

He didn't know what the hell he would do if he found out his little grasshopper was playing him, but tonight he was going to find out.

Chapter 19

"Baby, are you okay?"

Jason looked down at her and smiled. "I'm fine," he said, putting his arm around her, pulling her tightly against him as he led her towards her house.

Without a word he unlocked her door. Haley tossed her purse onto the coffee table and headed for her bedroom, more than ready to get out of her high heels and skirt.

"Haley?" Jason said, stopping her.

She leaned against the wall as she took her shoes off. "Yes?"

He ran a hand through his hair. "I....I was wondering if you wanted to go for a swim," he said, but Haley couldn't help but feel that wasn't what he wanted to say.

Ever since she came back from the bathroom, she couldn't help but notice that Jason was acting differently. He seemed genuinely upset, but denied it anytime she asked. Mitch and Brad were surprisingly tight lipped about it. Every now and then she caught both men sending killing glances towards her friends.

More than once she caught her friends watching them and laughing. She knew it was ridiculous, but she couldn't help feeling a little paranoid. It was probably nothing.

"A swim sounds like fun," she said, deciding that she'd rather forget about everything else but Jason. "I'll meet you at the pool in ten minutes."

"Okay," Jason said, sounding a little sad, at least she thought he had.

She was being ridiculous, she decided.

Fifteen minutes later she shut the sliding glass door behind her just as Jason broke the water's surface. Even in the dim moonlight Jason was breathtaking. She watched the muscles in his arms flex as he ran his fingers through his short hair.

"The water's great," Jason said, gesturing for her to join him.

She took her glasses off and wished she'd turned on the outside lights as her vision dimmed and became fuzzy. Trying not to stumble, she walked the five feet to the patio table, cautiously, and placed her glasses down.

Unfortunately for her, the time it took to put her glasses down hadn't helped her eyes adjust to the dim light. She didn't want to wreck a romantic midnight swim by throwing on the flood lights, but she also didn't think falling flat on her face was exactly romantic either.

Why couldn't she be a candidate for laser eye surgery?

She sighed heavily as she turned around, fully prepared to throw on the flood lights and wreck another romantic evening thanks to her poor eyesight when strong wet arms scooped her up.

"Don't worry, my little grasshopper, I've got you," Jason whispered, pressing a kiss to her forehead.

"Maybe we should turn on the lights," she grumbled unhappily. "I can't see a thing," she admitted quietly, feeling her cheeks burn with embarrassment. It was just another reminder that she wasn't sexy or desirable.

"Don't worry, I won't let anything happen to you," Jason promised as he carried her to the pool and helped her into the lukewarm water.

While Jason lowered himself into the pool she dove beneath the water to wet her hair. When she came back up ten feet away she smoothed her hair back and squinted.

"Jason?" she said, trying to separate him from the rest of the dim shadows. She really could not see a single thing out here. Maybe she should-

A small startled scream escaped her as warm arms wrapped around her from behind. Jason chuckled softly in her ear. "Did I scare you?"

"No," she lied.

"I'm sorry," he said, pressing a kiss to the top of her head. "Do you forgive me?"

She huffed out a breath. "No."

"What if I promise not to do it again?" he asked, sounding amused.

"I'd break out the fists of fury, because we both know you'd be lying."

"We wouldn't want that." He chuckled.

"No," she sniffed, "we wouldn't."

"Then perhaps you'll let me make it up to you with a kiss?" he said, already pressing wet kisses to her neck. Closing her eyes, she leaned her head back and to the side to give him better access.

"I suppose that would be acceptable," she said, biting back a small moan of pleasure as Jason ran his hands down her hips and over her thighs before bringing them back up again.

"That's very kind of you," Jason whispered hoarsely, tracing his tongue up her neck, taking her earlobe into his mouth and sucking it.

His hands skimmed up her sides teasingly, ending just below her breasts before they glided down to her hips. Haley reached up with one hand and gripped his wet hair, yanking him down for the kiss he promised her.

He devoured her mouth on contact. His tongue pushed its way inside of her mouth and she welcomed it, suckled it, loving the way he groaned with every little teasing lick and suckle.

Feeling a little daring, she reached up with her free hand and released the front knot that held her bikini top closed. Releasing his hair, she shrugged the top off, letting it fall between their bodies.

Her nipples hardened instantly from the mixture of water, cool air, and desire for this man. It felt so good, but she needed more. Placing her hands over his where they still rested on her hips, she gently tugged them up, gliding them over her wet body until they were where she wanted them, needed them.

Jason's long, pained moan sent shivers throughout her body. She arched into his hands, loving the way they weighed her breasts, squeezed, and caressed them. When he ran his palms over her hard nipples she sucked on his tongue, making him groan loudly as his hands closed around her breasts and squeezed.

"Jason," she mumbled desperately against his mouth. She needed more. Needed him.

He broke the kiss and turned her in his arms. His mouth slammed down on hers as he yanked her against him. She loved the way his warm hard chest felt against her breasts, but she loved the feeling of his hard erection straining against her even more.

She reached between them and cupped him, running her fingers teasingly up his long length until she found the large, velvety head poking out the top of his swim trunks. She cupped the large head in her hand, running her thumb over it and spreading the few drops of excitement that leaked out.

Jason broke away from her mouth with a groan and worked his way down to her breasts, licking, kissing, and sucking every inch of skin until his tongue was tracing circles around her nipple, making it harden almost painfully.

His hands came up to play, grabbing each breast and massaging them in a way that had her legs trembling and her breaths quickening. The fact that she couldn't see what he was doing only intensified each and every sensation that he was causing. Just when she thought she'd die if he didn't take her nipple into her mouth he moved onto the other breast and began the torture all over again.

"Jason!" she cried out when he finally put her out of her misery and took her over sensitized nipple into his mouth. He pinched and gently twisted her other nipple with his fingers. Haley was barely aware that he was backing her up against the side of the pool.

He kept her nipple in his mouth, suckling it hard as he worked her bikini bottom off. Haley was helpless to do anything but hold on tightly to his shoulders as he worked her into insanity.

His mouth left her nipple. "I need to taste you, my little grasshopper," he said hoarsely as he picked her up and sat her carefully on the edge of the pool. "Lie back."

Carefully, she lay back on the cool cement. Jason gripped the backs of her knees and pulled her legs open, spreading her wide.

"So beautiful," he said quietly.

She felt his warm breath tickle her thigh before he pressed a kiss right below the knee. A cool breeze ran between her legs, teasing her soaked lips. She couldn't remember ever being this turned on before or this wet.

She wanted him. Tonight. Now.

"Jason, please," she pleaded, trying not to squirm against the unforgiving cement surface.

"Shhh, it's okay," Jason murmured against her leg. He pressed another kiss against her inner thigh before running his wet hot tongue down her leg. He avoided where she needed him the most to run his tongue just below her belly button to her other leg.

"Please!" she cried, as another cool breeze teased her over sensitized skin, making her squirm desperately.

"That's not what I want to hear, my little grasshopper," Jason murmured against her thigh. He ran his wet tongue in a circle over her inner thigh before softly suckling the area.

He pressed a soft kiss against the thatch of soft curls between her legs, earning a loud moan. "So wet," he said, running the tip of his tongue between her folds. "So sweet."

His tongue traced her slit as he placed her knees over his shoulders. When she felt his thumbs separate her folds she ran her fingers through his hair, gently encouraging him.

He ran the tip of his tongue around her little sensitive nub and around her core in what felt like a figure eight, making sure not to touch the spots that ached for his touch the most. She spread her legs wider in silent invitation, making Jason chuckle.

"You want more?" he asked, pressing a delicious kiss to her clit.

"Mmhmm," she somehow managed to answer.

He flicked his tongue over her sensitive little nub as a reward.

She dropped her head back, moaning loudly. Her fingers knotted in his hair, urging him on.

Her breath caught in her throat when his tongue ran down to her core and slid in smoothly. His thumb gently circled her clit slowly, using her juices to heighten every touch.

In and out his tongue moved in a rhythm that had her gripping his hair, panting, moaning and half-screaming his name. Her orgasm caught her off guard. One minute she was panting and the next she was undulating her hips and screaming his name until her voice was raw.

Jason pressed a quick kiss to her stomach. "Come here," he said tightly.

Still trying to catch her breath, Haley sat up. Jason stepped between her legs, keeping them separated as he leaned down and took her mouth in a hungry kiss that stole whatever sanity she had left. She ran her hands through his hair and down his back only stopping to work his shorts off.

As soon as his erection was freed she gave up on the shorts and took him in hand. Jason moaned long and loud in her mouth as he worked to remove his shorts, careful not to dislodge her hand.

Without a word, he picked her up. Haley wrapped her legs around him, loving the way he felt. She shifted in his arms until his hard erection was pressed firmly against her wet core.

Jason gripped her bottom, teasing her slit with the tips of his fingers as he moved them through the water. Haley was so caught up in what they were doing that she didn't realize they were out of the water until he placed her on a lounge chair.

He released his hold on her to half kneel on the lounge near her face. "Open up, sweetheart," he said, casually stroking himself, rubbing the head across her lips.

Haley leaned over and took him into her mouth without hesitation. She reached up and gently gripped his firm balls as he leaned over and slid two fingers inside of her.

"That's it, my little grasshopper," he encouraged hoarsely.

She loved doing this for him, loved the way he felt, tasted and moaned. She pulled her mouth away so she could run her tongue up his cock and tease his slit. He hissed in a breath when she took him back in her mouth, sucking him harder. She was going to come soon and she was determined to take him with her. She added her other hand, knowing how much he loved that as she absently rode his fingers. This was so good....

"Not tonight," Jason said suddenly, pulling away.

"What?" she asked in a daze as he moved to lie down on top of her. Her confusion quickly turned to pleasure as he rubbed himself between her legs.

Smiling, she pulled him down for a kiss. He kissed her leisurely as he shifted on top of her. When she felt the hard velvet head of his erection tease her core she gasped into his mouth.

"Do you like that?" Jason asked as he teased her folds.

"Yes," she hissed when he teased her clit.

"Do you want me?" he whispered against her mouth, placing the tip of his erection against her core once again. This time he gently thrust his hips, teasing her.

Did she?

Yes.

She loved him and all this waiting was killing her. It no longer mattered what the future held. She wanted him now.

"Yes." The word was barely out of her mouth when Jason thrust forward.

Hard.

A small cry escaped her as he rammed all the way home. She was barely aware of the kisses he was pressing against her face or how he wrapped his arms around her and held her tightly. The only thing that registered in her mind was the pain from being split in two.

It hurt so much. She squeezed her eyes shut, hoping it would get better. It didn't. Jason continued to thrust into her, taking her cries and the way she dug her nails into his back as encouragement. Just when she thought she couldn't take any more he stilled on top of her and groaned.

Well, she thought as he pressed a tender kiss to her forehead, she knew the first time was going to hurt. Granted, it probably wouldn't have hurt if she'd talk to him about this before they did it, but they'd been caught up in the moment. It was better this way, more romantic. She liked the idea of her first time being a result of being out of control.

Okay, so it had hurt....bad, but it was over now and Haley was glad.

She pressed a kiss to his damp forehead.

Jason chuckled, leaning back to press a kiss to the tip of her nose.

"I knew it," he said, panting.

"Knew what?" she asked confused.

He brushed his lips against hers.

"I knew they were full of shit when they said you wouldn't sleep with me."

Chapter 20

Jason couldn't help smiling as he looked down at his little grasshopper. Not only had he proved that Haley loved him, but that had been the hottest sex of his life. She'd been so unbelievably hot and wet and so fucking tight he'd almost exploded when he'd entered her.

The last two months had definitely been worth the wait. Sex had never felt so good before. Just thinking about how good it was had his cock hardening for more.

"Get off me!" Haley said, shoving him away.

Confused as hell, Jason moved off of her.

"What's wrong?"

"You had sex with me because someone told you that I wouldn't have sex with you? You had sex to prove someone wrong?" she damn near yelled.

He held his hands up in a placating manor, hoping to calm her down, but dropped them when he remembered she couldn't see.

"It's not like that!"

"Oh? Then no one told you that I wouldn't sleep with you?"

He ran a hand through his hair, wondering how this had gone bad so fast. "Look," he sighed, "maybe we should go inside and talk about this."

"Now? Now you want to talk about this?" she demanded, trying to walk past him and almost falling into the pool. He quickly caught her. As soon as she was steady, she shoved his hands away and cautiously walked around the pool.

"I can't believe you did this!"

That caught him short. "What the hell do you mean? How exactly was this, a surprise? I'm your fucking boyfriend, Haley. This was bound to happen sooner or later with the way we were going at each other."

"Just because we're dating doesn't mean I was going to sleep with you!" she snapped.

Holy shit.....

They'd been right.

"You were never planning on sleeping with me were you?" he demanded, not bothering to hide how pissed he was.

"I wasn't sure yet! Up until ten minutes ago I hadn't made up my mind!"

He rounded the pool just as Haley found her glasses and put them on.

"You were fucking playing me?" he demanded.

When she didn't answer he continued. "Your friends were right. You were getting a kick out of playing me!" he yelled, for the first time since he met her not caring that he made her flinch.

"Did you brag that you brought me to my knees and kept me panting? Was this payback for all the bullshit I put you through over the years? Did you even care for me a little bit or was all this, a fucking game to you?"

"A game?" she demanded, wiping away tears that Jason wouldn't let affect him. She was upset? Too fucking bad, because he was pissed. She'd played him.

"You have the nerve to yell at me when you just took my virginity to prove something?" she demanded.

He froze.

A virgin?

She'd been tight, but.......

"Oh my God," he croaked.

"I don't know who you spoke to, well, I have an idea who, but they left out one very important item. I was saving myself for the man I thought I'd spend the rest of my life with. *That's* why I didn't sleep with you," she said, clearly trying to fight back the tears.

Just like that all the anger in him drained away. He reached out to pull her into his arms only to have his hands weakly slapped away.

"You were so damn eager to prove something that you didn't even stop to think about what you were doing!"

"Baby," he said, keeping his tone gentle, "if I had known you were a virgin I would have done this differently, but I can't regret this." He took a steadying breath. "I'm in love with you Haley."

"Ow!" he said when his little grasshopper kicked him in the shin. "What the hell was that for? I told you I love you and you kick me?"

"That's for being a jerk! You wait until you screw up to pull out the big guns? How about telling me that and making love to me because you love me and not because you felt you had something to prove?"

He nodded solemnly as he reached out for her. "That sounds reasonable. Let's go inside and I'll do this right."

"Are you crazy? You think I'm going to let you touch me after what just happened?"

"I'm really sorry about this," he said, reaching for her again.

"You actually thought I could hurt you? That's worse than anything you've done here tonight," she said, gesturing wildly towards the pool. "It should have been more than obvious that I loved you," she mumbled, wiping frantically at the tears streaming down her face.

Jason felt his heart break as he watched her. "Haley, I'm so sorry."

Haley ignored his apology and he couldn't say that he really blamed her at the moment. "You were so busy trying to prove that I wasn't playing you that you didn't think."

"What are you-"

"Jason, I'm not on birth control and you didn't wear a condom," she said, cutting him off.

"Oh shit," he mumbled. He'd fucked up in so many ways tonight, he wasn't sure where to start, but he knew which fuck up was the most important.

"Oh shit is right," Haley snapped, opening the sliding glass door and stepping inside.

He'd never forgotten to wear a condom before. Not once. He licked his suddenly dry lips. "Haley, we have to talk."

"You should have thought about that before," she said, turning her back on him.

"Haley, please don't do this."

"Just leave me alone, Jason," she said, shutting the door and locking it.

She was just mad, he told himself as he waited for her to come back and give him another piece of her mind. He'd fucked up big time, but they'd both known from the beginning that he was probably going to do that.

After a few minutes, he was sure she'd realize that he never really believed she could hurt him. He loved her. She had to know that he wouldn't love her unless he trusted her. She just needed a few minutes to cool off.

When a few minutes turned into thirty minutes he forced himself to move. He just needed to apologize to her. He hopped over the small picket fence separating their properties and made his way to her window more than ready to beg and plead if that's what it took to get her to listen to him when the sound of her quiet sobs caught his attention.

"Haley?"

No answer.

He stood there wondering what the hell he should do. Suddenly crawling into her room and pleading with her didn't seem like such a smart idea. She needed time to think, probably more time then he'd given her.

"I'll be in my room when you're ready to talk. So, just yell or call when you're ready," he said loudly, feeling like a useless idiot and not having a damn clue what to do. He left, hoping she'd come to him when she was ready.

* * * *

Haley spent half the night crying and waiting for Jason to crawl through the window and hold her. When she realized that wasn't going to happen she grabbed a pillow and a throw blanket and headed for the couch, unable to sleep in her own bed without Jason.

She couldn't believe how much this hurt. She'd been an idiot to think she could prepare herself for this moment. Losing Jason was hard enough, but the way he'd hurt her......

In one night she'd apparently lost so much, her best friend, boyfriend, her virginity and her heart. On top of that, it appeared she'd lost a few of her friends, which she really could care less about if truth be told. There was a reason after all why she kept putting off girl's night and it had very little to do with Jason. They'd been a part of the old Haley's life, the pushover version of herself where she never spoke up for herself and let others push her around. A few months ago when they started hassling her about Jason and letting her know they couldn't believe Jason settled for someone like her she should have cut them out of her life, but hesitated. She didn't like hurting anyone's feelings and apparently Jason didn't know that about her.

How could he have thought she would do that to him? She could just imagine what Amy and her friend Kate, well mostly Kate, could have said to upset him, but what she couldn't understand is why he didn't talk to her first.

Admittedly, it was a conversation they should have had in the beginning, but that didn't excuse his behavior. He'd set out to seduce her, consequences be damned. It hadn't mattered if she had her reasons for wanting to wait or how she felt for that matter. He'd only cared about himself.

She wished she'd realized that sooner, especially before last night. All these years wasted and for what? A horrible experience she could never take back. For that alone she would never be able to forgive Jason.

* * * *

"You're out of eggs," Mitch yelled.

"I don't care," Jason said, never taking his eyes away from Haley's front door.

Around three this morning he'd realized he'd fucked up this situation even more by not going to her. He spent the next two hours going over every single moment from the night before, trying to figure out exactly when he'd fucked up and made a list. After he made sure that he hadn't missed anything he folded the three page list, front and back, and stuffed it in his back pocket and came outside to wait for Haley so that he could start apologizing.

He contemplated waking her up, but then he'd have one more thing to apologize for, so he settled for waiting on his front step. A half hour ago, Mitch decided to join him after he spotted him waiting outside on his way home. It hadn't taken long for the other man to figure out that he'd fucked up.

"Are you going to sit out here all day?" Mitch asked, stepping out the front door. "I'm starving. Let's go get something for breakfast. By the time we get back Haley will be up and you can go grovel."

Jason stubbornly shook his head. "I'm not leaving until I talk to her. Besides, I'm not hungry."

"Holy Christ," Mitch mumbled, crossing himself.

He ignored Mitch and focused on Haley's front door. A few minutes later, it opened and Haley stumbled out. Jason was on his feet within seconds and heading for her. He really wasn't sure how much longer he would have been able to wait before breaking into her house and begging for her forgiveness.

"Haley, I....," he trailed off when he spotted the large duffle bag she was half carrying, half dragging. "What's going on?"

For the first time in months Haley's face didn't light up when she saw him. She pushed her glasses back up her nose and went back to pulling the bag.

"I'm going away," she said, sounding sad.

"For how long?" Jason asked, feeling as though his entire world was crashing down around him.

"A week," Haley said, walking past him as she dragged that damn bag.

A week? No, they couldn't be apart for a week. That was too much time. A week thinking over how badly he'd fucked up and how much better off without him she would be was not what they needed. They needed to work this out here and now so he could get on with the groveling.

"I don't think that's such a great idea, Haley," he said, automatically lifting the bag and placing it in her opened trunk for her when she began struggling to lift it. "Why don't we go inside and talk this over?"

She shook her head stubbornly. "I can't. If I don't go I'll be out a thousand dollars."

He waved that aside like it was nothing. "I'll reimburse you. Just stay here and let me explain about last night."

"There's nothing to explain, Jason," Haley said, shaking her head sadly. "I think it's for the best if we end things now."

Her words felt like a punch to the gut. "You're just mad, Haley. Maybe...maybe you're right. Maybe you just need a week to think things over," he said quickly, desperate to do or say anything that would make her take it back. "Take a week, think it over. We both knew I was going to fuck up at some point, my little grasshopper. After you think about it you'll realize that's all it was. Then you'll come back here and I'll grovel and we'll move past this."

She couldn't even look at him as she said, "I'm really sorry, Jason."

Jason couldn't move, could hardly breathe as Haley stood up on her toes and pressed a kiss to his cheek. "I'm sorry," she said, sounding close to tears. "We'll always be friends," she said, delivering the killing blow.

Chapter 20

Haley just barely stopped herself from looking for Jason when she stepped back outside and saw that he'd left. It was for the best she told herself as she threw her small backpack into the trunk. She closed it and walked slowly to the driver's side, hoping to catch one last glimpse of him.

Even though she'd always known they had no future, she couldn't stop herself from feeling disappointed. He'd given her up so easily. Maybe it was a good thing that they were over, she told herself. If he gave up so easily, then he really didn't care about her and it was for the best that she found out now.

At least that's what she tried to tell herself over the next three hours as she drove. Every five minutes she was either checking to make sure her phone still worked or stopping herself from calling him. She just wanted to hear his voice.

She knew it was over between them, but that didn't mean anything to her heart. All she wanted to do was pull the car over and curl up into a ball and cry, but she wouldn't allow herself that release, not yet. When she arrived at the cottage, then she'd allow herself to break down in privacy and use the week to mend her heart.

After this week was over she really didn't know what she was going to do. She'd told him they would always be friends, but she really didn't think she'd be able to see him day in and day out and survive after this. Worse, what would she do when a woman woke her up screaming Jason's name after he tossed her aside? Haley wouldn't be able to survive knowing Jason was with other women.

During the next week when she wasn't crying, or getting drunk into oblivion, she'd figure out what to do about work and her house. If worse came to worst she could rent out her house and find an apartment even if only temporary. Work would be another issue. Right now she worked at one of the most prestigious private schools in the country, but she knew if she left, she'd most likely end up working at a public school for a lot less money.

Her stomach's rumbling thankfully broke her out of her rather depressing thoughts. She took the next exit off the highway. Ten minutes later she was back on the highway and frowning down at her purchase, an extra large orange juice, three coffee rolls, two muffins and three apple pastries.

"Great, he's got me trained," she muttered with an eye roll. Either she'd have to break herself out of the habit of ordering for a small army or she'd become fat, she thought with a sigh. She picked up one of the coffee rolls and took a small bite before putting it down and taking a sip of juice. When a particularly annoying song came on the radio she spent a minute looking for a decent song. When she finally found one, she picked up her coffee roll and frowned at the half eaten baked item.

Apparently she'd eaten more than she thought. Great, she was eating out of depression and would no doubt be as big as a house by the time school started in a few weeks. She took a bite out of her coffee roll and placed it back on the passenger seat and picked up her now half empty juice.

"What the hell?" she murmured, taking her eyes off the road to look down at the insane amount of food she'd bought. Hadn't she bought two muffins and three apple pastries? There was only one of each now. She was starting to wonder if she was going crazy when a large tan hand suddenly appeared, scaring the holy hell out of her.

She let out a surprised yelp, jerking the wheel to the right and almost crashing into a tow truck. It took her a few seconds before her brain started to function again and when it did she narrowed her eyes on the hand that was blindly searching for the orange juice.

Glaring, she reached down and pinched the back of the hand, hard.

"Ow!"

Haley stole a quick glance back at the backseat and cursed. Somehow Jason had managed to fold his large frame onto the floor of her midsize car and cover himself with the large towel she kept back there.

"What the hell are you doing?"

Jason sighed heavily as he tossed the towel away and struggled to climb off the floor. Once he was comfortably seated in the back seat he reached forward and snagged her orange juice. "Having breakfast." He took a sip. "What does it look like?"

"Why are you in my car?" she demanded as she did her best to glare at him and keep the car driving in a straight line.

"How else do you expect us to finish our fight?" he asked, leaning forward to snag the last apple pastry. He took a big bite before holding it to her lips for her to do the same.

She shoved his hand away. "What the hell do you mean to finish our fight? We're done, Jason. I'm sorry, but it's over," she said, trying to remain calm.

"No, we didn't."

"Yes, we did."

"I don't think so," he said calmly, finishing off the rest of the pastry as if he didn't have a care in the world.

" Jason, I dumped you!" she snapped, feeling the last thread of patience snap.

She looked up in the rearview mirror when he didn't say anything for a minute only to find him frowning. Finally he shook his head. "No, I think I would have remembered that."

Her mouth dropped open.

"Anyway," Jason continued as if he hadn't just left her speechless with that little announcement, "after our talk I realized that you planned a week away for us and I really couldn't agree more. A week away is exactly what we need to work through our problems."

"Oh my God," she mumbled, "you're insane."

Another careless shrug.

"So, where are we going anyway?" Jason asked, getting comfortable.

"*We* aren't going anywhere. I'm leaving you at the next rest stop. You can hitchhike your way back home."

"That's really not going to work for me," Jason said, giving her a sexy smile when she glared at him through the mirror.

Her grip tightened on the steering wheel as she prayed for patience. "Jason, it's over. I'm sorry, but you have to accept it."

"No, I don't," he said calmly, irritating her even more.

"Jason," she said tightly.

"Haley," he mocked in the same tone, making her lips twitch damn him!

She sighed heavily. "Jason, you really hurt me last night. I don't think you-"

"I know I really fucked up, Haley, but if you remember I did tell you when we started that I was most likely going to mess this up," he said, cutting her off.

"Yeah, you did, Jason, and last night you proved beyond a doubt that you aren't capable of being in a relationship."

"No, last night I proved that I'm a fucking idiot," Jason said matter-of-factly.

She wasn't going to argue with that since she'd come to the same conclusion after hearing what happened, but that didn't mean she'd changed her mind.

"Jason, we're over," she said more softly.

He snorted. "No, we're not."

"Yes, we are! Stop saying that!"

"No, we're just fighting. You love me and you damn well know it."

She opened her mouth to deny it, but she couldn't. She did love him. More than anything on this earth, but he'd hurt her last night and she wasn't so sure that she could trust him not to do it again.

When she didn't say anything he settled back in his seat and said, "I'm coming with you so you might as well get used to it. The sooner we get the fight over with the sooner we can move onto the next phase."

"What phase?" she asked cautiously.

"Makeup sex," he said, grinning hugely as he wiggled his eyebrows.

* * * *

"What are we doing here?" Jason asked as he climbed out of the car, but not before Haley did. He wasn't an idiot after all. She was still pissed off at him and was probably still looking for a way to ditch his ass. In retrospect, he probably shouldn't have made that makeup sex comment.

The hour they spent at the rest stop had definitely proved that. She'd tried everything she could to get him out of her car, but he refused to budge. Finally when she was out of breath and exhausted from trying to drag him out of the car, it was a sad attempt, she gave up, slammed the door shut and drove off. She ignored him for the next two hours.

"I need groceries," she muttered unhappily, throwing another glare in his direction. When her eyes shot between the Super Wal-Mart center and her car he snatched the keys out of her hand.

"Hey!" She tried to grab them away from him.

"Sorry, my little grasshopper, you're not ditching me at Wally World," he said, pocketing her keys and heading for the store, leaving her to either fume at him or follow. He didn't bother looking back since he knew she wasn't going anywhere.

Although Wal-Mart wouldn't be his first choice, this solved one problem. He didn't have any clothes since he'd been in a bit of a rush to hide in Haley's car before she spotted him. But this would work out rather nicely for him and since he could smell the salt in the air he knew exactly what to buy.

"I hate you," Haley mumbled, storming past him to grab a carriage.

"You love and adore me," Jason informed her as he deftly snagged her carriage away from her and headed towards the men's department.

Along the way he stopped at the women's department when a little black bikini caught his eye, deciding that it would look great on Haley, he threw it into the carriage as well as the red one behind it. He wasn't too worried when Haley didn't follow him. He figured she was somewhere in the store trying to calm down or buying a baseball bat, to beat his ass into submission.

That was fine. They had a whole week to work their problems out whether she wanted to or not. She was his, plain and simple and the sooner she realized they'd be together forever, the sooner he could correct the mistake he made last night and show her how good it could be between them.

After he grabbed swim trunks, enough clothes for the week and a few toiletries he headed for the grocery section. When he spotted Haley's carriage he couldn't help but snort in disbelief. Did she really think buying single servings of food was going to feed them for a week? Clearly their fight had addled her brain.

He paused near her carriage, ignoring her cute little glare and dumped all his things into her basket.

"Hey!" she said, trying to stop him. "What the hell are you doing?"

"I need more room in my carriage for food," he simply said. He headed towards the dairy section, hoping she wouldn't just ditch his shit to get back at him. Then again, she should know that if she did he would take it as an invitation to walk around naked the entire week.

"Why do you need bubble bath?" she asked as she came up next to him in front of the dairy coolers.

He placed two gallons of milk in the carriage. "It's for you," he said in a tone that let her know it should be more than obvious. His little grasshopper loved taking long hot bubble baths to relax and he really needed her to relax if he was going to convince her to forgive him and forget about that breakup nonsense.

"O-kay," she said slowly, picking up a familiar black cardboard box. "And what about these? A twenty pack and magnum size no less, someone thinks awfully highly of himself."

Sighing, Jason reached over and snatched the box of condoms out of her hands. "Only one box? I thought I grabbed three," he murmured, making a show of looking in her carriage for the other boxes. Finally with a resigned sigh he threw the box back. "Remind me to grab a few boxes on the way out."

With that he headed over to the cookie section, knowing she was definitely going to follow this time.

"Why the hell would I remind you? We're not going need one box, never mind three!"

Jason really couldn't help but smile at that little announcement. "Okay," he said, grabbing the box of condoms and sticking it on the top shelf between some figs and jelly cookies. "I was hoping you'd say that."

The damage had already been done last night. Granted, if it had been any other woman he would have dragged her ass to the emergency room for the morning after pill, but with Haley he felt oddly calm about the whole thing. Actually, he felt a little excited at the idea of Haley having his child.

Up until a few hours ago he hadn't given much thought to the consequences of last night. He'd been too scared that he'd lost Haley for good, to really give it some thought, but once he found himself squeezed into his little hiding place he hadn't had much to do but think.

When he allowed himself to consider having a kid he may have freaked out just a little. Thankfully, Haley had been blasting the radio so she probably didn't hear him hyperventilating. After he finally managed to calm down, he allowed himself to think about Haley pregnant with his child. He'd been a little shocked when the idea didn't freak him out.

Soon he was picturing little girls with mischievous green eyes and pigtails asking him to play tea. Of course he'd bring real food to the tea party. None of that pretend food bullshit for his little girls.

By the time Haley had stopped for breakfast he'd been calmer about everything. He'd already decided to ignore that breakup nonsense. It was just ridiculous and he knew sooner or later Haley would realize that so they could get started on making their all girl baseball team.

"You were?" Haley asked, looking so damn confused and adorable.

"Damn straight," he said, grabbing several cookie packages and tossing them into his carriage. "Nothing should come between us when we're making love," he explained, loving the way her little face went bright red.

"We're not doing that again!" she hissed quietly.

Not doing it again? Puhlease. If there was one thing he knew about his little grasshopper it was that she was as insatiable in the bedroom as he was. He'd have her in his bed by the end of the day, guaranteed.

Chapter 21

"Can I have my keys back?" Haley asked, holding out her hand expectantly just as Jason placed the last bag in the back seat.

"Nope," he said, stepping past her and climbing into the driver's seat.

Sighing, Haley climbed into the passenger side, knowing there was no point in arguing with him and she really didn't have the energy. All she wanted to do was find the cottage, take a bath and sleep for the next day or two.

She pulled her hand away when Jason tried to hold it. Instead of arguing, he acted like nothing happened and focused on the printed driving directions. After a few minutes he took her hand into his again.

After a two minute tug of war, Haley gave up and let him have his sad little victory, mentally promising herself all kinds of revenge when he smiled smugly. She was too tired to argue so she sat back against the cool leather seat and tried not to doze off.

Her eyes darted to the rearview mirror and narrowed on the large pile of grocery bags. She turned her glare onto Jason. "I hope you don't expect me to cook for you." She decided that if he so much as pouted over that announcement she was going to break out the fists of fury on his ass.

He shook his head. "You're not allowed to cook this week," he said, surprising the hell out of her.

"What?"

"You're on vacation. I don't want you to lift a finger," he said, raising their entwined hands and pressing a sweet kiss to the back of her hand. When she felt herself starting to melt she reminded herself what he did last night and why.

After one last useless attempt to tug her hand back, Haley sighed and sat back in her seat, watching as they passed small houses, apartment complexes, and small businesses. Ten minutes later they passed through a quaint downtown shopping area and onto a scenic road that took them past several large hotels along the beachfront.

Haley was just about to drift off when Jason said, "I think this is it."

She forced her eyes open and watched as they drove past several small cottages. A minute later they were pulling onto the long driveway of a small one level cottage.

"Do you have a key?" Jason asked, throwing the car into park and shutting it off.

Biting back a yawn, she nodded. Without a word she climbed out of the car and trudged up the short crushed sea shell walkway and let herself into the house, deciding she'd handle Jason later. Right now she was too tired to do anything more than take a bath and nap. She looked around the cottage and noted that it was cuter than the pictures her grandmother's realtor sent her.

The wicker furniture in the living room was small, but looked surprisingly comfortable, she noted as she walked through the open doorway into the small eat-in kitchen and looked out the double glass doors. She frowned as she watched the waves crash against the smooth sandy beach. There was no way a cottage on a private beach was only a thousand dollars to rent for a week.

"Damn it," Haley cursed, stomping her foot. Once again her grandmother had tricked her. When Haley asked Grandma to see if her realtor could look into rental properties for her, she should have known Grandma wouldn't be able to stop herself from swooping in and taking care of it.

No one in her family understood why she wanted to make it on her own, least of all Grandma. Haley knew her grandmother meant well and that she was worried about her, but she really wished she'd stop pulling stunts like this one. There was absolutely no doubt in Haley's mind that her grandmother had paid for more than half the rental price.

Well, there was nothing she could do about it right now. More importantly, she was too damn tired to be pissed. Sometime this week she'd go into town and ask around to find out what a rental property in this area went for. Then she'd send her grandmother the difference.

"Are you sure this place only cost a thousand?" Jason asked, placing a half dozen grocery bags on the table.

Haley looked over her shoulder and sighed. That was one more problem to deal with. She pushed her glasses back up her nose and pulled her cell phone out of her front pocket. "Look, why don't you call one of the guys to come pick you up?" It would take a good five hours for someone to get here. Hopefully she'd sleep through Jason's wait.

"Why would I do that?" Jason asked, as he emptied the bags and started to put the food away.

"Because you're not staying here," she said bluntly.

He snorted.

"I'm serious, Jason," she said, stepping forward, blocking him from putting the ice cream away. He simply sidestepped her and put it away.

"I'm not going anywhere, Haley."

"Look," she said, taking in a deep calming breath, "I'll give you a ride right now to one of the hotels we passed along the way. You can stay there until someone can come get you."

"I'm staying right here, Haley, until we work this out," Jason said firmly.

"You're not staying here. First of all, I paid for-"

"Here," Jason said, cutting her of, as he slapped a check onto the white oak kitchen table. "I'm paying for the cottage so there shouldn't be any problems."

Jason was the only person, besides her grandmother, she knew that still carried checks in his wallet. She picked up the check and frowned when she saw that he intended to pay the entire amount.

She held the check out to him. "I'm not taking this."

"Yes, you are," he simply said, as he headed back into the living room. "If you tear that up I'll just write you another one when we get home."

Haley folded the check and stuck it in her back pocket. One more argument to have later, she thought miserably. Right now she was too tired to care. She walked into the living room and headed for the small hallway to the right, deciding she'd get her bags after her nap that would hopefully give her the energy to deal with this nonsense. She headed for the only door in the hallway and almost ran into Jason as he was coming out.

"Sorry," he said, stepping to the side so she could walk into the room. "I was just bringing in the bags."

"Thank you," she mumbled, feeling more exhausted than she could ever remember. She hadn't slept at all last night and the night before they'd stayed up late watching movies and cuddling.

"You look tired, baby," he said, reaching up to touch her face only to drop his hand away at the last second. "Look," he said, rubbing the back of his neck, "why don't you go relax. We can talk everything over later."

It was on the tip of her tongue to tell him there was nothing to talk about, but that would only start an argument so she simply nodded, closing the door behind her. She looked over the small Cape Cod style bedroom and nearly groaned. This place would have been perfect for a romantic getaway if Jason hadn't gone and ruined everything. She threw a look of longing towards the bed before heading for the bathroom. Although she'd like nothing better than to curl up on the double bed, she desperately needed to soak in a hot bath. It didn't matter that it had to be ninety degrees in the small cottage. She was still sore between her legs from last night and knew she wouldn't be able to sleep until she took some aspirin and soaked in a hot bath for a while.

It was just another reminder of what he did last night. She still couldn't believe he'd hurt her like this. Despite Jason's flawed dating past she'd trusted him, more than anyone. He was the only person that never took advantage of her "doormat" tendencies.

He'd been kind, sweet and considerate with her and never tried to manipulate her into doing something she didn't want to do. When they were intimate he'd never once pushed for more than she was willing to give him. That alone had made her love him even more. Too many times in her past men had gone out their way to coerce her into taking a step she wasn't ready to take.

When she refused they tried to sweet talk her, manipulate her, guilt her, until they finally got pissed. More than one man had ended things with her when she wouldn't sleep with him. She'd been called a bitch and a tease more times than she cared to remember. The fact that she'd been upfront about her sexual comfort level hadn't mattered.

There had been several men that ended things as soon as she told them she wouldn't have sex with them, but others thought she was lying, teasing them, or setting up a challenge. When they eventually realized she hadn't lied things would end, they'd turn cold and mean. Some had hung around a little longer hoping to change her mind, but she never did.

That is until Jason.

His reaction had been anything but typical or expected. Instead of arguing or questioning her, he'd readily accepted what she told him with a smile and a little teasing. Every time they became intimate she'd prepared herself for Jason to push her into having sex, but he never did. Not once. Even those times when she knew he was dying to take her, he hadn't. He'd grit his teeth and accept whatever she offered him, which was why she felt comfortable and ready to make love to him last night.

Taking the next step with Jason had felt so natural last night. It wasn't until after his little announcement, that she regretted what they'd done. He'd done it because he thought she was playing him, only to end up playing her. Last night he'd manipulated her into sleeping with him to prove something and then actually had the balls to announce it like it was no big deal.

She wiped away a tear. It was a very big deal to her. She'd waited all her life for the right man and the right time only to be used by the man she thought cared for her. He said he loved her last night, but he really didn't. There was no question that he cared for her a little, but love? No. Last night proved beyond a doubt that Jason wasn't capable of loving her. If he loved her he wouldn't have treated her so callously.

The simple truth was, Jason was stubborn. It was the reason why he slept with her, to prove something and the same reason he hid in her car and was being bullheaded about this breakup. She doubted he'd ever been dumped before and he probably wasn't handling it well. Jason liked to call the shots when it came to women and having his shy little neighbor dump him probably grated on his ego.

There was absolutely no doubt in her mind that if she took him back he'd dump her ass in a matter of weeks just so that he could be the one to make that decision. It was better for everyone that they ended things now. This way she was only disappointed in Jason and didn't hate him, although maybe that would be for the best as well.

She paused in the bathroom doorway and sighed heavily as she took in the steaming bubble bath Jason had drawn for her in the deep claw footed bathtub. He even set out a towel and her favorite tee shirt to change into afterwards.

"Stupid jerk," she mumbled, once again stopping herself from melting. She just had to remember that this was all a game to him and she'd be fine.

Chapter 22

"You fucking moron."

Jason couldn't argue with that. He'd seriously screwed everything up and desperately needed to find a way to fix it, which is why he called in the big guns.

His father.

"Tell me this is some sick joke," his father said warily.

"I wish I could, Dad," Jason said, looking over his shoulder at the small cottage as he walked along the edge of the water.

For the past three hours he'd been out here pacing, trying to figure out what the hell he should do. Finally he came to the conclusion that he was in way over his head here and needed someone with a history of charming his way out of fuckups with women and only one person came to mind.

His father fucked up more times with his mother than should be humanly possible. Not that his father screwed around on his mother. She'd simply kill the man if he ever even thought of it. No, his father could be an arrogant, hardheaded bastard that drove his mother to the brink of insanity countless times over the years.

"Let me get this straight, you let some dumb bar bimbo convince you that my poor sweet little Haley," his father said, making him shake his head ruefully. Haley managed to wrap his father around her little finger with those cupcakes and bought his undying love with fried chicken, potato salad and M & M cookies. The man's obsession with food was really pathetic.

Thank God he didn't have that problem.

"-could ever do something so heartless? Then you go ahead and screw it up instead of talking to her? What in the hell is wrong with you?" his father practically yelled, making Jason hold Haley's cell phone a good foot from his ear.

"I know I messed up, Dad," Jason said once his father stopped yelling. "Look, I need help figuring out how to fix this."

"You don't deserve my Haley," his father simply said.

Jason barely stopped himself from rolling his eyes. His father was such a food slut.

"Has it occurred to you that if I don't fix things with Haley that she'll never make you that Boston cream pie she promised you?" he said, knowing the way to get his father to focus was to threaten his food.

His comment was met with a short pause.

"Okay, this is what you need to do," his father said, all business now. *"You need to back off and stop apologizing."*

Jason frowned. "Stop apologizing?" That didn't sound right.

"Mmmhmm, no need to keep reminding her how big of an idiot you are. She already knows, trust me. Right now you need to work on being there for her. Don't pressure her. In fact, I would suggest you work on reminding her how much you care about her and how good you are for her."

He nodded slowly. "I could do that."

His father snorted his disbelief.

"I can," Jason stressed, promising himself that after Haley took him back that he'd get her to make him a Boston cream pie just so he could rub it in the old man's face.

"Just try not to fuck this up, because if you cost me Haley I will disown you," his father said before he hung up.

Jason placed the phone in his pocket and headed back to the cottage, deciding there was no time like the present to get started. He'd remind her how good they were together and why she adored him. It shouldn't be too hard. In fact, he was certain that one little problem was going to guarantee that she couldn't live without him.

He stepped into the kitchen just as Haley stomped angrily into the room wearing nothing but her "Geek" tee shirt. She threw him a glare and muttered something about his balls that he decided to ignore as she headed for the refrigerator. She grabbed an ice cold soda and sipped it as she glared at him.

She looked exhausted, he noted as he leaned against the counter. He had to stop himself from grinning. This was going to be so easy.

"Couldn't sleep?" he asked casually, already knowing the answer. She needed him and she damn well knew it. This was going to be the way he stayed close to her while he did his best to convince her to forgive him.

Haley pushed her glasses up her nose, took a sip of Coke and simply flipped him off as she walked out of the room.

Great. He was already fucking this up, he thought, walking after her. She slammed the bedroom door shut in his face. After counting to ten, twice, he knocked on the door.

"Go. Away."

Sighing heavily, he opened the door just in time to see the bathroom door slammed shut. He walked over to the bed and sat down.

"Haley, I-"

"Look, Jason, I really can't do this with you right now," Haley said, not bothering to open the door to face him, making Jason wonder if her pushover tendencies were once again showing up. That wouldn't be good for either one of them. He needed her to deal with him, not simply avoid him. "Let me finish getting dressed then I'll give you a ride to a hotel."

"No," he said firmly. There was no way in hell he was leaving. They were going to work this out whether she liked it or not and he had a feeling she didn't.

"Fine," she grated out. "Then I'm leaving."

Oh hell no.

If she left now, there'd be no stopping her from leaving his ass for good. There was no doubt in his mind that she didn't intend on giving him a ride home now, which would mean that he probably wouldn't get home until tomorrow afternoon. By then she could be anywhere doing her best to convince herself that she could do better, she could, but that wasn't the point. He couldn't let her walk away from him, not now, not ever.

He threw a quick look at the door before rushing over to Haley's little backpack that she liked to call a purse. He tore through it until he found what he needed. No doubt this was only going to piss her off more, but desperate times called for desperate measures. He pocketed her wallet and quickly checked her discarded pants, stealing the money she had in the front pocket, and her car keys, before rushing out of the room.

It only took him a minute to find the perfect hiding spot, one of the dozens of decorative baskets lining the ceiling. There was no way in hell Haley was going to reach it never mind find it. After a minute he decided to add her cell phone as well. He shut it off and added it to the pile and covered his tracks.

Knowing there was no way Haley could leave him until they worked things out, Jason relaxed for the first time since this whole thing started. He walked to the kitchen, feeling confident that his little plan was going to work.

He grabbed a cold soda from the fridge, wishing it was a beer, and headed for the beach. As long as his little grasshopper wasn't allowed to drink then he wouldn't drink. Not that he really expected her to be pregnant from one time, but he wasn't taking any chances.

Until he knew for sure that she wasn't pregnant with their baby, she wasn't so much as looking at a drop of alcohol, which was probably going to make it more difficult to deal with him. Granted it might help his case if he got her drunk, but he wasn't willing take the risk of harming any possible baby or having her throw it in his face later that she hadn't known what she was doing when she forgave him. He wanted her stone cold sober for this, especially since she was most likely going to be the one to figure out how to fix this since he was pretty sure he'd only manage to fuck this up more.

"You bastard!" he heard Haley yell from somewhere behind him.

He looked back at her and smiled, watching as she stormed over to him with her little fists swinging by her side. She shoved her glasses back up her nose, glaring at him against the bright sunlight.

"What did you do with it, you bastard?" she demanded, coming to a halt two feet from him.

"What?" he asked innocently, taking a sip of soda.

"You know what!" she snapped.

"Hmm, I really don't," he mused, trying not to smile when she growled in irritation.

"My wallet," she bit out through clenched teeth. "I need it back so I can leave."

"Then you're not getting it," he said, shrugging his shoulders. She thought he was going to help her leave him? Damn, his little grasshopper still had so much to learn.

"Fine," she bit out. "Give me my cell phone so I can call someone," she demanded, holding out her hand expectantly.

"Sorry, I can't do that either," he said, sighing heavily. Really, did she not know him at all?

"What about my car keys?" she asked, eyeing him cautiously.

He pursed his lips up in thought. It would be best for both of them if she was limited to the cottage and the center of town a mile down the road.

"No, sorry that's not going to work for me either."

"This is kidnapping!" she sputtered in disbelief.

"No, it's not."

"Yes, it is!"

"Nope."

"What the hell would you call it?" she demanded, snatching his soda from him and finishing it off.

"A romantic getaway?"

She snorted.

"If you really don't want to be here, then go inside and use the house phone to call someone," he suggested innocently.

She looked close to breaking out her cute little fists of fury. "You know damn well that I don't have any of the phone numbers memorized," she snapped. Yes, he really did know that. Haley, thankfully, depended heavily on technology. Once a number went into her contact list she never looked at it again. That little tidbit of information used to earn an eye roll from him, but now it pleased him immensely.

"Then I guess you're stuck here," he said, biting back a smile.

Her eyes narrowed dangerously on him.

"So," he said brightly, "do you want to go for a swim, go fishing," he gestured to the long rock wall that went out about three hundred yards into the ocean, "or are you hungry? I can whip some burgers up in no time."

With one last look that promised bodily harm, Haley stormed off back to the cottage.

Jason walked back to the cottage not even bothering to check the sliding glass doors. Haley's little smug smile had told him everything he needed to know. She'd locked him out. He'd allow her this little victory, he decided as he scooped up his shirt off the lounge chair and pulled it on and headed for town. There was probably no need to tell her that he snatched the cottage keys already.

She'd have to come to him sooner or later.

Chapter 23

Three o'clock in the morning and Haley was close to crying. She was so unbelievably tired. Her head was pounding and she felt sick to her stomach. She hadn't slept in five days.

Not one single wink.

Sadly it had nothing to do with the cottage. The bed was firm, just the way she liked it, the air conditioner ran perfectly, keeping the little cottage at a cool 68 degrees, and the only noise to be heard was the sound of the waves crashing against the beach. She really wished there was something to complain about, because that would mean going to one of the hotels down the road would provide her with the sleep her body desperately needed.

The reason she couldn't sleep was quite simple. The bastard who refused to leave no matter how many times she begged, pleaded or threatened was one hundred percent responsible for this little problem. Being this dependent on another person for sleep was not healthy or normal, but no matter how many times she tried to get that message across to her exhausted body it wouldn't listen.

She tried everything over the past three days. At first she thought relaxation would do the trick, so she'd taken about a dozen hot baths, read a few books, and even tried a relaxing moonlit stroll along the beach. When relaxation didn't work she moved onto vigorous activity. She tried swimming, long vigorous walks, and cleaning the cottage from top to bottom.

Absolutely nothing worked. There was no way she could handle another day without sleep, never mind that Jason was determined to keep her for four more days.

She sat up in bed and kicked the sheet away. Damn it. If she was going to be stuck with him, then she might as well get something out of it. She threw open her door and walked down the short hallway.

Jason looked over at her and sighed. She wasn't too surprised to find him awake. It seemed this little addiction went both ways, thankfully, because if she was going to suffer than so was he. Granted his inability to sleep might have more to do with the small wicker chairs he was forced to sit in all night.

"I don't know what you did, but you wrecked sleep for me and since you won't give me back my things I've decided that you will allow me the use of your body for *sleep*," she clarified, afraid he might get the wrong idea, "until we go home and I can get a prescription for sleeping pills from my doctor."

Jason simply looked at her through bloodshot eyes. "Okay," she said firmly, nodding to herself. "Move your butt," she said, gesturing for him to head to the bedroom.

"No," he said softly.

She narrowed her eyes on him. "Don't make me hurt you, Jason. I am way too tired for any bullshit tonight, so move your ass."

He stubbornly shook his head. "Not until you promise to spend the last four days with me."

"No."

They broke up and he really needed to accept that, especially since they returned to work in two weeks. She didn't want to have to deal with any of this nonsense at work. He needed to accept this so they could both move on. It was already hard enough being around him and not being able to touch him.

She loved him so much and this was killing her. The best thing he could do for both of them was to let her go now so she would have some time, even a few days, to mourn their relationship. She already knew she'd have to put her house on the market and look for a new job as soon as she got back.

After this, she knew she would never manage to be in the same room with him or spot him walking around outside without feeling her heart break. She needed to put as much space between them as she could if she hoped to survive this.

"We have four days left, Haley. If you want to sleep then you'll give me what I want."

"You need sleep just as much as I do," she pointed out.

He nodded his agreement. "I'm willing to go without if that's what it takes."

"We're not getting back together," she said, feeling more exhausted than she had five minutes ago.

"I'm not asking for that, Haley. I'm asking for some real time with you."

"You expect me to believe that?"

"Yes," he said, sounding as exhausted as she felt. "I just want time with you."

She considered him for a moment. At this point she was willing to fork over her kidneys if it meant getting some sleep. "Fine," she said slowly. "But just time. No kissing, sex, or touching."

He sighed with obvious relief as he got to his feet. "That's fine," he said, walking past her to the bedroom. She followed him, eager to finally get some sleep.

"Underwear stays on," she announced, as she walked into the room.

Jason yanked his underwear back up, probably too tired to argue, and flopped down on the bed. After a slight hesitation, Haley lay down and curled up against him. In a matter of minutes she felt her body relax and started to drift off.

* * * *

"Oh my God, no! It's going to bite me!" Haley squealed, jumping back as the small crab moved towards her.

Jason chuckled as he watched his little grasshopper run on her tippy toes, trying to get away from the small crab that did seem to have it out for her. Every time Haley changed direction so did the crab.

Now, Jason could very easily fix this little problem for his little grasshopper by picking her up, but he was following her rules. He only had four days left to convince her that she couldn't live without him, and if that meant he had to follow her rules to spend time with her then he was damn well going to follow them to a tee. He wasn't about to give her a reason to break their agreement.

That's why an hour ago when he woke up to find Haley curled up in his arms, he quickly jumped out of bed and away from her. She looked a little confused and hurt, and he almost ignored her rules and took her into his arms, but he forced himself to keep his head in the game. He said good morning and left her alone to take a shower, not joining her had almost killed him.

After lunch it had taken a little prompting and about a dozen reminders that she promised to spend the last four days with him. With a resigned sigh, she followed him to the beach. For the first time since he wrecked her flowers a heavy awkward silence rose between them.

He bit back another apology, remembering what his father said, and walked next to her, trying to figure out what the hell he should say to her. Unfortunately, Haley seemed to be just as uncomfortable as he was. He knew she was on the verge of suggesting that they go home again, when thankfully they'd found the little crab hell bent on attacking her.

Now they both laughed, watching the little crab's antics, the awkward silence forgotten.

"Jason!" Haley shrieked as the crab made a grab for her toes.

Sighing, Jason bent over and plucked the small crab up. He raised it so he could look at its tiny little buggy eyes. "It's kind of cute."

Haley squished up her face adorably. "If you say so."

He noticed that she didn't make any move to take a closer look. In fact, it looked as if she was trying to discretely step away. Jason bit back a smile as he held it out to her. She squealed, jumping back and almost fell on her ass in the ocean.

"Get it away from me!"

"Aw, come on, Haley. He just wants a little kiss," Jason said, shoving the crab towards her once again. "Just a little kiss."

Haley giggled even as she ducked out of the way.

"Come on, he likes you!" Jason said, chuckling as he chased after her.

"Go away!" Haley said, laughing so hard that she stumbled several times, but somehow managed to take off when the crab came within her personal space.

"I swear to God, I'm going to kick your ass for this!"

* * * *

Haley dropped her book as she latched onto Jason's arm and tried to drag him away.

"That's false advertisement!" Jason said, heading back for the door that they'd been unceremoniously kicked out of ten minutes ago. "The sign says, 'All you can eat.'"

Thankfully, the last several months in Jason's company had pretty much cured her problem of embarrassing easily. Otherwise, she'd probably be turning bright red right now and wishing for a hole in the ground to open up and swallow her whole as people stopped to gawk at them.

"They were closing," she pointed out softly.

"That's no excuse," he said, glaring at the wait staff that watched them nervously from behind the curtains.

"I think they ran out of food," Haley said, doing her best not to laugh when he pouted.

"Bastards," Jason muttered.

"Come on, I'll let you treat me to a late movie," she said, tugging on his arm. He reluctantly let her lead him away, only throwing the occasional look of longing towards the restaurant. Haley did her best not to roll her eyes. The man was way too obsessed with food. As they stepped into the long line outside the movie theatre a thought occurred to her.

"You never brought me to an all you can eat buffet restaurant at home," she pointed out. Now that she thought about it she was really surprised that he hadn't. It seemed like the perfect type of restaurant for Jason, heck, for Jason and his father. They both adored food, which is probably why his parents stopped with just one child. Just the thought of a bunch of little Jason's running around, eating their parents out of house and home was frightening.

Jason mumbled something.

"What?" she asked, tearing her eyes away from the list of movies playing.

"I said, I've been banned," he grumbled unhappily. "It's all political," he sniffed.

"Uh huh.......and your father?" she asked, already having a sneaking suspicion of what his answer was going to be.

"He's been banned since 1995," Jason said with a shrug.

"I see," she said, her lips twitching.

"In two years the ban in Las Vegas will be lifted. We're planning a big trip," he said, looking at her hopefully.

Haley opened her mouth to remind him that they weren't going to be doing anything together in two years when she realized what he said.

"You've been banned from Las Vegas?"

"Not from Las Vegas, just from all the buffets," Jason said with a shrug as if it was no big deal.

"All the buffets?" she asked, unable to hide her shock. There had to be hundreds of buffets in Las Vegas.

"I guess they had a meeting or something. As I said before, it's all political," Jason said, gesturing for her to move up in line.

She was too stunned to say anything for a few minutes. She knew they loved food, but wow......

"What movie do you want to see?" Jason asked, pulling her from her frightening thoughts.

Haley quickly scanned the list, about to tell Jason to go ahead and pick when she spotted a movie she'd been waiting to see for a while. How about *"To hell and back?"* she suggested.

Jason frowned. "The one with Edward and Dana Pierce?"

She nodded.

"Fine," he said with an exaggerated eye roll, earning a smile from her. "A chick flick it is." He bought their tickets and headed for the concession stand. "I just need something to eat before I pass out."

He reached out to take her hand, only to drop his hand away. His smile became polite as he gestured for her to go ahead of him. Haley forced a smile as she stepped in line ahead of him, reminding herself that this was exactly what she wanted. She wanted to go back to being friends, even if it was only for a little while, so Jason readily accepting that was a good thing, she told herself.

After they bought their snacks, well Jason's snacks since she was still full, they found two seats in the middle towards the front. Thankfully, the previews were already playing so Haley took the opportunity to get her head on straight. She really had to stop herself from wanting Jason to touch her, hold her, and kiss her.

They broke up. Jason obviously accepted it and so should she. It was for the best no matter how much it made her want to cry.

Chapter 24

"You didn't have to buy dinner. I could have cooked," Haley pointed out as they followed a waitress to the back booth in the fifties style diner.

"You're not lifting a finger while you're on vacation," Jason pointed out, again. It was just another thing they were going to have to discuss, but later. Right now he was too busy showing Haley how much he cared about her. Over the last two days he was pretty sure Haley had started to forgive him.

By now she probably realized they shouldn't be apart. Now all he had to do was work on not screwing up again, not that he really thought he would. He'd been acting like the perfect friend over the past couple of days. At night he allowed her to decide the sleeping position and in the morning he bolted from the bed and took a very cold shower or went for a swim in the ocean. Then he spent the rest of the day finding fun things to do and keeping his hands to himself.

It was more difficult than he'd ever imagined, but somehow he managed to treat Haley as a good friend. There was no doubt in his mind that she was ready to go back to the way things used to be. Thank fucking God, because he didn't think he could last another day with this friendship bullshit.

She was his little grasshopper, plain and simple. Not being able to touch her and hold her was just wrong.

"Can I get you a drink to start off?" the waitress asked, throwing him an appreciative look.

"We'll take two Cokes, please," he said, directing his attention to the menu in front of him. He wasn't about to do anything to encourage the woman. Right now he needed to be able to focus all his energy on his little grasshopper and not some waitress in a tight pink shirt two sizes too small that hoped to warm his bed tonight.

"I'll go get those right now," she said in a seductive voice. Jason snuck a look at Haley, wondering if the waitress' obvious interest bothered her. If it did, it didn't show. Apparently, once again Haley was too oblivious to care, which was probably for the best because he couldn't stand jealous women.

"I need to use the bathroom. Could you order for me if she comes back before I do?"

"Sure," Haley said, not bothering to look up from her menu. "What do you want."

"Two cheeseburger dinners," he said, not bothering to tell her how he wanted them or to ask for two extra sides. She knew what he liked.

Five minutes later he was walking out of the bathroom just as their waitress finished writing down their order. The waitress looked up from her writing pad and smiled at him. She said something else to Haley before walking over to him, smiling coyly the entire time.

"Your friend," she said, gesturing behind him to Haley who was watching them with bored interest, "said you might like the band playing over at TJ's. It's a Nickleback cover band. She said you could pick me up in two hours after I get off work, but if you give me fifteen minutes I could probably get the night off."

"Wait? What?" Jason asked, confused as hell. "She told you I was interested?"

"Mmmhmm," the waitress said, unconcerned that he was clearly pissed.

"Excuse me," he said tightly, stepping around her.

"I'll go ask about getting off early," the waitress announced, sounding giddy.

"Don't bother," Jason threw over his shoulder.

He walked over to Haley, placed his hands on the table, and leaned over until he was practically nose to nose with her.

"Tell me you didn't just try to set me up on a date with the waitress," he bit out, trying to stop himself from wringing her little neck.

"I didn't set you up per se, but I did tell her you might like the band and that you were single," she simply said, pushing her glasses up her nose.

"I'm single?" he repeated, his voice sounded hollow.

"Yes," Haley said, shifting her glance to the left and away from him.

He slowly pulled away from her and stood up. Swallowing hard, he asked, "Is that what you really want?"

"Yes," she said without the slightest hesitation, making everything suddenly crystal clear.

He pulled out two twenties and tossed them on the table. "Come on," he said, heading for the door.

"Where are we going?" Haley asked when she caught up to him.

"Home."

* * * *

"Jason? Jason, talk to me. You're really scaring me."

For the past six hours he'd been deadly quiet. When he said they were going home at the diner she thought he meant back to the cottage. She knew she shouldn't have encouraged that waitress. She didn't want to and had been on the verge of informing the woman that Jason was spoken for when she realized that seeing Jason with another woman might help her get over him sooner. She had no idea he'd be this pissed otherwise she wouldn't have said anything, but she needed to get over him before she finally gave into the pain threatening to bring her to her knees.

She loved him so much more than she should have allowed herself to.

Instead of answering her, he threw the driver's side door open and popped the trunk. She quickly climbed out of the car just as the motion sensor lights on her house turned on.

"Please talk to me," she said as she watched him grab the three shopping bags of clothes he'd bought and head towards his front door.

"Jason, don't do this!" she said, unable to stand the idea of ending things like this.

"You want to talk?" he asked, slowly turning around to face her.

"Yes," she said, relieved that he was at least talking.

He threw the bags to the side and walked over to her. "Fine. Let's talk, Haley," he said, getting into her face. "I fucked up, Haley. I shouldn't have let some bitch sell me a line of bullshit and I should have talked to you, but you know what? You screwed up, too."

"You never even bothered to tell me why you didn't want to have sex," when she opened her mouth to argue he spoke over her, "I know I could have asked you a thousand different times, but I was too damn happy to care. I wanted to be with you, no matter what. I loved you, Haley and I thought you loved me. So, when that woman told me that you wouldn't sleep with me *because* you didn't love me I panicked big time and did something I will probably regret for the rest of my life."

"You regret sleeping with me?" Haley asked, feeling her heart drop.

"Yes, because I obviously hurt you that night and it gave you the excuse you obviously wanted to break things off," he said, stepping away from her as he ran his hands through his hair in frustration.

"I wasn't looking for an excuse to break things off," she sputtered, taking a step towards him.

"Bullshit!"

"I wasn't!" she yelled right back. "You're the one who thought I was pulling a fast one on you! You're the one who just had to prove-"

"Oh give me a fucking break!" he shouted, causing her to jump back. "I fucked up, Haley. I admit that. Hell, I admitted it right when it happened and I even told you when we started out that I would most likely fuck up." He continued, not giving her a chance to speak, "You were happy that I fucked up. It gave you the little excuse you needed to drop me."

"No, it didn't! You hurt me, Jason! You should have-"

"I should have done a hundred different things, but you know what, Haley? I didn't. I fucked up, yeah, but you're acting like I fucked around on you!"

"Because you're going to!" she shouted back, wiping angrily at the tears that spilled down her cheeks. "We both knew this wasn't going to last, Jason! What you did proved it!"

"Wasn't going to last? I fucking loved you!" he shouted, getting closer. "I wanted to spend the rest of my life with you! But the entire time I was picturing a house, marriage and kids you were just using me!"

"I wasn't using you!" she cried, shoving him back.

"Then what the hell do you call it?" he asked, letting her shove him again. "I was good enough to hang around, date, sleep with, oh wait, no I wasn't, was I? The only thing you thought I was good for was a good time!"

"I can't believe you're complaining!" she said, shoving her hair out of her face. "That's exactly how you treat women! You're just pissed because someone did it to you!"

"I have never led any woman on. They all knew I had nothing to offer them, but you," he shook his head in disgust, "you made me think that you actually cared for me when all you were was a bitch looking for a good time."

She slapped him, hard.

"You're a fucking snob just like your family," he said coldly.

"I hate you," she bit out, ignoring the stinging pain in her hand. She hadn't used him, she knew that. She'd been the only one of them who went into this relationship with a level head. He might think that he loved her today, but she knew that would change one day and she wasn't going to feel bad because she got out before that day came.

He wiped a small drop of blood off his lip as he watched her. "You came to me for a good time so I'm going to make sure you get just that."

"Wha-"

He cut her off with a firm kiss. She tried to pull back, but he wasn't having that. He cupped the back of her head, holding her to him as he brushed his lips over hers, coercing them to cooperate. When he ran the tip of his tongue between her lips, demanding entrance, she was helpless to refuse.

She moaned when his warm tongue slid into her mouth, gliding over hers, and then tangled together. Her arms wrapped around his neck, pulling him closer, unable to stand the thought of being apart.

No matter what he thought, she hadn't been using him. She loved him so much and even though she knew she would wind up hurt in the end she hadn't been able to pass up a chance to be with him.

When he picked her up in his arms she didn't fight him. No, she fisted his hair, tilted her head, and deepened the kiss. Several minutes later they were in her living room and he was kicking the front door shut. He placed her on her feet only to grab behind her thighs and lift her back up. She wrapped her legs around his waist, loving the way he grabbed her ass and ground her against his hard erection.

She released one hand from his hair to reach between them and yank his tee shirt up. Jason turned in the hall, leaning her against the wall as he reached back and yanked his shirt off, only breaking the kiss to pull the shirt off. He kept her pressed against the wall as he worked her shirt off.

He raised her above him so he could lick his way down to her breasts. She hugged his head against her chest as he traced the cups with his tongue and moaned when he suckled her hard nipple through the thin lace.

"Mmmm," she moaned softly as he suckled and kneaded her breasts. Her hips gently rolled against his stomach, searching for relief. She arched her back when she felt his hands leave her breasts and move to her back. In seconds he had her bra undone and his tongue running over her breasts, flicking her hard nipples.

Haley licked her lips as she worked her bra off the rest of the way. She wrapped her arms back around his head, holding him against her as she leaned over and pressed a kiss to the top of his head.

Jason groaned as he wrapped his arms around her, keeping her breasts where he wanted them and pulled her away from the wall and walked down the pitch black hallway to the bedroom. Somehow he managed to walk them into the bedroom without stumbling.

He laid her on the bed. Bending over her, he ran his wet hot tongue from one hard nipple to the other as he undid her shorts. He slid his hand beneath the waist of her shorts and under her panties. He cupped her in his hand, making her squirm against him.

With one last flick of his tongue against her nipple he sat up and helped her out of her shorts and panties, while Haley toed off her canvas sneakers. She opened her arms to him, expecting him to come back for a kiss. In the dim moonlight she saw him shake his head.

"Roll over onto your stomach," he said, already helping her turn over. "On your hands and knees," Jason said softly.

"That's it," he crooned when she did what he asked.

Haley gasped, gripping the comforter tightly in her hands when she felt Jason press a wet kiss to one cheek and then the other. Without a word she spread her legs more and arched her back. He continued to press kisses against her back and bottom as he slid one finger inside of her.

Haley moaned, licking her lips. The few times they'd fooled around in this position had been so good. He always took her hard with his fingers or mouth like this, making her scream. Once he ran his cock between her lips. When she realized he was pleasuring himself against her she'd come harder than she could ever remember.

Just the thought of him teasing her folds with his cock had her riding his finger.

"You like that?" Jason asked, adding another finger.

"Yes," she moaned as she pulled forward until only the tip of one finger remained in her, then slowly slid back, loving the way he filled her. She loved the way he felt, the way he touched her, the way he made her so crazy with need that she could only think about having him. She just loved him.

Over the past week she'd been stupid and so damn scared that Jason would hurt her one day that she almost made the dumbest mistake of her life. She wasn't letting him go. They belonged together. On some level she'd always known that, but she'd been so damn scared that she hadn't seen it.

For the first time she allowed herself to imagine the future she always thought was out of their reach. She imagined falling asleep in Jason's arm every night for the rest of their lives, imagined little boys smiling when she made cookies and little girls wrapping Jason around their little fingers, and she knew she would never be happy without him.

"Then you're going to love this," he murmured softly.

She licked her lips in anticipation when she heard the sound of his zipper being pulled down. A second later she felt his jean clad thighs press up against the back of her legs and his warm stomach press down against her back.

He licked a line up her neck to her ear, taking her earlobe into his mouth and gently suckling it as the tip of his erection pressed against her core.

"You remember the day we were in your flower garden?" he whispered in her ear.

"Yes," she managed to say.

"You have no idea how badly I wanted to take you that day, just like this," he said, sliding slowly inside her.

"Oh God!" Haley cried out at the sensation of being filled. Thankfully it didn't hurt like last time. It felt so good being filled by him like this, so right.

"I've imagined fucking you like this at least a dozen times a day since, my little grasshopper. I think it's only fitting that we end this the way we started it, don't you?"

"Jason, what are you-"

He cut her words off with one long, deep thrust. It was followed by another, and then another. His hands covered hers, fingers entwining as he took her slowly. His low groans in her ear and the way he rubbed against her clit every time he slid back in her had her screaming her release. Jason groaned in her ear minutes later as she felt his hot release inside of her. It felt so good that it set off another orgasm. Jason gently thrust in her until her arms gave out and she collapsed on the bed, gasping for breath.

Somehow she managed to rollover to make room for Jason, but he wasn't there. She looked up to find him pulling his zipper back up.

"Jason?" She slowly sat up. The hurt expression on his face twisted her stomach. She reached out to take his hand, only to find him stepping back.

"Goodbye, Haley," he said softly.

"Jason? Jason!" she cried as her bedroom door shut with an ominous click behind him.

Chapter 25

"Jason?" Haley said, gasping for breath.

"Haley?" said the last person on earth she expected to call.

"Dad?" Haley said, sitting down on the arm of her sofa and doing her best to calm her racing heart. She'd been outside weeding her garden and trying to make it through another day without crying when she heard the phone ring. Afraid that it was Jason calling she ran into the house desperate to hear his voice.

One whole week and not a word and that wasn't from a lack of trying either. She called his phone about a dozen times a day, sent him text messages and harassed the hell out of his friends and family looking for him. So far, no luck. Nobody had any idea where the hell he was. Up until yesterday, she'd convinced herself that he just needed some time and that he'd be back, but that was before the realtor, the same realtor that failed to sell her house for her, pounded a "For Sale" sign in his front yard.

Now Haley was desperate to find him. She needed to explain some things to him and probably grovel. Jason wasn't the one that screwed up. She needed him back here so that she could fix this before it was too late.

"Do you have a moment?" her father asked.

Frowning, truly confused and shocked that he'd called, Haley nodded woodenly, then remembered that he couldn't see her and answered. "Yes. What's going on?" she asked, wondering why he didn't just have his secretary call to relay whatever message he needed to give her.

"Your grandmother told me that you took a vacation last week. How was it?" he asked casually, but Haley couldn't help but feel there was more to it. This wasn't like him to actually take an interest in her life.

"It was fine," she said, wanting to kick her own butt all over again. It could have been great if she hadn't overreacted in the first place. Yeah, Jason had screwed up, but it hadn't deserved the level of drama she'd created. If only she'd made him grovel for a few hours they could have had a great time.

Man, she was such an idiot.

"I heard that Jason went with you," he said, followed by a short expectant pause.

"Yes, Jason went with me, Dad. I told you we were dating," Haley said, walking over to the bay window and looking out. Her eyes narrowed to slits as she watched Barbara, her ex-realtor, gesture for a middle age couple to follow her into Jason's house.

"It's nothing serious I hope," he said, drawing Haley's attention back to the conversation.

"What?"

"You and Jason. Your grandmother said that you were serious, but I didn't think you'd be so foolish to waste your life on a man like that," her father said, stunning her into silence. Although by now, one would think there was very little her family could say or do that would shock her.

"What do you mean, a man like that?" Haley asked, insulted on Jason's behalf.

He let out a tired sigh. *"Haley, do we really need to get into this? We both know you could do so much better."*

"No, I really couldn't, Dad. I love Jason."

"Sweetheart, I know that you think you love him right now, but in time you'll realize that...well, he's not good enough for you."

"And why is that, Dad?" she asked tightly, for the first time in her life she didn't bother to hide what she was feeling from him. "Because he works for a living?"

"You know I don't have a problem with someone working, Haley. I work for a living," he pointed out.

"Then I don't understand the problem," she lied. She knew exactly what her family's problem was from the first moment they laid eyes on Jason.

"He's not one of us, Haley. He'll never fit in. Surely you realize that, sweetheart. When you stop pretending to be someone that you're not, you'll come to realize that Jason just doesn't stand up to our expectations for you," he said soothingly.

She laughed without humor. "Oh, now you have expectations for me? Isn't that convenient? The one time you show concern for me just happens to be when you're worried that I'll sully up the bloodlines and marry someone who might embarrass you."

"Haley, that's ridiculous and you know it. I love you and care very deeply for you," he swore. *"I'm just watching out for your best interests, sweetheart. In a few years you'll see that. Maybe you should give Robert another chance so that the two of-"*

"What do I do for a living?" she bit out between clenched teeth, cutting him off.

"Excuse me?"

"I asked if you knew what I do for a living," she repeated.

"You run a day care," he said with such conviction that even she almost believed it.

"I teach history at Latin Scribe High School," she informed him, trying not to cry. She had absolutely no doubt that if she asked what committees Rose or Martha were on, he would know, mostly because they were a reflection of him.

"Oh," he said, sounding surprised. *"Congratulations, sweetheart. Why didn't you tell me you got the job? We would have held a dinner to celebrate."*

She opened her mouth to remind him that they did in fact celebrate her job at her grandmother's insistence five years ago, but what was the point? He was never going to change and was truly never going to care about her until she started living the life that he wanted.

He'd start giving her attention and his precious time if she decided to ask for a trust fund and live off him and date men like Robert. It wouldn't matter that Robert was a cheating bastard and would drop her as soon as she slept with him. Her parents only cared about their image. It was kind of funny that her father started out in life by sharing a room with his two brothers in a small two bedroom cabin, or that his parents worked their asses off so they could go to college and never have to worry about money. He'd been spoiled and she knew that was Grandma's biggest regret in life.

"I got the job two weeks ago when I turned thirty," Haley lied, wondering if her father was going to remember this time. Of course he didn't.

"Oh, um, did you get my birthday card?" he asked, before he covered the phone with his hand from the sounds of it. She heard him mumble to someone, probably his secretary, to send her birthday card out right away.

Looked like she'd be getting three grand in a few days, she thought with an inward shrug. She'd keep it without putting up a fuss this time. She already had an idea of what to do with the money.

"Look, sweetheart, the reason that I'm calling is that your mother is having a dinner party next week and we'd like you to come," he said, not surprising Haley that her mother hadn't bothered to call her. It just wasn't worth getting upset about.

"I'll think about it," she said, not really sure she wanted to put Jason through that nonsense again.

"We'd really like you there. Robert is very excited to see you again. You know he's been trying to call you, don't you? I really think you should give him another chance, Haley."

Since Haley doubted that her father knew that his precious Robert had been calling up and leaving messages offering to take Haley away for a weekend and "have some fun and prove that his theory that she was wild between the sheets was correct" she hadn't bothered to call Robert back. Then again her father would probably just laugh it off if she did because it was someone he approved of.

"I'm not interested in him, Dad," Haley said firmly, hoping he'd just let it go. "If I can make it I'll be bringing Jason."

"He's not good enough, sweetheart," he said, sounding tired.

"Then neither am I," she said, hanging up.

She took one last look at the couple walking into Jason's house before walking over to her stereo system and turning it on. She found a heavy metal station, cranked it up all the way until she could actually feel the base vibrate throughout the house. She pulled off her shirt, threw on a very revealing bikini top, grabbed a beer and dumped half of it out before heading for her front door.

After mentally promising herself aspirin for the headache that was already forming, she pasted a huge smile on her face and yanked open the door in time to see the couple and realtor stumbling out of Jason's house with their ears covered.

When they glared in her direction she held up her beer and said, "Who's thirsty?"

* * * *

"If anyone has a problem with the new computer system, please let my office know immediately," Headmaster Jenkins said, reaching for his briefcase. "Have a good first day, everyone."

Jason grabbed the pile of handouts Jenkins had swamped him with and headed for the door. He wasn't too surprised when Haley jumped in front of him. She was a persistent little thing.

For two weeks she'd been hounding all of his friends and parents, looking for him. Nobody would tell her where he was, not because they were on his side, oh hell no. They were all on team Haley and they made damn sure he knew that when they managed to get him on the phone. A week ago he finally had enough and threw his phone out his driver's side window somewhere in New Jersey.

When he left Haley he'd been on the verge of a nervous breakdown. He knew if he'd stayed he would go back to Haley on his hands and knees, begging her to give him a chance, and he almost had. The only thing that stopped him was knowing that Haley would never want him the way he wanted her.

"You've put your house up for sale," she said accusingly, pushing her glasses back up her nose as she glared at him.

He simply stepped around her and walked out of the teacher's lounge. Of course that didn't stop Haley. In seconds she was walking beside him.

"Jason, we need to talk."

"I think we said everything we had to say two weeks ago, Haley."

"No, we didn't, Jason. You left before I could talk to you. Look, would you slow down?" she asked, doubling her efforts to keep up with him.

"No."

He didn't want to talk. Hell, he didn't even want to look at her, but he had no choice in the matter. Until his house sold, he was stuck working here and seeing her every day.

"Jason, we really need to talk."

"No."

She somehow managed to catch up with him and jump in front of him just as he reached his classroom.

He pinched the bridge of his nose and sighed. "Move."

"No," she said stubbornly.

He didn't have the patience for this shit. "Move out of the way, Haley."

She shook her head.

"Fine," he said, stepping away from her and heading for her classroom, intending on cutting through her room.

"Fifteen people have looked at your house and not one offer. That's kind of funny, isn't it?" Haley asked in an offhand tone, stopping him dead in his tracks. It was the gist of what his realtor had told him last night over the phone when he got in.

"What the hell are you talking about?" he demanded, turning around to glare at her.

Haley made a show of examining her fingernails. "Just that it's kind of funny that no one has made an offer on your house, especially after all the work you've put into it over the past few months." She looked up from her nails, giving him a smug little smile.

"And how exactly do you know that no one has made me an offer?" he asked, narrowing his eyes on her as he took several steps towards her.

Her brows arched up adorably. "A little birdie told me?"

"Uh huh," he said, tilting his head to the side to study her. "And what else did this little birdie tell you?'

"That you won't get one offer on your house until you give me what I want," she said firmly. There was no doubt in his mind what she wanted.

Friendship.

As much as he would love to be able to stay in Haley's life and make sure that whatever lucky bastard ended up with her took care of her, he couldn't. Not when he knew he should be the lucky bastard who was allowed to hold her, love her and be there for her. She was *his* little grasshopper.

"I can't give that to you, Haley," he said hoarsely. "I wish I could, but....but I just can't. I'm sorry."

"Then you're not going to sell your house," she simply said, shrugging.

"I'm sorry, Haley," he said, walking back to his now unguarded door.

* * * *

"Last chance, Jason!" Haley yelled through the front door.

Great, he thought, sitting back on the kitchen chair. This was just what he needed. It was bad enough that he was forced to cut Haley out of his life, something that was going to take him a long ass time to get over, but he didn't need her going psycho on him.

Haley was smart and level headed. He never really expected her to land on his doorstep at eleven o'clock at night, demanding to talk to him like so many women before her. At least she didn't sound drunk and wasn't screaming a bunch of bullshit for his neighbors.

"About time," he mumbled, rubbing his hands down his face when he didn't hear anything for five minutes. Although he was glad that Haley had given up, he couldn't help but feel a little insulted. Women he'd only fucked once or twice were a lot more persistent and demanding than a woman who claimed she loved him.

Then again, she only loved him as a good friend, one that she'd apparently wanted to screw around with for a little while, but a friend nonetheless. He'd known the entire time they were together that he wasn't good enough for her, he just never expected Haley to so readily agree with that assumption.

It figures, he thought acidly, tossing his red pen down on the stack of essays he was grading, that the one woman he wanted only wanted him as a fuck buddy. A year ago he probably would have been flattered that his shy little neighbor saw him as a stud. Now he just wanted to put his fist through the wall.

He fought back a yawn as he picked his pen back up and started going through the essays again, wondering what the hell had possessed him to give an essay quiz on the first day of school. The answer was easy. Haley and of course the new biology teacher, Mark Armstrong, who wouldn't leave her alone all day, were responsible for this simple act of stupidity.

Jason had been forced to watch as Mark flirted with *his* little grasshopper. When Haley had dropped her notebook in the hallway before first period and bent over to pick it up, it had taken every last ounce of control to stop himself from ripping apart the bastard who licked his lips while he watched Haley's pert little bottom wiggle. Since Jason needed the job and a good reference he refrained from killing the bastard and took it out on his students, who now hated him.

He didn't give a shit.

The only thing he cared about was getting the hell out of here with his sanity intact, he doubted that was going to happen if he was forced to see Haley everyday and watch as other men drooled after her. He'd have to find out from his realtor tomorrow what the hell Haley was doing to scare people away.

Right now he was too damn tired to think of the possibilities. He hadn't been able to sleep much over the past couple of weeks, another thing he was going to have to fix. He felt himself start to doze off as his head dropped forward. This time he didn't fight it.

* * * *

"Wake up, Jason," Haley's sweet voice had him groaning as his eyes slowly opened. "Good boy," she said, pressing a kiss to his forehead.

"Haley?" Jason asked groggily as his eyes slowly focused on her cute little smiling face.

"Mmmhmm," Haley answered absently as she slowly walked around him, letting her finger glide over his shoulders.

He went to cover a yawn with his hand only to frown when he realized his hands were pulled back behind him and.....yup, cuffed. He tried to move his feet and sighed when he realized his legs were also bound to the chair. Great. She really had gone off the deep end.

"Untie me," he said, sighing.

"Nope," was Haley's reply.

"Haley," he warned through clenched teeth. "Untie me right now."

"Sorry, I just can't do that," she said, stopping in front of him and leaned back against the table, smiling sweetly at him.

Jason tried to yank his arms and legs out of their bonds with no luck.

"Unfucking tie me! Now!" he roared.

"Sorry. I can't do that," she simply said, pushing her glasses back up her nose.

"Haley, I swear to God if you don't untie me-"

"Why don't we get started?" she asked brightly, cutting him off.

He closed his eyes, praying for patience he sure as hell didn't have. "Haley, it's over. You need to accept it and let me go. *Please*," he all but begged. She was killing him. Losing her was the hardest thing he'd ever experienced. He needed her to let go so he could find some way to cope with the loss without losing his sanity.

"No, it's not."

"Yes, it is," Jason said, opening his eyes, to find Haley studying him with her head tilted to the side.

"You know," she said, pushing away from the table, "you don't look very comfortable."

"That's because I'm not. Untie me, Haley," he snapped, yanking on his handcuffs again to no avail.

She kneeled in front of him, ignoring the glare he was sending her way and laid her hands on his knees. Jason watched as she licked her little pouty lips and smiled sweetly up at him.

"Did you miss me?" she asked as she gently caressed his knees.

"No," he lied. He'd missed her so goddamn much. Those two weeks away from her had been a living hell and one he knew he'd be reliving again soon.

"Well, I missed you," she mumbled softly, running her hands over his thighs slowly, almost distractedly.

Jason shook his head in regret. "Haley, we can't be friends."

She shrugged delicately. "I know." She ran her hands down the inside of his thighs, letting her nails lightly scratch him. He sucked in a breath as she ran her nails all the way back to his knees and then back up his thighs.

"I don't want to be friends," she said, running her hands up and over his shirt covered stomach and chest. He had to force himself to focus on their conversation and not on how good her hands felt on him.

"I'm not going to be your fuck buddy," he bit out angrily. Even though he knew he should happily accept anything she was willing to give him, he couldn't. He wanted all of her.

"That's not going to work for me either," she said, slowly loosening his tie and pulling it away from him. She met his eyes as her nimble little fingers unbuttoned his shirt.

"Then what the hell do you want?" he asked, trying not to lick his lips in pleasure as she ran her nails teasingly down his chest and stomach. When she reached his navel she flattened her hands against him and slid them up until she was pushing his shirt away, exposing his chest to her greedy eyes.

She ignored his question, instead tracing her fingers softly over his muscles and chest. When she ran her thumbs over his hard flat nipples he had to bite back a hiss. Haley gave him a knowing smile as she leaned forward.

"Have I ever told you how much I love your body?" she asked softly against his stomach as she pressed a kiss against his skin. He watched in shock and pleasure as she licked a trail from his navel to his left peck. He hissed as she ran her warm wet tongue over his nipple.

His head dropped back with a loud groan as she licked her way to the right and teased his other nipple. When she flicked her wicked little tongue over the flat nipple his dick went from half mast to steel in seconds.

He licked his lips as he shifted to make some room in his suddenly tight pants. Haley's hands slid back to his thighs as she kissed and licked her way to his neck. When she pulled his earlobe between her teeth he couldn't help but moan.

"Did you miss me?" Haley asked as she suckled his ear. "Even a little?"

Christ, he couldn't think, never mind answer her.

"Hmm, why don't we see what else we can do to make you....more comfortable, shall we?" she asked, smiling against his neck.

He raised his head when he felt her move away from him. Panting, he watched her sit back on her haunches as she ran her hands over his inner thighs. Every time she ran her hands mere centimeters away from where he needed her, he groaned in frustration.

"Fuck!" he gasped when Haley leaned forward and pressed a kiss against the bulge in his pants.

"Tell me you missed me," Haley said quietly as she leaned back slightly and ran her hand over the bulge, lightly gripping it before reaching for his belt.

He stubbornly shook his head. As much as his body screamed for her touch he couldn't do this. Haley deserved to be with someone she loved and who made her happy and as much as it pained him to admit it, it wasn't him.

"Stop."

Chapter 26

"Stop!" Jason begged.

Haley finished pulling his belt loose, unbuttoned his pants, and had his zipper down before he could say it again. She sat back, leaving his pants open revealing the large bulge now hidden only by his gray boxer briefs.

"Okay," she said soothingly. Jason sucked in a deep breath and visibly relaxed.

She knew she was pushing him, but she had no choice. Jason was being so damn stubborn and wouldn't listen to her. She mentally tsked him as she stood up. If only he'd stuck around two weeks ago, he'd know exactly how much she wanted him and how sorry she was that she'd hurt him.

There was no doubt in her mind that she'd hurt him and she hated herself so much for it. Months ago when she'd welcomed Jason into her life she'd been so foolish to think she was done with categorizing people into safe little groups to protect herself. All she managed to do was hurt both of them and push Jason away.

When she told herself there could never be anything more with Jason she'd been so foolish and so frightened to let herself truly love him and hope for a future she told herself was impossible. She'd been so damn selfish and hurt the man she loved.

Now he was hurting and trying his best to take care of her by protecting her. As much as it warmed her heart that he'd do anything to make her happy, even suffer, she was actually pretty pissed. His stubbornness was only delaying the inevitable. She'd break out the fists of fury to knock some sense into him, but she didn't want to hurt him.

So that left only one thing.......

Biting back a smile, she stood up and leaned back against the kitchen table. She'd never done anything so bold in her life, but this was for Jason. It didn't hurt that he was handcuffed and couldn't stop her.

"Are you sure you want me to stop?" she asked coyly.

"Yes," he hissed, still panting.

"Hmmm, then perhaps we should just talk?" she suggested as she stepped out of her high heels.

Jason's eyes narrowed on the action as he absently nodded.

"I think we should forget about being friends, Haley, and go our separate ways," he said, looking up, but not quite meeting her eyes. "Once my house sells, I'm moving away for good."

"That's really not going to work for me," Haley said, reaching up and slowly unbuttoning her silk blouse.

"That's too damn bad, Haley! I'm moving. You need to move on," he snapped, clearly trying not to watch as she revealed a black lacy bra.

"Have you moved on?" she casually asked, gently shrugging out of her shirt.

"Yes," he said without any hesitation.

"I see," Haley said, biting back a smile, as his eyes practically devoured her.

She reached back and released the fastenings on her skirt and watched as Jason followed the skirt as it hit the floor, hesitating at the matching black panties. Haley stepped out of the skirt and kicked it aside before leaning back against the table.

"So," she said, tracing the top of her bra with the tip of her finger, "you're over me?"

"Yes."

"I guess this means you want me to get dressed and leave," she said, having absolutely no intention of leaving until he was hers.

He hesitated, making her smile. "Yes."

"That's a damn shame," Haley said, reaching up between her breasts and undoing the front clasp. She held the cups together as she studied him. He couldn't seem to stop shifting in his chair or take his eyes off her.

"What is?" Jason asked distractedly.

"Well, what if I don't want it to be over?" she asked, slowly peeling away each cup, revealing tight hard nipples.

Jason cursed softly as she let the bra drop to the floor. "You don't care," she started to ask as she spread her legs to give him a better view of what waited for him, "if another man touches me?"

She watched a large muscle in his clenched jaw twitch while she absently ran the tips of her fingers of one hand over her breast and down her stomach.

"No, I don't," he bit out coldly.

"Really?" she asked, turning so she could lean over the table and grab the Tupperware bowl she'd brought with her. She looked over her shoulder and bit back a smile when she caught Jason licking his lips hungrily as his eyes ran over her bottom.

"I guess then I should tell you that Mark, the new biology teacher, asked me out tomorrow night. Dinner at his house," she said offhandedly, popping the top of the container as she watched his reaction.

His eyes snapped up to hers and she couldn't help but notice all the muscles in his neck and chest going taut.

"It's none of my business," he ground out.

She picked up the bowl, turned, and knelt in front of him.

"What the hell are you doing?" he asked, shifting nervously.

Haley pulled her bottom lip between her teeth as she placed the bowl on the floor. She reached over and pulled his boxer briefs down, releasing his rather angry looking erection. She resisted the urge to run her fingers down it.

"There, that looks more comfortable," she murmured as she picked up the bowl again.

"Oh God.....is that buttercream frosting?" Jason asked in a strangled voice

"Mmmhmm," she said, dipping her finger into the buttercream and making a show of licking it off. "Mmmm." She dipped her finger in the delicious frosting again. "I believe I owed you," she said, reaching up and smearing the frosting over one of his nipples.

He hissed in a breath when she leaned over and licked it off. "The deal was that I got to lick an entire bowl off of you," Jason said between clenched teeth.

"But this is so much more fun," Haley said, scooping up more frosting. She gave him a sly smile as she reached over and smeared the frosting over the underside of his hard cock. "A lot more fun."

* * * *

Jason groaned long and loud at the first swipe of her tongue. Christ, it was a lot more fun than he imagined. Granted, it would be a lot more fun to lick it off her breasts and off her round little bottom. He watched as Haley traced her tongue over his cock, slowly licking off the buttercream frosting.

He should stop this. It wasn't right to lead her to believe that he'd stick around, but when she took the large head into her mouth and sucked hard, he couldn't do anything more than moan and pant.

She took her time licking him clean, clearly enjoying herself. Finally when she'd licked all the frosting off, she released his cock with a loud *pop*. With a soft grip, she ran her hand down his length.

"You'd be fine with me doing this for another man?" she asked.

His breaths came quicker as he imagined his little grasshopper doing this for anyone else. He couldn't deal with it. He knew he'd fucking kill any man that so much as touched her never mind this.

Fuck it.

She was his.

He didn't care if she didn't love him the way he loved her. It didn't matter. He'd more than make up for it. He'd spoil the hell out of her and keep her in orgasmic bliss so that she wouldn't realize that she was settling.

"No one else touches you, Haley. No. One."

"What about you?" she asked shyly, rising to her feet.

"Only me," he promised as she shimmied out of her panties. She grabbed something off the kitchen table and walked around him. He heard the *click* of the handcuffs as she released each hand and foot.

When she was done, she tossed the key onto the table and walked out of the room towards his bedroom. Jason wasted no time in pulling his pants and underwear off the rest of the way. He walked into his room and nearly sighed with content when he spotted his little grasshopper waiting for him on his bed.

He walked over and climbed onto the bed. Without a word he picked up her left leg and pressed a soft kiss to her calf before setting it back down to the side. He did the same for the other leg, exposing heaven on earth. He leaned over and pressed a kiss against her swollen wet lips, earning an enticing moan.

"Just so we're clear," he said, running the tip of his tongue between her slit, "you're marrying me."

"Just so we're clear, I decided *that* two weeks ago," she said, earning a pained chuckle from him. "I'm in love with you, Jason," she said softly, running her fingers through his hair.

He raised his eyes to watch her. "You're not in love with me," he somehow managed to say. He knew she didn't love him the way that he loved her, but it felt like a physical blow to have to say it out loud.

"Ow!" Jason hissed. "What the hell was that for?" he demanded.

Haley sighed heavily as she released the lock of hair she'd just yanked and gently rubbed the sore spot she'd created.

"How the hell can you say that I don't love you?"

"Easily!" he snapped, moving away from her and sitting back on his haunches.

Haley quickly got to her knees and glared up at him. Well, as best as she could since she'd taken her glasses off. She poked him in the chest, hard.

"Listen to me, buddy! I am head over heels in love with you and if you think that you're going to pull another snit and get out of marrying me then you're crazy!"

He shifted closer. "I'm pulling another snit?" he practically roared. "I'm not the one who started all of this bullshit!" He grabbed her by the back of her neck and held her as he leaned down closer. "But I can damn well promise that I'm going to be the one to fix it."

"What the hell does that mean?" she asked, mimicking his hold on her. She drew him closer.

"It means, my little grasshopper," he said, releasing her neck abruptly so that he could reach down and grab her by the back of her thighs. With a quick flick of his wrists, he sent her falling back onto the bed.

Before she could scramble away he was kneeling between her legs with his still painfully hard erection in hand and running it between her pouty wet lips the way he knew drove her crazy. She squirmed against him almost desperately.

"It means that I'm not taking a chance on you changing your mind. You're marrying me this weekend and that's final!" he snarled, licking his lips as Haley rubbed her wet pussy over the underside of his cock.

Her answering smile stole his breath away. She looked so damn beautiful. He knew he'd fucked up his proposal, but that didn't really faze him since he had a tendency to fuck this kind of thing up. Besides, he wasn't going to ask her to marry him. That would have been fucking stupid since it would have given her a chance to say no. She was marrying him no matter what. It really was the only way to keep her safe, he decided as she rolled her hips and took the tip of his cock inside of her.

"Are you going to make love to me, or do I have to break out the fists of fury?" she asked, moaning.

He leaned over and covered her body with his. "Definitely going to make love to you," he said against her neck as he rolled his hips, feeding her his cock. He took her mouth in a hungry kiss, tangling his tongue with hers as he gently thrust into her, inch by inch. She was still so damn tight and felt so fucking good wrapped around him.

"I...I...oh God!" Haley moaned loudly.

"What do you want, baby?" Jason asked, pulling his cock out almost all the way before sliding back in slowly. He groaned as the sensation of a thousand hot wet little tongues licked his cock.

"I love you!" she cried out as he ground himself against her. He pressed a kiss to her shoulder as he continued to grind himself against her. "I love you, too," he said, turning his head to look down at her. "More than anything."

She fisted his hair and yanked his mouth down to hers. He reached between them and slid his thumb between her slit and over her swollen clit. Haley cried out into his mouth as he quickened his pace and rubbed the nub harder and faster.

"Oh fuck," he ground out as she clamped down tightly around him and squeezed unmercifully, leaving him gasping for breath and pounding into her without any finesse or reason. He was barely aware of her nails digging into his ass or her little blunt teeth biting into his shoulder as she screamed her release. His release came on him so damn hard and fast that he couldn't hold back his roar of ecstasy as Haley squeezed him dry.

He collapsed against her, careful to keep most of his weight off her and to the side. He pressed a kiss to her damp shoulder.

"Just so you know," she said, panting just as hard as he was, "the next time you try to leave me. I'm going to kick your ass."

Jason had to bury his face against her shoulder to stop himself from laughing out loud. She was just so damn cute.

"Stop laughing at me! I'm a threat, damn it!"

Jason pressed a gentle kiss to her lips.

"No, you're my sweet little grasshopper."

Epilogue

Ten years later.....

"But, Dad, we're going to starve!" Cole complained, again, as he sagged to the ground, doing his best to look like he was dying. Of course eight year old Elizabeth and five year old Joshua copied their older brother, dropping to the ground right beside Jason's feet and doing their best to out pout the other.

Jason chuckled as he added more burgers and chicken to the large stainless steel grill he'd bought and set up yesterday.

"Don't you love us, daddy?" Elizabeth asked, adding just the right amount of lip trembling, while Joshua over did it. Jason sighed, throwing more hot dogs onto the grill. He was going to have to work on looking pathetic with his youngest son again it seemed. An amateur pout like that could mean the difference between Haley feeling sorry for all of them and baking some delicious treat to shut them the hell up or her rolling her eyes and ignoring them.

"I so hungie, daddy," Joshua said, using the baby voice that he knew his parents were suckers for.

Jason looked down at his children and did his best not to laugh at their over exaggerated pouts. They were so damn cute, but that was to be expected since they were his kids. All three of them took after him in height, dark hair and appetite, but they all had their mother's beautiful emerald eyes, cute little noses and the ability to brighten up a room with their smiles.

Pursing his lips in indecision, he looked around their large backyard for his little grasshopper. When he didn't find her among their guests, he stepped back and craned his neck to look through the kitchen's double glass sliding doors. He spotted his parents, a few cousins and uncles, but no little grasshopper.

When he looked back at his kids he wasn't too shocked to find them already back on their feet, looking ready to pounce. They knew the drill after all.

"Take this plate," he said, grabbing a plate off the large picnic table he had set up as his work station, "and go hide. Make sure you share, because if I hear any whining I'm not doing this again." He threw another cautious look over his shoulder before loading up the plate with three large barbeque chicken legs.

"After you're done, make sure you get rid of the evidence and, Cole," he said, looking over his shoulder at his oldest son who was licking his lips hungrily, "make sure your brother and sister remember to wash up this time."

The last time they snuck food at a party, Cole innocently denied eating the double chocolate birthday cake. Haley would have probably bought the story if Elizabeth and Joshua hadn't been covered from head to toe in chocolate frosting. Then again he wouldn't have been caught if the kids hadn't ratted his ass out.

He handed the large plate to Cole. "Pick a better spot this time," Jason warned his son.

Cole nodded. "Can we have some-"

"Jason Bradford!" his mother said, drawing their attention towards the house. They all swallowed noticeably when they spotted Haley standing next to his mother with her arms crossed over her chest and her cute little brows arched.

"Please tell me you're not already sneaking food," his little grasshopper said on a tired sigh.

"No, of course not--*run kids! Run!*" Jason yelled even as Cole took off towards the woods with his brother and sister hot on his heels.

His mother let out a long suffering sigh as she walked over to the table and picked up the small box of baby wipes and three juice boxes from one of the large coolers and headed for the woods.

Jason gave Haley the grin that still got him out of parking tickets and earned him unlimited free samples at the grocery store. Haley simply stared at him, pushing her glasses back up her nose with one finger.

"I love you?" Jason said, trying not to laugh as Haley tried to look stern and failed miserably.

"They're my cupcakes, you greedy bastards!" they heard his father yell from the kitchen.

Haley's lips twitched as she said, "Between you, the kids, and your father, I don't think there will be enough food for everyone."

"But they were starving, my little grasshopper. The poor things were barely able to move from hunger," he said, trying to look and sound innocent as he shifted closer to the grill so that she wouldn't see the plate of chicken bones he forgot to hide.

"Those *poor things* conned Mitch out of the two plates of peanut butter cup bars that Mary brought, twenty minutes ago," Haley informed him, chuckling.

"They what?" he yelled, causing everyone around them to jump. He ignored them as he turned a glare in the direction his children headed. The sense of betrayal hit hard. Not only had they conned the soft hearted Mitch out of delicious baked goods that were meant for him, but they failed to give him his customary cut of the action, fifty percent.

"Yup," Haley said, walking past him to grab a cold soda from the cooler. She rolled her eyes when she spotted the chicken bones and perched her cute little ass on the end of the picnic table. "As soon as he walked in and put the baby down they hit him with 'I love you, Uncle Mitch' and hugs and he was a goner."

Jason's glare shifted to his best friend who was lounging in a chair with his wife, Mary, Haley's best friend, on his lap. Their baby played in the sandbox close by as their two oldest children ran around with the other kids playing tag.

Ten years ago Mitch would have simply taunted and teased the kids with the baked goods until someone hit him upside the head and made him share, but that all changed when Haley asked the bastard to do her a favor. Back then Mary was a struggling single parent of a newborn and was barely getting by on less than an hour of sleep a night.

As a favor to Haley, after much manipulation on Haley's part, Mitch reluctantly volunteered to run some food, formula and diapers over to Mary's small apartment. Mary opened the door with messy hair, dried spit up on her clothes, looking exhausted, holding a screaming baby girl and Mitch fell hard.

Almost overnight, the old Mitch was gone and the new soft hearted family oriented man appeared. He started spending all his free time helping Mary, making sure she got enough rest, and taking care of little Tabitha much to everyone's shock. Everyone knew that Mary had fallen equally hard for him, but she held back, too afraid to end up hurt again. It took some time, but Mitch eventually wore her down and within a year they were married and expecting their second child.

"Did no one try and stop him?" Jason demanded, turning his attention back on his little grasshopper, who was helping Brad's son, Aaron, make up a plate of food.

Haley chuckled softly as she sent the little boy on his way. "Everyone was too busy laughing."

"Those were my peanut butter cup bars, woman!"

"But," Haley said with an innocent little pout, "the *poor things* were starving."

"You're mocking me, aren't you?" he asked, lips twitching as Haley walked into his arms. He put an arm around her shoulders and pressed a kiss to the top of her head.

"Yes, yes I am," Haley said, sounding proud as she snuggled closer.

He held her for a few minutes, simply enjoying having his little grasshopper in his arms before he asked the question he hated asking, "Did they show up?"

"No," she mumbled against his chest.

Jason leaned back and cupped her face in his hands. "I'm really sorry, my little grasshopper," he said softly, pressing a kiss to her forehead. He hadn't really expected them to show up to celebrate their ten year anniversary, but he had hoped for Haley's sake.

No matter how many years passed, he still couldn't rid himself of the guilt he felt every time her family disappointed her. After they announced their elopement her family had gone a bit hysterical. They'd screamed, ranted, and begged Haley not to throw her life away on a loser like him. They hadn't cared that he'd been in the room at the time.

Finally, Grandma had put an end to the bullshit and started swinging that cane of hers. Ten minutes later while Mr. Blaine was rubbing a sore knee he wrote a check in Jason's name for a hundred thousand dollars and all he had to do was walk away from Haley. Turning down that money had been the easiest decision he'd ever made. He just wished Haley and the kids weren't the ones to suffer as a result.

They completely cut Haley off and refused to have anything to do with the kids. He knew it hurt Haley, but she never let it show. Thankfully, he had enough family to more than make up for the loss.

"It's okay," Haley said, forcing a smile.

"The hell it is!"

They both looked down and smiled as Grandma glared up at them from her new electric wheelchair. With a flick of her hand she gestured for Jason to load her up. With a smile he did just that.

Having Haley's grandmother move in with them five years ago when Chris retired and they finished building this house had probably made up for her family's neglect. Haley and the kids loved having her with them and Grandma loved having her own in-law apartment and the freedom to harass them any time she felt the need arise.

"I don't know why you keep inviting them, Haley," Grandma said, gesturing for Jason to add another hot dog. "They don't deserve you."

Haley shrugged. "It wouldn't feel right if I didn't."

Grandma gave Haley a sad smile. "I know, kiddo."

"Here you go, Grandma," Jason said, placing the plate on one of the tables the guys had set up that morning. She reached out and gave Haley's hand a squeeze before she rode over to the cooler and grabbed an ice cold beer. With a long suffering sigh, Jason grabbed the beer away from her, ignored her glare, and handed her an ice cold root beer instead.

Haley couldn't help but smile as the two got into a bickering match over Grandma's right to have a beer at a barbeque. Jason reminded her that her doctor said no alcohol and Grandma reminded Jason that she'd take him over her knee if he didn't give her the damn beer.

In the end, Grandma grumbled as she went to eat her meal with an ice cold Coke. She threw Jason a fond smile when he wasn't looking. Five minutes later, the kids were happily skipping out of the woods with an exhausted Megan pulling up the rear.

"Grandma!" they said excitedly as if they didn't see their great grandmother every day. Grandma didn't bother hiding her pleased smile as all three children sat down with her and shared their latest adventures with her. Megan grabbed a beer and headed for the pool, muttering something about needing a vacation.

Haley leaned against Jason as he flipped burgers. "You okay, my little grasshopper?"

She wrapped her arms around his waist and snuggled into his side. "More than okay."

"I love you, my little grasshopper," he said, leaning down to brush his lips against hers.

"I know," she said, smiling against his lips.

He pulled back to grin down at her. "You know?"

"Mmhmm," she said, absently as she ran her fingers through his hair, smoothing it back.

"*Mmmhmm*?" he repeated back, sounding amused. "You love me and you damn well know it."

"Maybe," she said with a shrug.

"Maybe you should just admit that you're crazy about me," he said, leaning in to kiss her again.

"And why would you want me to do that?" she asked, still smiling.

"Because I'm playing for keeps, my little grasshopper."

The End.

5191595R00125

Printed in Great Britain
by Amazon.co.uk, Ltd.,
Marston Gate.